FRAILTY

By
Betsy Reavley

www.bloodhoundbooks.com

ISBN: 978-0-9956212-0-6

Printed and bound in Great Britain by Clays Ltd, St Ives plc.

For Alexina

*Not even the brightest future can make up
for the fact that no roads lead back
to what came before – to the innocence
of childhood.*
Jo Nesbø

*What is tolerance? It is the consequence
of humanity. We are all formed of frailty
and error; let us pardon reciprocally
each other's folly – that is the first law
of nature.*
Voltaire

Prologue

I look around and try to see in the dark. Everything feels strange here. Far away and yet close. I'm scared. I'm really scared. Hello. Is anyone there?

'Mummy?

'Mummy, can you hear me? I don't know where I am. I don't like the dark any more. Please let me out. Please. I'll be a good girl. I'm sorry. Please.

'Mummy?'

And I wait for a sound. Anything. An echo. The sound of my own voice but there is nothing.

I keep waiting for my eyes to see something. Anything. But that doesn't happen. I am still surrounded by the blackness. It sits on my skin like rain. Close and muggy. I expect there to be wind. Normally there is wind. From somewhere it just appears and rustles through the trees. But not here. Not in this place. Here things are different and I don't understand.

How did I get here? What have I done to deserve this? I try and remember. I try to get a picture of my life in my head. I try. I keep trying really hard. It makes my brain hurt, the way trying to do my times table would. I close my eyes and for a moment lock out the darkness. Normally I would hear myself breathing but there is just silence. This place has no sound. Trying to understand what is happening to me I hug my arms around my legs. But I'm not cold. I don't think I am feeling anything.

'Daddy?'

Wanting to move, to search this place I reach out my hands in the bitter blackness and try to feel something. My brain is telling my feet to put one in front of the other. I don't know if I can, though. There is nothing to see. Nothing to aim for.

Walking, at least I think I'm walking; I go on and on, hoping to find something. Hoping that a chink of light will appear and light the way. That my hands might feel something that tells me where I am.

After hours or seconds, I don't know which, I give up and let the darkness swallow me. I can't escape it. It is like the universe that is never ending. That's what my teacher said. He said it went on and on. I couldn't understand it. Nothing goes on forever, does it?

All of a sudden everything I thought I knew, everything that was real, seems suddenly far away and the fear comes creeping back, as if it is a living monster that hides in the dark and waits for me. Tucking myself into a little ball I try to hide. But I feel it growing closer. It's here in this place. Whatever it is. It's closing in and it is going to get me. I call feel it and it knows I am here. But I can't get away. I have nowhere to hide. 'Mummy, please help me.'

I wait for her to answer but she doesn't and the silence comes nearer.

Holding onto my head I try to remember where I should be. But I can't. So instead I scream and scream and scream.

AUGUST 2013

Libby

'She's gone. I'm telling you. I don't know where she is.' My breathing is frantic and the woman on the other end of the line doesn't seem to understand my concern.

'When did you last see your daughter, ma'am?'

'I just told you, a few hours ago. She should be home by now. She doesn't wander off. Something's happened. Please, just send someone over.'

'Could she be with neighbours, or a friend?' The flat voice on the end of the line is starting to wind me up.

'She is eight years old. She knows that she must come straight back when she goes to the shop. That was,' I look down at my wrist watch, 'nearly two and a half hours ago.' I look down at Gracie who is sitting on the sofa digging into a fromage frais with her fingers and making a mess. 'I've been to the shop, I've asked the neighbours, I've called her friends. No one has seen her. She's eight. Something has happened to her. I'm telling you.'

'I'll send someone over shortly, ma'am.'

'Tell them to hurry up. It's Mill Cottage, Frogge Street, Ickleton.'

'Please try to remain calm and stay by the phone in case someone calls to tell you her whereabouts. An officer will be with you soon.'

I place the receiver down, hands shaking, and turn to look at Gracie again. Her round blue eyes are filled with concern. She doesn't understand fully but she knows something is wrong. I move over to the sofa and sit down next her, trying to avoid the smudges of yoghurt on the fabric and wrap my arm around her skinny shoulders.

'Are you sure you haven't seen Hope?' I try to keep my tone light.

'No, Mummy. Hope go to the shop.' She sucks on her yoghurt covered fingers and looks into the empty pot. 'Can I have more yoghurt, Mummy?'

'Yes.' I sigh. 'I'll get you one.' I stand up and make a move towards the kitchen.

'Rawberry, please.' Gracie calls out.

'Yes. Rawberry.' I feel the tears begin to well up and take myself off so my three-year-old daughter won't see me cry.

Once in the kitchen I open the fridge and stand there for a while letting the cool air stroke my skin and dry my eyes. It is August and stiflingly hot for the time of year. England is in the grip of a rare heat wave. I've been living in my cotton dress and flip-flops for the last week.

As I reach into the fridge to remove a small yoghurt pot I notice how brown my arms look. Then I remember that we have booked to go on holiday to Brittany in a week. I hope we won't have to cancel it now. Or maybe when she gets home that's exactly what we will all need.

My thoughts turn strangely calm and I close the fridge door and fetch a teaspoon from the kitchen drawer. Gracie won't use it: she prefers to eat with her hands, but it doesn't stop me going through the motions. One day she'll use the spoon.

I take her yoghurt back into the sitting room and offer it to her. In the corner of the room an electric fan spins furiously, doing little to cut through the warm air.

'Tee-tee?' Gracie takes the yoghurt pot from me and plunges her little fingers into the creamy contents.

'OK. Just for a little while.' I smile and pick up the remote control. As a very small child Gracie could never say television. She called it 'tee-tee' so that is what is has become known as. Even Danny and I referred to it as 'tee-tee'.

When I know that she is engrossed in an episode of Mr Tumble, I get up and return to the kitchen, clutching my mobile phone in my hand.

For the fifth time, I try to reach Danny on his mobile.

'Hi. I'm not able to answer your call right now but if you leave a message I'll phone you back.' Beep.

'Please call me. It's really urgent. Call me back.' I leave my message and hang up.

Danny left just after lunch to go and play tennis with a friend. I'd been to the courts looking for him when I realised Hope was missing but no one was there. The game must have finished and he'd forgotten to turn his phone back on. He was probably in a pub enjoying a pint in the sunshine.

For a moment I thought about going to look for him but then I remembered what the emergency operator had said. I needed to stay at home and wait for the police to show up. Where were they?

Not knowing what to do with myself I stand in the kitchen doorway watching Mr Tumble fool about, not hearing anything he is saying. I am in a daze and the world is on mute. Even Gracie's little chuckles are lost to me. All I can do is wait for that knock on the front door. Surely it can't be long now.

I nearly jump of out of my skin when my mobile phone starts ringing.

'Hello?' I answer in a panic and do not check the name on the screen.

'Hi Lib. What's wrong? Is everything OK? I just got your messages.' Danny's rich voice travels down the line.

'I've been calling and calling. Come home. You have to come home now. I can't find Hope.'

'What do you mean, you can't find her?'

'She's missing. She went to the shop a few hours ago and hasn't come back. Just come home.' The tears start to fall again.

'Have you looked for her?' He is trying to remain calm but I can hear the fear in his voice.

'Of course I have! I went to the court to see if she'd come to watch you. I've been to the park and I've called around her friends. No one has seen her. The police are on their way. Just get home now.'

'OK. I'll be back in ten.'

The line goes dead and as I slip the phone back into my dress pocket I notice Gracie's little face peering over the back of the sofa at me. The sunshine flooding in through the French windows is bouncing off the faded peachy pink wallpaper and reflecting on her face, lighting it up.

'Where Hope gone?' her yoghurt covered fingers are curled around the back cushion.

'Hope will be home soon, sweetheart. Don't worry. You just watch Mr Tumble.' My attempt at a smile fails. Gracie remains looking at me for a moment before deciding that the TV is more interesting.

I return to the kitchen to get a glass of water. It's so hot and a wave of dizziness hits me. Checking my watch again I notice nearly twenty minutes have passed since I called 999. It takes every ounce of self-control I have not to dial it again and beg them to hurry.

Doing all that I can to fight the shock that is flooding my body, I lean against the kitchen table and take small regular sips of the water. I can't afford to fall apart. I have to think clearly. I have to find her.

A sudden knock at the door makes me spring into action. I put the glass down on the table and rush into the hallway. Taking one deep breath in an attempt to calm myself, I turn the handle and pull the door open.

Standing on the front step in the bright sunshine are two police officers.

'Mrs Bird?'

'Yes, come in.' I step back and let them pass. 'Go through there,' I indicate to them with my head, taking one last look out along the road hoping that I might see her walking home.

Gracie comes running up to me and grabs hold of my dress, smearing pink yoghurt all over the white cotton. She looks at the officers warily and I pick her up.

'Hello,' says the policewoman, smiling at Gracie.

'It's OK, girlie. They've come to help find Hope.' Gracie gives a nod of acceptance and I lower her back down to the floor. 'Why don't you go and watch Mr Tumble and I'll go into the kitchen and talk to the nice police?'

She shrugs and skips off back to the sofa as I lead the uniformed man and woman into my kitchen.

Sinking down onto one of the farmhouse chairs I put my head in my hands. Their arrival has made the situation all the more serious.

'I'm Sergeant Hughes and this is Sergeant Larkin. We need to ask you a few questions to get an idea of what's happened. Can you please tell us when you last saw your daughter?' The fair-haired officer pulls out a notepad and hovers his pen over the paper.

8

'At about one fifteen she asked to go to the shop and buy a treat. I'd told her this morning that if she tidied her room she could have a magazine. She's been to the shop on her own lots of times. It's only at the end of the road.'

Suddenly guilt catches in my throat. Am I a bad mother for letting her g o alone?

'Has she ever been late back before?' Sergeant Larkin has a kind face that puts me at ease.

'No. Never. It's only a few minutes down the road. It should have only taken quarter of an hour. When thirty-five minutes had gone by and she hadn't come home I put Gracie in her pushchair and wandered down to look for her. The shopkeeper, a nice man, said he'd seen her a while ago. She'd bought a magazine and left the shop earlier. So I went to look for her at the playground. She wasn't there either so I thought maybe she had gone to watch her dad play tennis. He'll be back soon. I called him. But there was no one at the court. Then I started to panic so I rushed home and called around her friends. No one has seen her. I've searched the house, in case she came back while I was out looking for her. She's not here—'

'Would you mind if I had a look?' the male officer interrupts. 'Sometimes kids think it's funny to hide. Best we check.'

'Go ahead.' I wave him out of the room. 'But I know she's not here.'

Sergeant Larkin sits down on the chair opposite me. She looks hot and sweaty in her uniform so I offer her a drink.

'Oh yes please, some water would be great.'

'She's not the type to hide or run off. Something has happened to her. I know it.' With a shaking hand I pass the officer her glass of water.

'We have to check.' She smiles kindly before taking a long drink. 'So she's never disappeared before?'

'No. She's not like that. She's a good girl. She's nervous of strangers and being on her own.'

'And there aren't any problems at school or home that could be worrying Hope?'

'It might be Saturday to you but it's the school holidays for us. She's a happy kid. There's nothing wrong at home.' I feel myself growing defensive.

'I have to ask these questions.' The officer shifts in her seat.

'She's definitely not in the house.' Hughes reappears in the kitchen looking hot and bothered. I notice the large sweat patches on his white shirt.

'I told you that already.' My misery cuts through the air.

'Right, Mrs Bird, we need a description of Hope. Can you tell us what she was wearing?'

'I've got a photograph if that helps,' I start to leave the room but Larkin reaches out to stop me.

'That will be great but first can you just describe her to us?'

'OK.' I feel all my energy leave my body as I return to sitting at the table. 'She has mid-brown shoulder-length hair. It's straight. She always wears it down.' I smile at the thought of her silky hair. 'She has blue eyes.' I put my head in my hands and rack my brain to try and think what she was wearing. 'She had a white and green strappy cotton top on. It was decorated with little green flowers around the hem that look a bit like clover and she had blue denim shorts on that were just above her knees. She's got lovely brown skin. Her grandmother is Indian and Hope is lucky to have a few of her genes. On her feet she was wearing her pink plimsolls.'

'Did she have a bag or anything else with her when she left?' Larkin leans towards me.

'No. I don't think so.' I try hard to remember. 'I gave her a five pound note that she put straight into her shorts pocket.'

'OK. Those details are good. They will help. You've done well,' Larkin reassures me. 'Now, what happens is we will pass a description of Hope out to all officers in the area and I will inform the control room officer that she is missing. Officers will be dispatched to look for her and will start the search in and around the village. Can you please direct me to the shop that Hope got her magazine from? We need to speak to the shopkeeper.'

OCTOBER 2004

Libby

When I discovered I was pregnant it felt as if my world was falling apart. I was twenty-four, reckless and selfish. All I wanted to do was get drunk with my friends and sometimes I spent the pittance I made working as a waitress, on coke. But I was just a normal girl. I wasn't a hooker or a coke head. I just liked having fun. We all did. The boring days were tolerated because of the promise that came with the nights. I lived in a shared house with three male friends, all of whom were as ready and willing to lose themselves in a drink or drug haze as I. That's what university taught me: how to have fun.

I came away from Oxford Brookes with a distinctly average 2:2. My parents were disappointed. If only I'd applied myself… But I didn't. At least not where my work was concerned. I concentrated on making friends and going to parties. It was all harmless really. Self-indulgent but harmless.

Oxford had been the only place I'd wanted to go after my A levels because my best friend wanted to go there. We'd been friends since we were thirteen and he had set his sights on Oxford for some reason. I just wanted to be where he was.

Over the four years spent living in Oxford I collected more memories than I could hold onto. I'd had a few boyfriends and one-night stands but nothing serious. I wasn't a serious girl. I wasn't looking for love or romance like some of them were. Even if I had, it would have been difficult since most of my friends were men and that tended to put would-be boyfriends off.

I'd always enjoyed the company of men more than women. It was partly because, like me, they were always joking around. Women my age, when they got together, seemed to spend all their time worrying about men. I didn't understand that. I liked the banter. It was as if I had ten brothers. Sex got in the way sometimes, usually fuelled by one substance or another, but we always got over it in the end.

Once in a while things would get complicated. One of them would try it on or I'd be drunk and make a fool of myself. I'd had my heart broken a handful of times and avoided looking for love for the time being. It was easier that way.

Then, one September, I met Danny. He was a friend of a friend and our paths had never crossed before. That sunny afternoon a number of us were sitting in a pub garden recovering from a two-day bender. He sat in a corner with his beanie pulled down so that it shadowed his eyes. He was wearing an olive-green linen granddad shirt and I remember watching as he fumbled with the cuff, picking at it with his fingers. When he looked up at me I was taken aback by the colour of his blue-green eyes. He had a rich suntan that made them stand out even more. I smiled over at him and knocked back my tequila before returning to the conversation I was having with my housemate about planning a holiday to Mexico.

By that evening the party had reignited and moved back to my house, which was often the hub of the action. I found myself sitting on our flea-bitten navy sofa talking to Danny. He explained how he'd spent a year away travelling around India and Nepal. I was impressed. The most I'd ever done was spend a couple of weeks on a Thai Island and all I'd gained from that experience was severe sunburn and a trip to the STD clinic when I returned to UK soil.

Danny puffed on a joint while telling me about some of his experiences. I was in awe. He seemed so grown-up and I felt like a child in his presence, so when he put his hand on my knee and bent his face to kiss my neck I went with the flow.

The next morning when I woke up to find him in my bed snoring, I crept out of the room and took myself downstairs, wearing an old baggy T-shirt and just my pants that I'd picked up off the bedroom floor.

Downstairs was an open-plan kitchen-diner-cum-living room. On the sofa a couple of familiar faces were dozing. Another guy I didn't recognise was curled up in a foetal position in the armchair.

The kitchen smelt of stale beer and smoke. I couldn't see a clean surface for empty cans and bottles. Padding over to the fridge I removed half a bottle of flat coke that had the top missing and the remains of a bottle of whisky. I needed hair of the dog.

Putting the bottles down on a chair I picked up one of the dirty glasses and rinsed it in the sink before mixing the whisky and coke in the glass. It was cold and sweet and strong. Opening one of the drawers in the kitchen I searched for cigarettes and came across half a packet wedged at the back behind the cutlery. I always kept an emergency pack.

The sun was pouring into the room through the sash window and I opened it to let the warmth in and the smell from the party out. Then I lit a cigarette with a shaking hand and took a long drag. Looking up at the kitchen clock I saw that it was only half past seven. I'd only been asleep for a few hours.

The silence in the house was quickly making me feel uncomfortable. I longed to crawl back into my own bed and pull the duvet up over my head but knowing Danny still lay there prevented me from doing so. I didn't want him in my bed. I wanted him gone. I was already regretting sleeping with him. We'd not even known each other for twelve hours.

Throwing the rest of my cigarette out of the open window, I rubbed my eyes with the palms of my hands and tried to bury the feeling of shame. A drink- and drug-induced panic was setting in so I did what I always did when faced with it, and started to clean the kitchen. It helped me feel like I had some control.

Tearing a black bin bag off of the roll I set about filling it with empty cans, bottles and the contents of ashtrays that lay dotted about. I didn't care if I woke the sleeping people in the living area. I just needed to get rid of the evidence. I needed it gone. Looking at it and smelling it was making me feel ashamed.

The stranger in the armchair opened one eye and glared at me before rolling over and burying his face into the fabric of the chair, trying to shut me out. When I was sure he couldn't see, I gave him the finger. No one looked at me like that in my own house.

By the time the second bin bag was full I was starting to feel better. Then Danny appeared in the doorway wiping the sleep out of his eyes. He looked as awkward as I felt.

'Morning.' I busied myself tying the sacks and refused to look him in the eye. He just stood there and didn't say anything as if he was expecting me to say more. I returned to the kitchen and finished my flat coke and whisky. Seconds later I felt his presence behind me, looming like a dark shadow.

'What are you up to today?'

'Sleeping.' My tone was cutting and as I turned to look at him I felt guilty. His face was forlorn and I was the cause.

'Oh.' He started to fumble with his shirt again and looked down at the floor. 'Do you want to get some breakfast or something?'

'No. Not hungry. I never eat breakfast.' I put the glass into the sink and moved towards the corridor. 'See you around.' I turned and tried to smile at him but couldn't manage it.

Danny remained in the kitchen looking lost as I rushed up the stairs and into the comfort of my bedroom.

Things went on like that for a while. He chased and I backed away, apart from when we got pissed and then I let my guard down. Danny was determined. He texted me and kept up his pursuit despite my knock-backs. We suffered a number of false starts before I finally realised what I had.

The following June we got together properly. We went on dates like other couples. It was lovely. We planned holidays and chatted, putting the world to rights. He was so clever. His mind impressed me.

Danny had just finished a philosophy degree and, like me, was hanging around Oxford trying to figure out his next move. Unlike me he had come away with a very good degree and would no doubt do well in life.

By August we were head over heels in love and inseparable. After a week spent lying on a beach in Brittany, we decided to move to Brighton. We had only been together for a few short weeks but it felt right. Both of us knew it was a risky move but it was one we were prepared to take. He had inherited some money from a grandparent and we dreamed of buying a bar and running it together on the seafront.

Danny was as keen to take a leap into the unknown as I was. I'd met my soul mate.

Then in October everything changed. My period was late. I'd been ignoring it for a few weeks but inside I knew. I went home to visit my parents and brother for a while and only when I was far enough away from Oxford, and Danny, could I entertain the idea of taking a pregnancy test. I remember that moment as if it was yesterday.

My mum and dad had gone out for supper with some friends and my younger brother, Alex, was downstairs in the kitchen drinking wine with his girlfriend.

I went into the bathroom and made sure the door was locked before removing the pack from my slouchy hoodie. It was a double pack. I wanted to be sure of the result.

Sitting down on the cold loo seat I placed the white stick between my legs and peed, trying, but failing, to keep my hands out of the stream. When I was certain the stick had absorbed enough urine, I balanced it on the edge of the bath, flushed the loo and washed my hands.

It was the longest minute of my life. I paced backwards and forwards watching the clock on my phone and counting the seconds. Finally, the timer went and it was time for me to look at the test. Not wanting to touch the pee-covered stick I peered down at the indicator window. Two pink bars meant I was pregnant. One meant that I wasn't.

Two bright pink lines sat clearly in the window. Quickly reaching for the box that contained the second test I removed it, tore the foil wrapper off and returned to my squatting position on the loo, urinated again and repeated the whole process. Three minutes later I was looking at the results of the second test. There were two pink lines.

Feeling sick and beginning to shake, I made my way downstairs to the kitchen where Alex and his girlfriend Daisy sat sharing a bottle of red and some olives. Alex looked up at my ashen face and asked what was wrong.

'I'm pregnant.' I blurted out. 'I'm fucking pregnant.'

Daisy, who I didn't know very well, remained very quiet as I began to sob. Alex got up out of his chair and came and put his arms around me. He was two years younger but six inches taller.

Apart from the physical presence of my brother, all I can clearly remember is the fear. A gut wrenching fear that gripped me and made me shake.

Maybe I was pregnant or maybe I was ill. It was hard to tell the difference.

I was in love for the first time, with someone who gave a shit about me. The idea of losing him scared me more than anything I could have possibly imagined. I couldn't think straight. Every little process my brain tried to undertake caused me further pain.

When I woke up two days later it all became clear. I wanted him. I wanted Danny. We didn't want a baby. Not yet. Not that way. So I went and saw a doctor and I made an appointment. It was suddenly simple. And when I'd settled it in my own mind then I was ready to confront him.

None of it played out the way I expected it to.

'So, I'm pregnant.' I said down the phone, feeling a million miles away from him. 'But it's OK,' I interrupted before he could object or hang up. 'I've got an appointment and I'm dealing with it.'

Still silence.

'Please say something. Anything. It was a mistake,' I continued.

'Sorry, it's not a good time. I'll call you later.' And that was it. The phone line went dead. I held the receiver in my hand and remember looking down at it in horrified shock.

'He hung up.' I looked over to my brother and Daisy. 'He just hung up.'

The next twenty-four hours were agony. I cried, I screamed, I cursed and then I collapsed. I almost prayed. Almost.

What I held onto was that I had a plan. I was dealing with it in the only way I knew how.

My parents remained in the dark. I couldn't cope with their opinions or disappointment.

Alex was my sounding board. He always has been. Never judgemental. He has the ability to see through the shit and give an unbiased opinion.

On the day I had the doctor's appointment I'd finally sorted my head out. Did I believe in abortion? Probably not. It was all new to me. The only think I knew for sure was that I wanted Danny in my life. The prospect of losing him was unthinkable. I did my best to bury the image of a little life growing in my tummy.

He took me by surprise, turning up in his parent's aging Toyota estate unannounced. I was prepared to do it all without him. I didn't want him there. But he appeared, knocking on the front door looking sheepish.

'What are you doing here?' My words were crisp and I did my best to hide my terror.

'I need to talk to you.' His large eyes were hooded by the shadow from the hat he wore.

'A bit late for that.' I crossed my arms across my chest and tried to feign disinterest.

'Look I'm sorry, OK. I was a bit shocked.' He sounded so reasonable. It hadn't occurred to me that it was that simple. I'd felt abandoned.

'I'm dealing with it. I don't need you here. It's all taken care of.'

And that is how it went for all of twenty minutes. After I'd let him into the house and explained his impromptu visit to my folks, we scurried upstairs to my teenage bedroom and lay on the bed, both staring up at the beamed ceiling, debating the existence of the peanut that had made itself at home in my womb.

An hour later we were in his car on our way into Cambridge, leaving behind the comfort of a quiet village.

Neither of us spoke. I think the radio was on. I doubt either of us could have handled the silence.

Finally, we arrived at the soulless concrete car park, which had sprung up out of nothing and now dominated the south side of the city. He parked and we both made our way towards to Cineplex in silence. We didn't hold hands. The physical contact would have been too much.

Once at the bowling alley we both stood, like gormless kids, gawping at the girl behind the desk who was chewing her gum furiously. Neither of us said anything. I think we were waiting for her. But she just stared.

'You want a game?'

We looked at each other but didn't speak to her.

'Do you want a game?'

'No.' I blurted it out. 'I want a beer.'

She smiled through her thin lips, showing her bright pink bubble gum. 'Bar's over there.' She nodded with her head and rolled the gum around her mouth. 'Next.'

Danny and I moved aside.

'Come on. Let's go to the bar.'

By the next morning it was all decided. We were going to be parents.

AUGUST 2013

Hope

This is such a strange place. Everything smells funny and weird. Mummy says I have a nose like a dog because I'm always talking about smells but here they are different. Nothing is what I am used to. My head aches and I feel sick all of the time.

If I wasn't so frightened I could pretend I was on holiday because it is a bit like that, in the way that everything is so different from what I'm used to. But this isn't a holiday and I am frightened.

When I curl up into a ball I get scared by the touch of my own hands, as if they aren't mine and they might be someone else's. That is what the dark does to me. It makes monsters and Daddy told me that monsters aren't real but now I know they are because I'm in this place, whatever it is, and I can feel the monsters creeping around me.

'Daddy, are you there?'

When I had a bad dream and I thought there was a witch under the bed mummy made me look. I just knew I would see that witch hiding and I stood behind mummy while I ducked down. But there was no witch there. Mummy was right. But it isn't like that here. I know if I looked here I would see something horrible so maybe I should be happy I am in the dark, but my imagination keeps coming up with really bad stuff.

I don't understand any of this. It is so fuzzy, not like when I had the dream about the witch.

When I move I hear a jiggle sound but a loud one like pots and pans and I know that the sound is made by me.

It is a bit like the sound of when Mummy uses a metal spoon in a saucepan she is cooking in. Like scrapping. The noise sounds cold. That is the only way I can describe it.

'Mummy, I want to come home.'

After I start to understand that the noise happens every time I move I spread my fingers out and feel about in the blackness and when my hands touch the thick chain it makes me want to cry.

Someone is keeping me here attached to this chain that is fatter than my arm and I am terrified I will never get away.

I am too scared to try and escape. I don't know where I am or if there is somewhere for me to go so it is best if I just wait for someone to come and get me. Maybe I am in here by a mistake. Maybe this place is like Narnia and I am trapped in a wardrobe.

I don't know why I am in here. I don't want to be. I just wanted a magazine. How did I end up in this place? Why can't I remember?

Please don't let me be stuck in a nightmare. Don't let the witch or the monsters be real.

Or maybe I am like the child in the story about the boy who cried wolf and ended up stuck in a well. This smells a bit like a well, all wet and sweaty. But if this was a well I would be able to look up and see light and I can't. I can't even see my own hands.

'Mummy?

'I keep thinking I hear you but I can't. It's just me here. Only me.'

JULY 2005

Libby

Danny had a different experience to me. He was never dosed up to the eyeballs with gas and air and he didn't have an anaesthetist plug drugs directly into his spinal fluid. He also didn't have midwives talk to him about discharge, or strange women show him what an expanding pelvis looked like using a skeletal diagram. We were on different sides of the fence, looking over at one another and trying desperately to find a common ground.

And looking back I see it so differently now.

The first time I saw her on a screen – that was when things changed. Until then it was surreal. His parents, my parents all nodded – despite their reservations – and promised to help us through it all. The power of the promise of a grandchild is a strong thing. I didn't know that until then.

I was never very close to my parents. My relationship with my mother was always strained. When they announced that they were moving to Cornwall I wasn't in the least bit surprised. Their first grandchild was about to be born and they were going to live on the other side of the country, taking Alex with them.

Danny and I made our minds up, sort of, and the next week we were announcing our good news to the world. *Did we believe it? Did it matter?*

Suddenly two families, who were virtual strangers, were thrown together. Both did a noble job of supporting the other but suspicions were rife.

He led my daughter astray.

She is a hussy.

They were easy assumptions. Nobody meant any harm. They were just wary and I think that uncertainty was what pushed Mum into wanting to move so far way. She couldn't bring herself to stick around and watch me fail.

When Hope was in my belly, twisting and turning, kicking me in the ribs, I made her a promise that I would always protect her and do my best. I didn't know her then. I didn't even know I was expecting a girl. I couldn't picture her at all. She was a child. A feeling. But not real. Not really. Not in those days.

I remember collecting scraps of pretty fabric to make a quilt with. I was no earth mother, I didn't buy organic veg or worry about the state of the planet, but having a person growing inside me compelled me to do something homely and honest to celebrate the arrival.

Danny was working so hard to make sure our little nest had everything it needed. He hated his job. It sucked the life out of him but he kept on. He never complained. He was my rock.

While he sat behind his desk, tapping away at the keyboard, I spent time at home preparing the nursery. A nursery intended for a child nobody had ever met. Pink, blue or yellow? Those were the extent of the worries I had. And when he came home, trying to smile and hide his frustration at life, loosening his tie and wanting nothing more than to sink into the sofa with a cold beer, I'd bore him with my colour scheme conundrum. That was how we came round to the idea and adjusted.

We were kids ourselves. Apart from our parents, who seemed far too grown-up, we didn't know other parents. He and I were the first out of our group to have a baby.

My brother used to joke that she was the product of tequila and cocaine. He wasn't far wrong. I borrowed the joke for myself. But as time went by it became less acceptable. She was more than that. So much more.

I realised I'd used the joke as a way of taking the pressure off myself. If I said it was light-hearted, then maybe it would become so. Part of me was willing for the cover that self-fulfilling prophesy offered. It was a get-out-of-jail-free card; imply everything is easy and comfortable and it shall be.

There were moments during the pregnancy when I wondered if I was ill instead of being pregnant. She weighed heavy in my skeleton. Had the doctors made a mistake? Was it cancer? What was the alien growth in my stomach? But then I would feel a gentle kick and I'd know she was turning around, trying to make herself comfortable. Then, when no one was around to see, I'd rest my hand on my tummy and talk to her. Sometimes, I'd even sing. She loved rock and roll. She would start to dance whenever there was a good beat. I loved that. It made me smile and I started to feel like I knew her. But I didn't know she was a she. For a while I was certain I was expecting a boy.

Danny and I were fumbling about in the dark. It made sense to me that we would have a son. For some reason a son seemed an easier option. But it's so long ago now and so much has happened, I can't link back to that way of thinking. I'm a different person. Nothing is the same.

After she was born I would swear I knew she was a girl. Whether I did or not, who knows. Or who really cares. History was rewritten.

It was then that I learnt how we all lie to ourselves. Motherhood brings with it a whole new set of lies and I was just finding my feet.

The three of us were plunged into the deep end and all it took was sex. That was it. Yes, there was love and attraction and excitement but it was the sex that changed the course of our lives. It created a life. A perfect, strange, little life.

That was the focus of it all. My nightmares would consist of so many things. There was dread of childbirth and the tangible fear of the pain and danger of the unknown. Would my body ever be the same? Would she be born alive? Could my body do her justice? Would I survive? Perhaps medical advances meant nothing. I was going to find out whether I was ready or not.

The pregnancy was horrible, the labour worse. It was a car crash of flesh and blood and doctors. Then she was here. When she arrived, crying, blue, pink and covered in blood, Danny was ready. He'd always been ready. I wasn't. I prayed my animal instincts would kick in and make sure I did my best. Ultimately they did.

He held her wrapped in a bloody blanket in his arms and I watched the tears fall, as if in slow motion. For a little while it was just the two of them and I was the outsider, lying on the hospital bed, tired, panting, confused and full of drugs.

I was still terrified. For the first time I had proper responsibility. Not like looking after the family Labrador, when my parents went away on a golfing holiday, but proper life and death weighing on my shoulders. But when he put her in my arms, wrapped in that bloody blanket, I held onto her and promised her the world. Any fear I had disappeared and what took over was something much rawer.

Frailty

Without any real warning, I was a mum.

The next day he collected us from the hospital. It was that same god-damn awful bloody Toyota, which was covered in dents. Now I can admit I hated it. Now I confess that I resented it.

Carrying her, as if she were made of porcelain, I slipped her into the car seat. The government insisted all children had them by then. You couldn't just strap a kid to your lap and make your way to the shops any more. It was so much more complicated.

Neither of us could work out how to attach the baby seat to the seatbelt. It was worse than a Rubik's Cube. It was designed to trip people up. Danny and I both felt our hackles go up. Neither of us wanted to admit that we didn't have a clue what we were doing. So, like a pair of rabid dogs, we went for each other.

They do say that the birth of a child ruins your marriage. We made up quickly, but something had shifted between us.

People were taken in by her. She was such a beautiful child. Even our parents forgot to doubt each other. They stopped looking at one another like they were adversaries and started to work as a team.

Danny and I sat in the middle of the confused mess and let it unfold around us. We wanted it to work and they made it possible.

Of course the fact that she was intoxicating made it easier. Her blue eyes were like deep pools. I watched people get lost in her stare. But it was pure. She was just a pretty little girl with a heart-shaped face, beautiful skin and a smile to die for. Without a doubt her name would be Hope.

I knew that before she was born. Danny and I didn't discuss it. Like a lot of things.

When we got her home we took her out of the car and put her gently down in a corner of the room, which was padded with more cushions than was necessary. Then we both took a step back and stood looking down at the tiny fragile creature that squirmed beneath the cotton blanket. My body ached but it was strangely tolerable.

Danny removed a packet of cigarettes from his pocket and we stepped outside into the cool summer's night air and had a few precious minutes to ourselves. I relished the taste of the hot sticky nicotine. Nine months of abstinence left me wanting more. The only thing missing was a measure of Scotch.

I was wearing a pair of pyjama bottoms and a loose top. It could have been any day spent in Oxford. The morning after the night before. But it wasn't. Everything was different. She was there, just a metre away from us, inside, sleeping peacefully.

He and I didn't speak. We just sat on the back door step looking out at the stars, allowing the drama of childbirth to settle.

Then she started to cry and we were brought crashing back to reality. A moment of confused terror passed between us before we both threw our cigarettes away and went to tend the unhappy bundle. In a split second he and I stopped existing. Hope was all there was.

I was proud, so proud but it took me time to reach that point. For a little while I was intimidated. She shone and I wondered how I'd ever be able to support her. To nurture such a delicate creature would not be easy. I wasn't sure I was cut out for the job. She deserved a different mother; a better mother.

But time went by, without either of us noticing, and we worked out how to co-exist.

Her little hand always reached out for mine and one day it all clicked. I realised that whatever happened I was her mum and I had a job to do. She never doubted me. I hoped that she would never grow up and discover what a disappointment I was.

It took Danny a while but eventually he proposed. Everything had happened so quickly that neither of us had really had a chance to stop and think. Then, one day when he came back home after work and, while we sat eating our supper at the kitchen table, Hope glued to my breast while I fought with one hand to cut my chicken, he suggested we got married.

I'd thought about it. I liked the idea of being his wife. Hope already had his surname. So, happily, I agreed. She was four months old at the time and we planned to marry six months later. That would give me time to plan the party.

Neither of us was religious so it wouldn't be a church affair. We decided to have a small service in a registry office followed by an almighty party for all our friends and family. We wanted to celebrate our marriage and the birth of our daughter. I wanted the world to know how proud I was of them both and it was the perfect excuse for a knees-up.

Danny was happy to let me take the lead. He didn't want to concern himself with the minor details like choosing the flowers or deciding what colour the table cloths would be. Those things mattered to me – though I will never know why. I look back at that time with confused amusement. How did he put up with all my lists and the endless phone calls backwards and forwards to his mother. His tolerance was remarkable. It was one of the things I loved most about him.

AUGUST 2013

Libby

The next two days pass in a blur. There is still no sign of Hope and now the national press have arrived in our small Cambridgeshire village. I see them through the window, talking to our neighbours, waiting for a glimpse of the worried parents. They remain on the periphery. As if we aren't real. As if our pain shouldn't be private.

For most of my life I felt as if something was missing. My twin sister died on the day we were born and until Hope was born I'd always felt incomplete. Now that feeling has returned again.

I try to spend as much time indoors as I can, away from the prying cameras and questions. Danny insists on joining the police and the droves of kind strangers who have volunteered to help scour the area. If it weren't so horrible I'd take the time to stop and thank the public for their support. But I can't step outside of my personal horror. I can't think about them. I can only think about her.

Today we have agreed to take part in a press conference. Inspector Will King is taking us through it step by step. He says it will help. People keep talking at us, advising us and trying to keep our focus on the search. I'm trying to stay calm. I'm trying to hold it together.

I cling to her pillow all the time. I won't put it down or let it out of my sight. It smells of her, her unique scent that nobody else has. Gracie doesn't smell like that. She smells of something different. But Hope has a sweet musky scent that I'm certain only I know. It's a secret we share. Our smells. She knows my scent and I know hers. So I keep her special pillow close. The one she hugs in bed when she's tired or after school when she is sleepy on the sofa watching cartoons.

In amongst the blur of drama sits Gracie. She's so small and skinny. Her little blue eyes are searching the faces of all of the adults around her, trying to make sense of what is happening. But she's so little. How can a three-year-old be expected to understand what is going on? I don't.

Danny's parents showed up yesterday and have been helping take care of her. My father-in-law, Paul, has been great. He's kept a cool head the whole time. He's a practical man and his influence has been soothing. Paul has taken over cooking and making sure that we all still eat. But even he, when he thinks no one is looking, allows the horror to show on his face. We have all aged ten years in the last two days.

My mother-in-law, Clare, spends most of her time trying to keep Gracie entertained. She's tearful but doing her best to be brave for us. I find it hard to watch her with Gracie. It hurts too much so I leave the room when they start playing.

I keep going over that afternoon in my head trying to make sense of it and trying to see if there is a little detail I've overlooked that might hold the key to her whereabouts. But there is nothing that stands out. Nothing was different that day. And despite the original speculation that she might have run away, I am certain that she didn't. I understand that the police had to explore the possibility but there is no way she would ever go off on her own.

Her father and I taught her about stranger danger. Hope knows never to talk to strangers. She is a wary child, unlike Gracie. She wouldn't like speaking to someone she didn't know. That leads me to suspect maybe she does know the person who has her. It was broad daylight. Surely she would have screamed or cried if an adult grabbed her on the street? I can't bear thinking about it but I have to. I need to work out where she is.

The police have been speaking to everyone we know. The phone never stops ringing. Everyone is trying to be supportive but I don't want to talk to them. I just want my little girl to come home.

Our little cottage has turned into Piccadilly Circus. We have had scene of crime officers rummaging through Hope's belongings. Earlier today they took our computer away for examination, since we told them we let Hope use it from time to time.

A family liaison officer has been appointed to us. Kerry is very nice but I find her presence stifling. She keeps offering me tea. I don't want bloody tea.

Then there are all the other officers, and my in-laws and friends who keep popping in to show their support. I can't breathe.

As I sit on my bed, trying to find a place away from all the people who now fill our house, there is a knock on the door. It seems I can't get five minutes to myself.

'Come in,'

'Libby?' Inspector King puts his head around the door. 'Can I come in for a moment?'

'Yes of course.' Under any other circumstances it would be strange, having a man that isn't my husband in our marital bedroom, but nothing feels normal any more.

King shuffles into the room and stands awkwardly with his hands in his grey trouser pockets. The room is hot and stuffy and the fan that sits on my dressing table rotates, blowing warm air in his direction.

'I want to talk to you about the appeal.'

'I've said I'll do it. Danny and I agreed. We'll do anything to get her home.'

'Right. I've spoken to the press and we have arranged for an appeal tomorrow lunchtime. If you would rather, I will take the lead and do most of the talking but, to be honest, the public normally respond better to a direct appeal for help from the parents. I know this is a very difficult time for you both and if you think you won't be able to cope then I will speak on your behalf.' King cocks his head slightly to one side and looks at me with his dark brown eyes. 'What do you think, Libby?'

'Either Danny or I will talk. It's fine. We can handle it.'

'You are being incredibly brave.'

'Just find her.' A lump forms in my throat.

'We are doing everything we can.' In that split second something passes across his face but it's gone before I can determine what he was thinking.

'I'll be down in a minute. Is Danny back?'

'Not yet. They have expanded the search out towards the railway track.'

'She wouldn't play there!'

'I'm sure you are right–' he stops before saying anything else.

'Are you looking for a body?' The realisation suddenly dawns on me.

'We are looking for any sign as to her whereabouts.' He cannot look me in the eye. I hug the pillow tighter than ever and curl up into a ball on the bed. 'I just need five minutes.' I close my eyes, not wanting to look at him anymore.

'OK.' I hear his footsteps and then the sound of my bedroom door being shut and when I am sure he is far away enough I scream into the pillow.

Hope

How long have I been here? 'Come on. Someone. Anyone, please.'

It's so, so dark. 'Mummy, are you there?'

And then my skin starts to crawl. At least that's what it feels life. There is a tingling sensation close to my ankle and the flesh feels tight over my bones.

I'm still alone. Am I? 'Please! Hear me. I can feel you, or someone. Who is it? Where are you?

'Mummy?

'I'm here.'

It's so black and dark. 'Help me. I want to find you. Call out and I'll follow your voice. Just shout...'

You said I shouldn't be scared. Please help me not to be scared. I want to be brave.

I want to open my eyes. I'm trying, really. Maybe if I count like you said I should. Do you remember? Count sheep? That's what you said. Just pretend they are clouds and let them float by but don't forget to count them. Make every one count. That's what you said. And I still remember. That's what I listen to. Your words are the only thing I can hear. The echo around the living darkness stops me, for a little while, feeling so alone.

'Daddy?

'I know that when I see some light then everything will be good again. All I want is cuddles. Can I have my bear? I left him on the sofa, sleeping under a blanket. It was hot but he was cold so I tucked him in. If I can just get him then I will be quiet. I promise. Can I?'

But there is no answer and I think maybe I am asleep or just talking to myself again.

I feel my head turn as I search from one side to the other. But this place doesn't have sides. I'm trapped in a black bottomless pit.

How did I get here?

How can I get out?

'Mummy, please. I'll be good from now on. I promise I'll be good.'

Libby

I haven't had a wash since she went missing. I'm frightened that if I'm in the shower I might not hear the phone ring. It's silly, I know, because there are so many other people crammed into our little cottage but I feel responsible for her. She is my daughter. Not theirs.

Nothing else exists at the moment. The business Danny and I run together has ceased for now. We frame artwork from home. He is good at it. I deal with the orders and he does the actual labour. It's good being involved with people who like art. We have a few artists we work with, as well as buyers and dealers. No day is ever the same. We are lucky that we enjoy what we do. The money isn't great but it keeps us ticking over and allows us to work together. He stays at home and helps me with the kids. No more office hours or the tedious task of ironing shirts. We are a team.

But now even that feels different. We can't look at one another. Since she disappeared all communication between us has dried up. I feel like he blames me. As if he thinks I am responsible in some way.

And I'm angry with him too. *What if she went to try and find him at the tennis court and he wasn't there? What if that is the place that someone decided to grab her?* I know it's irrational but the thought keeps crossing my mind.

It's nearly six-fifteen and I'm sitting at the kitchen table alone staring at a cold piece of toast that I'm never going to eat. The sun is already making its climb and a warm beam of light is coming through the window making patterns on the stone floor. I've been awake for hours. I like the peace when everyone else is sleeping. Danny is in our room. I can't stand to sleep in there with him but I don't know why. I'd rather be in her bedroom surrounded by her belongings.

Gracie has been sharing a bed with her grandparents. She wants to be close to someone but I can't bring myself to cuddle her. I feel guilty that she is being loved and protected when Hope is out there, alone and probably afraid. It doesn't make sense that I am punishing Gracie for not being Hope but I don't have enough space in my head to concentrate on them both at the moment. And Hope needs me now more than Gracie.

I stare at the space on the fridge where Hope's school picture used to be, held in place by a ladybird magnet. The police took this and handed out copies to the press. She looks so pretty in that picture and I worry that is the reason she is gone.

Today I have to face the cameras. Danny and I have agreed to go on live television and ask people to help us find Hope. Subconsciously I touch my face. Normally I'd be worried about my appearance but today I don't give a toss. My dark brown hair is pulled back from my face in a messy bun and I am wearing one of Danny 's T-shirts and a pair of cotton shorts that just cover my bum. It's too warm to be modest.

I push the toast away across the table and take myself back upstairs towards her bedroom, creeping quietly past the master bedroom where Danny is lying alone and then past our spare room where Gracie is sleeping, tucked up between her grandparents. Normally she shares a room with Hope, but Hope isn't there and Gracie doesn't want to be alone.

The bedroom is a mess. I gave her the five pounds to buy the magazine because she at least tidied up all the bits of Lego that kept digging into my feet every time I entered the room. Hope has never learnt to tidy up after herself, despite all my nagging. But I suppose I'm not exactly a good example. I can't remember the last time I dusted. I don't even know if we own a duster. Have I ever bought one?

The laundry basket is over flowing with pink garments. When the girls were little I tried to tell myself I would not conform to making them wear the colours associated with their sex. I dressed them both in blue as small babies but I kept coming across old women in the street who said, 'What a lovely little boy.' So I gave in and succumbed to the norm. Neither their father nor I ever wanted them to be the same as everyone else but we didn't want them to stick out like a sore thumb or, god forbid, be bullied. The decisions one makes as a parent aren't always in line with philosophical ideals we hold dear.

Sitting down on her single bed, and lying back down on the sheet I push the fairy decorated duvet away down the bed with my feet. The window is open, as if I think she might climb back in. I don't want anything to stop her from coming home. Perhaps, like Peter Pan, the girl will return to her world through the window. The thought makes my heart ache.

The memory of the press conference stops me from allowing myself to sink into the mattress. Hope has been asking for a new duvet cover but I told her she didn't need one and refused. If she came home now I'd get her whatever she wanted.

Despite it being early in the morning I am already beginning to feel the distinct sprinkle of sweat on my brow. This oppressive heat is only exacerbating my feeling of claustrophobic panic. I decide the only answer is a cold shower.

Leaving the bedroom in the same mess it's been in for days, I gently close the door and tiptoe along the landing into the bathroom. The window is closed and the small tiled room feels like a sauna already.

Desperate for some fresh air I throw the window open and hang my head outside. Below, the silent garden looks up at me. The grass is too long, the borders are wild and the apple tree has grown too large. Suddenly every single thing in my life appears to be out of control. There is an urge to go into our bedroom and shake Danny. He should have mown the lawn and he should keep the tree pruned. He should have protected Hope. Then, remembering my numerous failings, I sink onto the floor.

I should not have let Hope out of my sight.

She wasn't outgoing like some of the other children. She was never far from my side. She liked everything to be just so. For hours she would spend time putting her toys into size order. I used to worry that she was obsessive compulsive. But as she grew and the mess spread, I learnt to relax. She was more like me than I first thought. It made her easier to understand. Suddenly we had a common ground. But her failings only reminded me of my own and in reality I wasn't so forgiving. Now I wish I had been. I wish I'd ignored all the silly rules that made me bug her to tidy her room, and sit at the table when she was eating her dinner. What does any of that actually matter? Would it make her a bad child if she had a messy room and sat eating pizza while watching TV? These are just stupid things people do. Everyday things. It's not *who* we are.

Dragging myself up off the floor I reach over the bath and turn on the shower. Even the cold water doesn't feel as cold as it should. Nothing is right.

A few hours later and I am clean. Sort of. The close air still tickles my skin threatening a new outbreak of sweat at any moment.

The house is alive now. My in-laws flap about in the kitchen trying to get Gracie to have some breakfast. Upstairs I hear the familiar drum from the shower as Danny prepares himself for the difficult day ahead.

Sitting on an old armchair that used to belong to my grandmother and still smells of her, I slowly nurse a cup of tea that someone gave me to drink. For the first time in a few days I am not wearing that old T-shirt and shorts. I've slipped into a pair of fresh shorts and a clean green T-shirt. Clare suggested I change. She is right, of course. Appearances are important. The press will hang me if I give them any reason to. Not that I give a shit what they think. But I need their help to find Hope. If they don't like me, it might impair their judgement and ability to assist the search.

I can smell croissants warming in the oven. The scent carries on the warm air and fills the downstairs of the house. Hope loves croissants. If I buy a pack from the supermarket she finishes the lot before anyone else has had a chance to eat one. They never last more than a few hours in this house.

Putting the cold mug of tea down on the coffee table I wander over to the French windows and look out. The garden is so still and I am reminded of how Hope and Gracie both recently tried to persuade Danny and me that we should get a dog. I can picture their little faces now. We laughed, Danny and I. Never have two children tried so hard to manipulate their parents. But we found it funny and charming and promised we would consider getting a dog next year.

As I remain staring out of the window, lost in another world, I feel a hand come down and touch my right shoulder. It feels alien having another person touch me. I've avoided all human contact since she disappeared. It feels as if I am cheating on her by being close to anyone else. Silly, I know.

When I turn around, expecting to find a member of my family, I am surprised to find Kerry, the family liaison officer, standing behind me.

'What are you doing here?' I cannot stop myself from sounding clipped.

'We've had a development in the case.' Her cheeks are flushed red and I can't help thinking she looks as if she needs a poo.

'What is it?'

'A search was done on the ViSOR offenders register,'

'Sorry, but you forget I don't speak your language. What is that?' My frustration is tangible and I watch her shift on the spot.

'Yes, right sorry, the Violent and Sex Offenders Register. It's come up with a name.'

'Who?'

'Mr Chadrad.'

'You mean Amit? The man who runs the village shop?'

'Yes. He is at the station now, helping us with our enquiry.'

Libby

'You still want us to go ahead with the appeal?' Danny and I sit at either end of the sofa looking at Kerry who is perched uncomfortably on a chair opposite.

'At this stage, Mr Chadrad is only answering questions. He has not been arrested.'

Danny and I look at each other.

'But you must think he knows something if you hauled him down to the station.' He grips his bare knees with his hands. His shorts have ridden up his brown thighs. Instinctively I reach over and rest my hand on his. He looks at me and his face softens for a moment.

'Can you tell us why Amit was on the sex offender list?'

'I am not at liberty to say.'

'Well that's helpful.' Danny puffs his cheeks out and sinks back into the sofa.

'The press appeal will take place at one-thirty. Are you still happy to go ahead?'

'Yes of course. If you think it will help.'

'Someone out there knows what happened to Hope. It's possible your appearance will help jog a memory.'

Danny and I both nod silently as Kerry stands up and excuses herself.

'Amit. I just can't believe it. He was always so sweet to her,' he leans forward and puts his head in his hands. 'God help him if he's hurt her.'

'We don't know that.' I can't help thinking that the longer it takes us to find her the less likely it is that we will find her alive.

'It's so fucking hot in here.' Danny stands up and marches over to the French windows, throwing them open and letting out a long, loud sigh. 'I just feel so helpless.' There is a crack in his voice. I want to stand up and go over to him. I want to put my arms around him and tell him everything will be fine. But I don't. I can't.

'Let's just get this appeal out of the way. We don't know anything for sure yet. Maybe the police are wrong.'

'Maybe they're not.' He turns to look at me, his eyes filled with tears.

The next few hours leading up to the appeal pass by very slowly. I spend most of my time in the garden watching from a distance as Gracie splashes in the padding pool in her pants. Her nakedness makes me feel uncomfortable and I have a desire to make her put her clothes on, but I don't because I know it's irrational. She is playing happily while Clare sits in the shade of the apple tree and watches her fondly.

I examine my mother-in-law's face. She is an attractive woman with good cheekbones and pretty eyes but her expression is sad, even when she smiles. The worry is etched into her brow. I decided there and then that I need them to leave. Having Gracie in the house is too difficult. She shouldn't be subjected to the heavy anxious atmosphere that cloaks our home.

As Gracie rips handfuls of grass up and drops them into the water I approach Clare and rest my hand on her shoulder. She turns and tries to smile.

'All OK?' she cannot hide the fear in her voice.

'Yep.' I pause for a moment trying to work out the best way to ask her to leave. 'You and Paul are being amazing. I know this is agony for you both.'

'We all love her.' Clare swallows hard.

'I know you do and I don't know what I would have done over the last few days, if you hadn't been here.' In tandem we both turn as Gracie lets out a little scream. But it's not a terrified scream; it's full of joy. 'Clare, this is really difficult for me but I need to ask you a favour.'

'What, sweetheart?'

'I need you and Paul to take Gracie away for a little while.'

'What do you mean?'

'Please go home, Clare. Take her away from all of this. It's not right that she should have to be subjected to it. She's so little. I don't want her here.' Clare looks at me for a moment and processes my request. 'I know you and Paul want to be here and be involved but there's nothing you can do. Christ, there is nothing any of us can do, is there? Please take Gracie back to your house. Spoil her, let her have fun. Remove her from this nightmare.'

She nods.

'There is one condition.' Her steely brown eyes fix mine. 'You keep us up to date with every little thing that goes on. I don't give a damn what time of night it is – you call us.'

'Yes. Of course.' I want to cry.

'I will go and tell Paul then we will pack our things and get going.'

'Thank you, Clare.' I watch as she gets up from the garden chair and carries a towel over to Gracie.

'Come on, poppet. Time to get dry. You are coming to stay with Nana and Papa for a little while. Isn't that exciting?'

'Can we go to swings at Nana house?' Gracie stops splashing and stands in the sunlight, dripping wet, her hair clinging to her delicate pale neck.

'Yes and get ice cream.' Clare grins at her granddaughter then wraps her in a baby blue towel and lifts her out of the water.

'Icing! Icing!' Gracie still can't pronounce some of her words properly, just like Hope couldn't at her age. Then for a second she stops squealing with excitement and looks across the garden at me. 'Mummy coming Nana house?'

I get up from resting on my heels and approach my daughter.

'Not this time, trouble. You are going on a special big girl adventure. Mummy and Daddy stay at home.'

'And wait for Hope?' the question makes me catch my breath.

'Yes, piglet. And wait for Hope.' Clare quickly wipes a tear away and makes her way back towards the house carrying Gracie. 'You be good girl for Nana and Papa, OK?'

'OK Mummy,' she waves with her little hand as the distance between us grows before wrapping her arms around her grandmother's neck and disappearing back into the house.

When I am certain they are safely inside I collapse on the ground and cry and cry and cry.

I cannot bring myself to wave them off. We say our goodbyes in the house. I kiss Gracie and hold her tight not wanting to let go. *Am I doing the right thing?* I don't trust myself any more.

Danny picks up their luggage and carries it out to the car for them, ignoring the few reporters who linger outside the house like a bad smell.

When he returns we hold each other in the living room for a long time.

'Have we done the right thing?' I prise myself away from his grip and look up at his sad face.

'Yes.' Danny wipes a piece of hair, which has worked its way loose from my bun, out of my eyes.

I know he's right but everything I do makes me feel guilty.

'The house is so quiet.' We stand together alone in the living room for the first time in three days.

'We'll get her back, you know.' Danny sounds so sure of himself and I secretly wonder if he really believes it. 'Let's get ready. The car will be here to pick us up soon.' He checks the time on his mobile phone.

'Will you do most of the talking?'

'Yes. I'll do it.'

'Thank you. I'm not sure I can hold it together.'

'No one expects you to, Lib.'

Half an hour later there is a knock at the door.

'Ready?' Danny looks at me and takes me by the hand.

'Nope, but that's beside the point.' I smile as best I can trying to ignore the growing whirlwind of butterflies in my stomach.

We step out into the heat but the sun has temporarily hidden behind a large grey cloud that lingers low over the village.

No one speaks and the atmosphere in the car is stuffy as we make our way to the police station, where a room has been set up for the appeal.

Danny and I get out of the car and follow Inspector King into the building.

'We will wait to be called in to the room. They are just gathering the press.' King looks nervous. None of us are used to going on television.

'They are ready for you, sir.' A sergeant pops his head into the room.

I am still holding tightly onto Danny 's hand as we follow King into the conference room where rows of press sit facing a table. King sits down and arranges some papers in front of him, fiddling self-consciously with his uniform. Danny sits in the centre between us. He keeps hold of my hand under the table.

At the back of the room a row of cameras and bright lights point at us.

King clears his throat and addresses our audience. 'Thank you all for coming.' His voice sounds far away and his hands are shaking. I hope his nerves won't make the press think badly of us. 'I am going to make a statement and then the family want to say a few words. Please refrain from asking questions until we have spoken.' He sorts the papers in front of him, busying his hands.

'This in an appeal for information about missing eight-year-old Hope Bird, who disappeared on Saturday afternoon from the village of Ickleton. Hope left her house at approximately thirteen fifteen to go to the shop to buy a magazine. The shopkeeper has confirmed Hope went into the shop and purchased the item. That is the last time anyone has reported seeing Hope. She was wearing a green and white cotton top, blue denim short and pink plimsolls when she left the house. We are increasingly concerned about her whereabouts and ask anyone with information to contact Cambridgeshire police. A search of the surrounding area is underway and I would like to thank all the volunteers who have come forward to help with the search.' I notice that the nerves King started off with have now disappeared. He is looking confidently down the lens of a camera and I admire his stoic resolve.

Before Danny has his turn to speak a reporter cuts in, holding a Dictaphone out towards us.

'Tom Daler, from *The Mirror*. Inspector King, can you tell us more about the man you have arrested in regards to the case?' Horrified both Danny and I turn to look at King. 'And do you believe this was a sexually motivated abduction given that the suspect has a criminal record?'

King, who appears flustered, answers the question as calmly as he can. 'I am afraid that your information is wrong. We have not made an arrest. A man is currently answering questions and helping us with our enquiries but that is all. Next question?'

'But isn't the man the owner of the shop where Hope was last seen alive? Sources have confirmed that Mr Amit Chadrad, is listed on the sex offenders register for having had sex with a minor. Is that not correct?' The smug look on the face of the journalist makes me feel sick. *How can he be enjoying this?*

Before Danny has a chance to get to his feet and release his rage, we are both ushered out of the conference, the clicking of cameras drowned out by the barrage of questions thrown at us.

Hope

I'm so cold. My leg is stiff and sore. It feels like there is metal wrapped around my ankle but I still can't see anything so I don't know.

Then I think I hear a sound and I freeze tucking my legs up so my body is in a ball. I listen in the dark, waiting to hear it again. What was that sound? I was like the echo of a door banging shut. But I don't hear it again. I'm still alone in the silence. The only sound I can hear now is my own breathing.

I keep trying to think about things that make me happy. Like playing on the swings with Eva. She's my best friend. We are in the same class at school and we always do everything together. She's really funny. I wish she was here. Mummy isn't coming and I've called for Daddy but they can't hear me. No one can. I'm locked in this dark place all on my own and I don't understand why.

As well as the cold I'm really hungry and thirsty. My tummy aches and my mouth feels as if it's full of glue. I'd even eat lettuce if I had to. That's how hungry I am. But I'd rather eat pizza. It's my favourite; the one with pepperoni on it. Then I'd have a big bowl of chocolate ice cream and some Coca-Cola.

That's what I had on my birthday, at my party. Mummy said it was a special treat to have ice cream and coke. And even after eating all that I had another piece of chocolate cake. Daddy gave it to me with a wink and told me not to tell Gracie because she would be jealous. So I went into the Wendy house at the end of the garden and ate it quickly so she wouldn't see me. That was a good day. Not like today.

I don't like today or anything at the moment. It is bad.

Sitting in this black space I realise that my pants feel wet. I can't remember when I last went to the loo so maybe I have made a mistake.

I'm embarrassed. Eight year olds don't wet themselves. That's what babies do. I don't want to be a baby.

Moving my hand in the darkness I feel my front bottom and wince. It's painful and sore and damp. When I take my hand I way I feel the wet stuff still on my fingers. Then I realise there is a smell but it's not wee-wee. It smells like metal.

And now I feel really scared again. I've forgotten the happy memory of my birthday party. It's gone. All there is now is pain.

How did I get here? Why does my front bottom hurt? Where are my family? I want my Mummy and Daddy. 'Please can someone let me out of this place? I want to go home.'

Libby

'Is it true, God damn it?' Danny stood towering over Inspector King who suddenly appeared small.

'He is on the register but I am not at liberty to discuss why.'

'The fucking press are happy enough to talk about it. Is that how this is going to be from now on? We get our information second hand through some low-life journalist?'

I'm sitting in a chair holding my head in my hands as the world spins.

'We are doing everything in our power to find Hope.' The inspector is clearly as upset by the revelation as we are.

'If he took her then that means you can find her now.' I look up at the blank faces looking down at me.

'I want to make it clear that we have not arrested Mr Chadrad.'

'Why not?' Danny growls. 'If a sex offender is living on our doorstep and my daughter goes missing it doesn't take a genius to link the two.'

'We require evidence. There is none at this stage.'

'Except he was the last person to see her alive.' My comment hangs in the air.

'This is pointless.' Danny comes and puts his hand on my shoulder. 'We are wasting time being here. Let's go home.'

I stand up weakly and follow him out of the room without saying a word to anyone.

Once outside Cambridge police station I look up and down the busy road wondering how we are going to get home. On the park opposite I see a group of young boys being coached football.

'I'm going to find that reporter.' Danny speaks in a hushed voice. 'He knows things that might help us find Hope. Here,' he puts his hand in his pocket and removes his wallet, 'take this cash and get a cab home.'

'No,' I push his hand away. 'I'm coming with you.' Realising that he is in no position to argue, he slips the money back into his wallet and nods. 'So how do we find the reporter?'

'He said he worked for *The Mirror*. We'll call them.'

'OK but let's go home. I hate not being there at the moment. What if she turned up and we weren't in?'

'Yes, OK.'

We sit in the back of the silver Mercedes in silence. The black leather seats are hot and sticky against my skin. The smiley, round-faced African driver hums along to a song on the radio. Cold air blasts from the vents in the front filling the car and making the hairs on my skin stand up. The space smells of sickly sweet air freshener that hangs from the rear view mirror, swinging in time to the music.

After the dreadful pop song comes to an end the DJ introduces the news.

'The search for Hope Bird continues today. The eight-year-old has now been missing for seventy-two hours. Police are searching the area around the village of Ickleton where the child was last seen. A man is helping police with their enquiries...'

Both Danny and I freeze in the back of the car. It is so strange having our situation broadcast for the world to hear.

'Animal.' The driver mutters looking at us in his rear view mirror. 'If I's got me hands on dat man, well less just say he would not be hurtin' dem kids egain. Dem paw parents. Days never find dem kids alive.'

Suddenly I want to be sick. I fumble with the switch on the door trying to open the window and get some fresh air. Danny, sensing my panic, puts his hand on my knees and gives it a gentle squeeze.

'So do you folks know dem people? You's going to Ickleton, right?'

Danny and I exchange a look.

'No, we don't know the family.' Only I recognise the tremble in his voice.

'Me's want to go and lay some flowers for dat lil girl.'

'She's not dead.' I speak through gritted teeth.

'Just coz dey don't find no body yet.' The driver tuts and kisses his teeth.

I want to scream and shout and punch the back of his seat but I sit frozen. It is the first time I have heard anyone actually say it out loud. For these past few days I have willed myself not to entertain the idea but here it is in its inescapable ugliness.

Danny and I turn to look at each other. Both our eyes are fill with tears, the silent despair we feel is almost tangible.

'She's alive,' he chants quietly.

'Which number does yous want?' The driver raises his eyebrows and starts to slow the car down as we turn into the village.

'Drop us by the church please.' Danny thinks on his feet.

'Will do, boss.'

As the car takes the left hand turn onto Church Street we pass by Amit's shop. It is closed and outside members of the press have gathered in their droves.

'Dat must be de shop de animal owns.' The driver scowls at the harmless building as we crawl slowly past.

'Just here will be fine.' I sense Danny's desperation to get out of the car as he removes a note from his wallet and thrusts it at the driver who is craning his neck to get good looks at the action. 'Keep the change.'

We get out of the car and watch as the driver pulls away.

'That was horrible.' I bury my face in my husband's shoulder and feel overcome by exhaustion. 'When is this going to end?'

Danny puts his arms around me and clings on to me. 'She'll be home soon. They'll find her. I'm sure of it.' But we both know that he isn't.

We walk the long way around the village and across the field into the back of our house so that we can avoid the journalists. The sun is high and beating down on our shoulders.

Around every corner, and as we pass every tree and shrub we stop to look for Hope. Maybe she is hiding after all. But there is no sign of her.

Once back in the house I pour us both a tall glass of cold lemonade.

'I'll ring *The Mirror* now.'

'They are bound to want an interview, you know.'

'Then we'll give them one. Just as long as the reporter tells us everything he knows.' Danny shrugs and removes his mobile phone from his green shorts pocket.

Less than two hours later Tom Daler is sitting on our sofa sipping a cup of tea. He is a distinctly unlikable man, with a thin face and little round glasses that sit on the end of his pointy nose. There is an air of self-righteousness he carries with him and a smug grin that is ever present. It is only the second time in my life that I have been in the same room as him and already I am wishing I wasn't.

He puts his teacup down on the coffee table, leans back and crosses his legs.

'I know this must be a difficult time for you...'

'Cut the crap.' It comes out before I've stopped to think what I'm saying. Tom sits up looking rather shocked. 'You are after a story. You don't give a damn about the agony my husband and I are going through. You want a story and we want the information you have. Let's just get this over and done with. We don't have time to play games.'

Out of the corner of my eye I see a small smirk pass over my husband's face.

'Yes, right.' Tom shifts awkwardly on the sofa before adjusting his glasses. All at once he is no longer the cocky prick that walked in. 'How much do you know about Amit Chadrad?'

'He's the local shopkeeper. He's always been friendly enough. That's about it. I never thought much about him until you made your statement at the press conference.' Glaring at Tom still, I sit back in my chair and refasten my hair back into a shaggy bun.

Tom looks at me over his glasses. 'Eleven years ago he was arrested for having sex with a minor. He was thirty-two at the time. The case did not go to court because the victim did not wish to make a statement. He was given a suspended sentence and put on the register.'

'How does a grown man who has had sex with a child get away with it? He ended up on the register so they knew he was a danger. It doesn't make sense.' Danny rubs the sweat on his brow away with his fingers.

'I cannot answer that. You would have to speak to the police.'

'But they won't tell us much,' I groan.

'You mean that they are withholding information from you that might tell you the whereabouts of your daughter?' Tom's eyes light up.

'Is that the angle of your story then?' Danny speaks through gritted teeth.

'I am here to report the facts.' His pointy nose sticks up towards the air.

'Get out.'

'What?' The confusion on Tom's face is priceless.

'You heard me,' Danny takes a step forward, 'get out of my house.'

'But the interview—' Tom looks like a deer caught in the headlights.

'I have nothing to say to you except get the fuck out of my house. You've told us nothing we didn't know already. You know nothing.'

'You're a weasel.' I get out of my chair and go and stand beside Danny. 'My little girl is out there somewhere.' Danny puts his arm around my shoulder for support.

'I'm not going to say it again. Leave or you'll regret it.'

'I'm going.' Tom picks up his iPad, slides it into his bag and then slips out of the room in a hurry.

The pair of us slump down into the sofa.

'So what now?' I turn to my husband hoping he might have the answer.

'Honestly Lib, I don't know.'

'You don't think Amit has her, do you?'

'I don't know. I wouldn't have thought he was a nonce but I guess you can't always tell.'

'It must have come as a shock to Simran. You don't suppose she knew her husband was a…' I couldn't bring myself to say the word.

'Doubt it. No woman would stay with a man if they knew something like that.' Danny closes his eyes for a second and rests his head on the back of the sofa. 'This heat isn't helping.'

'But they said he hasn't actually been arrested so maybe it's not related.'

'Maybe, but where there's smoke…' Danny stops and doesn't finish the sentence.

Just then the phone rings cutting through the uneasy atmosphere in the room.

'I'll get it,' I spring up and dash over to the bookcase the phone is resting on. 'Hello?' My heart is going at a thousand miles a second.

'Lib?'

'Mike.' His unmistakable Australian accent echoes down the phone and my heart sinks.

'Any news?'

'No. Still nothing.'

'I was helping with the search this morning but they called it off so people could get some lunch. It's so bloody hot. It's like being back in Oz.'

There is a long pause. I have nothing to say.

'Is it a bad time to call? Just that Eva is awful worried.' Eva, Mike's daughter, is Hope's best friend. Father and daughter moved into the village four years ago after his wife died battling cancer. Eva joined Hope's school and within no time the two children were as thick as thieves. Mike had met Emma, his wife, when she was travelling after university and the couple had moved back to England. Two years after Eva was born, Emma was diagnosed with bone cancer. She fought the disease bravely for nearly two years before it got the better of her. I never met her but the way Mike talked about her charitable escapades suggested to me that she had been a lovely woman. They had been living in the large village of Linton, ten miles away from Ickleton, when Emma died and Mike decided it would be best for Eva if they moved to a new house. He couldn't stand living with the painful memories the house held.

'I'm sure she is. She must be so frightened.' I wonder if I am talking about Eva or Hope.

'Well, you know, if there's anything I can do, you just let me know.'

'Thanks Mike. You're a good man.'

'Any time. See you.' The line goes dead.

'What did he want?' Danny asks.

'Nothing really. Just checking up on us I think.'

'He's a good bloke. That little girl is a credit to him. How he managed to bring her up after her mother died is a mystery to me. I'd fall apart if anything ever happened to you.'

'Or Hope.' Our eyes meet.

'Right,' he stands up, 'I'm going to have a cold shower and then I'll go and join the search again.'

'You look so tired.' I step towards him.

'I'm not going to stop.'

'Let me come with you.'

'Why? It's hot and the press are still hanging around. Just stay here and wait for news.'

'I'm going mad being in this house. I need to do something proactive.'

'One of us has to stay here in case she comes home.' We both know that is unlikely but neither of us say it. 'And Kerry will be around. So you won't be alone.'

'Maybe I'd rather be alone.'

'Don't pick a fight now.'

'I'm not.' He's right, of course, but I'm not going to admit it.

'Fine. I'm going for that shower.'

'OK. I'll get onto Twitter and Facebook and try and stir up a shit storm. Someone, somewhere, has to know something.'

Libby

A week has gone by and there is still no news on Hope. Amit wasn't arrested and was sent home after answering the police questions. But King says there is no evidence that he had any involvement in her disappearance. It was routine to speak to him, apparently, because of his history.

The press have been all over him. I can't bring myself to read the papers or watch the news any more. So much speculation. So many awful things being suggested. No doubt Danny and I are being dragged through the mud too. I'd rather not see or hear any of it. It's not helping find her. It's making money for the papers and giving reporters something to do, that's all.

When all of this started it never occurred to me that we would put under the spot light. Naively I expected the press to be on our side and for the attention to be on finding Hope. But, as I am learning, it doesn't work like that.

Danny is at his wit's end. They have stopped the search after ten long days. Just like the taxi driver we encountered, everyone seems certain she is dead. But I don't think she is. I'm her mother and I would know if something like that had happened. She must be alive. I feel it and I won't give up.

The appeal didn't turn up anything. King muttered about time wasters and a few dead ends but that was all.

How can a little girl vanish into thin air? None of it makes any sense.

My brain aches and my body is running on autopilot. I can't eat. I can't sleep.

Our local GP has visited – that was kind of him because they don't do home visits very often but because of the situation he agreed to come to our house. He prescribed a low dose of Valium, to help with the shock he said. Dr Marcus Vogler is a skinny man in his forties with rimless glasses that sit at the end of his broad nose. He's nice, but I find myself looking at everyone differently. What if he took her? Everyone is a suspect.

I keep replaying that day over and over in my mind and the one thing that keeps coming back to haunt me is that Danny was playing tennis when she disappeared. If only he'd been at home, maybe he would have gone to the shop with her, or perhaps he would have watched Gracie so I could have walked with Hope. A few unfortunate coincidences have left us in the dark searching for our missing child.

Kerry is still lingering around the house, trying to offer her support. But she's a stranger and it feels odd having her so involved in something so private and personal.

The phone never stops ringing. If it isn't a bloody journalist then it's friends wanting to offer their support and find out what's happening, or family. I speak to Clare at least five times a day. She is eager to be kept up to date. I wish I could give her some good news but nothing is happening. It's like living in limbo and every time that damn phone starts to ring it acts as a harsh reminder.

Gracie is better off out of it. I miss her terribly. I've gone from being a mother of two to having no children. It physically hurts but I have to protect her. I didn't manage to do that with Hope. I won't make the same mistake again.

When Gracie is handed the phone and begins talking to me I have to cover the mouthpiece with my hand so that she doesn't hear my sobs. The poor little girl is so confused and I wish I could comfort her – but at least she is safe. That's what I have to remind myself constantly.

Just as I am about to pour myself another glass of pinot the phone rings again and I groan. It's nearly ten at night. Danny is in the office on the computer. We have started a campaign, Bring back Hope. We have to do something to stop ourselves from feeling so utterly helpless.

Reaching across the table I pick up the phone and answer.

'Hello?'

'Lib, it's Mike.'

Even though I know it's unlikely to be news about Hope I can't stop myself from holding my breath every time the phone rings.

'Hi Mike.' I let out a long sigh.

'Sorry to call you guys so late but I walked past your place a minute ago and I saw the lights were on. I wondered if it would be OK if I came over. I've got a bottle of red that needs to be drunk.'

I want to say, "Of course our lights are on!" but I don't.

'Go on then.' I'm too tired to try and come up with an excuse. 'Isn't Eva sleeping though?'

'She's gone to Abby's house for a sleepover, so I'm alone.' Remembering what a lonely man he is I soften. 'Bring the red, that would be good.'

'See you in a jiffy.' Hanging up the phone I consider that it might be nice to have a distraction, if only for a little while.

Leaving my glass of wine abandoned on the pine kitchen table I head towards the office to warn Danny that we are going to have company. When I push open the door I see he is asleep in the armchair in the corner of the room. Gentle orange light from the table lamp fills the room. Quietly I go towards the bright screen to see what he's been working on but what I find is not what I am expecting. He has been doing research into child abductions. There are pages and pages of news stories open on the desktop. Sliding into the leather swivel chair I flick through each of the open tabs.

To my horror there is story after story of children who have been taken and never returned alive. I turn to look at my husband sleeping in the armchair. He is frowning and looks pained even though he is sleeping.

So this is what he's being doing.

Danny internalises everything. He's not an open, heart on his sleeve type of man. Most people find him difficult to read. He can be aloof and some mistake that for rudeness. Actually, beneath his cocky exterior he is a shy and gentle person.

Trying to block the horrible stories that I've just seen out of my mind, I turn the computer off, get up and leave the room. He needs to sleep. We both do but I can't shake the image of the little girl from Linton out of my mind.

I return to the kitchen table and go back to nursing my now warm glass of wine. Maybe when Mike arrives I'll explain that I need to sleep and tell him to come back another time. I'm not sure I can face him now.

Danny and I have always been kind to him. We appreciate how difficult it must be raising his daughter alone. Our kids are friends, so it has always made sense to be friendly. But tonight, I am not sure I have the energy to paint a smile on my face.

Just as I am gearing myself up to turn him away there is a quiet knock on the front door and in less than a second I have lost the will to make an excuse.

Still clutching my glass I open the door and usher Mike in. He is wearing a pair of old khaki shorts that cover his knees and a faded orange T-shirt.

'Danny is having a nap so let's keep it down.' For some unknown reason I feel like a teenager sneaking in a friend.

'Damn, Lib, I can leave if it's a bad time.' He scratches the back of his neck and stands looking awkward.

'Relax. If I didn't want you here, I'd say.'

'Here's the merlot,' he hands me the bottle.

'Thanks.'

We go into the kitchen and he sits down at the table while I search the drawer for a bottle opener.

'How are you guys doing?'

'I don't really know.' I pull the cork from the bottle. 'This is like a bad dream I keep thinking I am going to wake up from.'

'I can't imagine what you guys must be going through. If anything ever happened to Eva–' he stops dead, taking the glass I hold out to him.

Sitting down opposite Mike, I let out a long tired sigh.

'I am so sick of this worry. There's a knot in my stomach that just won't go away. Nothing I do seems to help. The only thing that is going to make it disappear will be getting Hope back. But I don't know when that's going happen.' I rub my eyes with my fingertips in an attempt to keep them open.

'Is there no news at all? Nothing?' Mike can't believe it either.

'Nothing.'

'Except they were talking to Amit Chadrad, right?'

'Yes, but they don't think he's involved.'

'Why were they talking to him then?' Mike looks sceptical.

'Because of his history. He's got a record.'

'Yeah, I read that in the papers. I've received the odd parking ticket, doesn't mean the cops come knocking when there's been a hit and run.' His Australian accent is strangely comforting. The way he says the words make them sound somehow less daunting.

'It's more complicated than that.' I don't want to go over this again.

'Because he was done for sex with a kid.' Mike's face is serious and grey.

'Please, Mike. I can't keep torturing myself. I have to be hopeful and think the best. I have to.'

'Yeah, of course. Sorry Lib. Me and my big mouth.' He sips his wine and sits back quietly. Neither of us says anything for a while.

'I just keep thinking, especially at night, like now when it's so dark out there, that she must be so scared. She hates being in the dark outside. How is she going to cope in the dark, on her own?'

My hands are trembling and Mike leans across the table and rests one of his large hands over mine.

'They've got loads of cops out looking for her. I'm sure they'll find her soon.'

'But what if they don't?' I sniff a nose full of snot away and wipe the tears off my cheeks.

'You can't think like that, Lib.'

'I'm thinking all sorts right now. No one has seen a trace of her. It's like she just disappeared into thin air. How is that fucking possible?' My anguish begins to subside and I feel rage taking over of me. Mike shrugs meekly. Seeing his reaction I immediately soften again. 'I'm sorry Mike. I'm all over the place.'

He nods and finishes his glass of wine quickly.

'I shouldn't have come. You need to get some rest. Finish that glass of wine then go to bed.'

'I won't be able to sleep.'

'Maybe not, but drinking any more isn't going to help you or Hope. Lie down, close your eyes, have a long bath, whatever. Just try to clear your mind.'

'You sound like a tree-hugging hippy.' I smile, realising it's the closest I have come to making a joke in days.

'Just give me a joint and call me Skippy.' Mike winks and stands up. 'I'll let myself out. Call me if you need anything, OK?' he squeezes my shoulder as he passes. 'I'm here for you, and Dan.'

I hear the front door open and gently close and I am alone with my thoughts again.

Hope

I wish I could see. Mummy and Daddy told me that if I ate my carrots I would be able to see in the dark. So I did, but it isn't helping. I fall asleep for a little while but I don't dream. Then I wake up and I'm still here in this dark, dark place.

My ankle still feels funny. I want to touch it but I'm scared in case it hurts.

I want to scream but I don't bother. My throat is so sore and I know that nobody can hear me. Otherwise they would have come by now. But Mummy and Daddy will come. They won't stop looking for me.

I miss them and Gracie. She's really annoying and I know I call her poo face sometimes, but she can be really funny. I like having a sister except when she breaks my toys. At night she always crawls into my bed and sleeps next to me after the lights have been turned out. She has her own smell, like washing and milk and even though she wriggles in the bed I like sleeping next to her, especially when it's raining. I don't like the noise on the window and we feel safer together. I wish she was here now. But she is probably with Mummy and Daddy and that makes me sad because I want to be with all of them, too.

When I try to think how I got here, I can't. There is just a big blank space in my head and it hurts. Everything hurts. So I start to cry, sobbing into the blackness. But then I hear a noise and I stop crying instantly. It sounded like breathing. I hold my breath and listen really carefully again.

There it is. That noise. And I start to feel really afraid. Is it the person who put me in here coming to get me? I try to back away from the sound not knowing what direction it is coming from. But it is getting closer.

'Leave me alone.' I call out through my tears.

Then the noise stops and I wait, listening for it again.

'Hello?' My words echo through the darkness. 'Is anyone there?'

Nothing.

Then suddenly a scurrying noise from somewhere, like rats running across the floor. And the terror returns. I hate rats. They have sharp teeth and claws and long fleshy tails. Mummy likes rats. She had a pet one when she was a little girl but I don't like them. They are scary. What if they are hungry? There isn't any food here. They might try and bite my feet. I don't want the rats to eat me and the thought of it makes me cry out.

Then the noise comes again, even closer to me than before. I swivel my head trying to work out where it is coming from but it's no good. I still can't see a thing. And without realising it is happening I wet myself and it stings. It stings so much I wince and try to move away from the pain. But I can't get away from it. It follows me around.

'Go away,' I beg through the tears.

'Shhh.'

I freeze.

'Who said that?'

'Shhh.' I hear it again.

'Who's there?' I've stopped crying. I'm too shocked to be scared.

'It's OK.' The voice sounds like it belongs to an angel. 'Don't be frightened.'

'Who are you?'

'I'm your friend.'

'Where did you come from?'

'I've been here for a long time.'

'Why didn't you say anything before?'

'I couldn't reach you. I didn't know you were here. Now we've been put together.'

'I don't understand. I want to go home.'

'So do I.' The angel begins to sob.

'Please don't cry.' I can't bear the sound of someone else's tears.

'I'm sorry.' The angel sniffs and stops crying.

'Why are we here? How can we get out?'

'I don't know.'

'How did you get here?'

'I can't remember.'

'Me neither.'

'What's your name?'

'Zoe Jones.'

'Hi, Zoe Jones. I'm Hope Bird.'

'Hi, Hope.' I can feel the angel's presence but have no idea where she is. I think she feels close.

'Are you an angel?'

'No. I don't think so.'

'Oh.' The disappointment comes over me. 'Can you get us out of here?'

'I've tried.' The words trail off.

'Me too.'

We remain together in the silent darkness wondering what we can do.

'How old are you?' Zoe asks.

'I'm eight.'

'I'm seven.'

'You're a child?' I'm so surprised.

'Yes.'

'Well, because I am older than you, I am in charge.' I tell her. 'I'll look after you. I've got a little sister and I look after her too.'

'Do you have a plan, Hope?'

'Not yet. But I think we can make one together. If we can just find a door, then we can escape. A bit like Scooby-Doo.'

'OK.' Zoe sounds hopeful and I realise how pleased I am to have a friend.

'Do you have any food?'

'No. I haven't eaten since I got here.'

'Me neither. I'm hungry.'

'Me too.'

'What's your favourite food?'

'Jelly, and cheese sandwiches.'

'I like jelly.' It feels good to have something in common other than both being in this place.

'Well maybe we can have some jelly when we get out of here. You can come to my house for a play date if you like?'

'OK.' Zoe sounds pleased and it is nice thinking about getting away from this place.

'Where do you live, Zoe? I live at Mill Cottage, Frogge Street, Ickleton.'

'I live in Linton. At number 43. Our house is white and has a red front door.'

'I like red but my favourite colour is pink.'

'My favourite colour is purple.'

'My sister, Gracie, likes purple. Do you have a sister?'

'No and no brother. It's just me and my mum.'

'Where's your dad?'

'He lives in Cambridge and mum says he is a waste of space.'

'My dad is nice. He's funny. He always makes silly faces and takes me out on my bike.'

'I wish my dad was like that.' She sounds sad and I don't know what to say to her.

'Well my dad will come and find us. He will get us out of here.'

'I hope so.' Zoe doesn't sound positive.

'He will. I know he will.'

Libby

I wake up with a slight hangover. I know it doesn't do any good to lose myself in drink but it is the only thing that helps me to sleep, and if I don't sleep I am no use to anyone.

Last night I slept on the sofa. When I wake up there is a furious banging on the door. I stumble off the sofa, still wearing the clothes from the day before and make my way towards the racket.

'OK, OK.' I call fumbling with the Chubb lock.

As I open the door I am surprised to see Mike standing there looking flustered.

'You'd better get down to Amit's.'

'Why?' I rub the sleep out of my eyes, squinting in the bright sunlight.

'The cops are crawling all over the place. I think something is happening there. I thought you'd want to know.' He steps back and looks at me. 'I'm sorry, Lib, did I wake you?'

'Yes but that doesn't matter. What time is it?' My head is a jumble of thoughts.

'Nearly ten o'clock.'

'Jesus!' the throbbing in my head is beginning to kick in. 'Right, sorry, come in Mike. I'll just get Danny.' I step back into the house and let him pass.

'Danny? Danny!' I call up the stairs wondering why he didn't wake me. Then I spot a note left on the coffee table.

Left early to join the search. I've got my mobile. Thought I'd let you sleep it off. Call me when you wake up.

He has not left a kiss.

'Shit.' I mutter to myself bunching up the note and throwing it into a wastepaper basket, trying to ignore the feelings of guilt.

'Come on, Lib, I really think we should get down there.'

'Right, yes.' I am trying to think clearly. I've never been a morning person. 'Let me just have some water then we'll go.' I head into the kitchen. 'What did you see? What's going on?'

'I dunno. Just saw a cop car rushing past the house and ducked out to see what was happening. I followed it round and saw it had stopped outside Amit's shop. There were cops banging on his door and then a team showed up in white suits. Something's happened.'

My stomach does a somersault and I finish the glass of tepid water.

'Let's go.' I grab my keys and sunglasses from the kitchen table and lead the way.

We step back into the bright morning light and I pull the door closed with a thump before we set off towards the scene.

Amit's shop is about seven hundred yards from my front door and we race along the street half walking half running. My heart is going at a thousand miles an hour and I feel sick.

As we near the corner of Frogge Street and Church Street I see a police car pulling away with Amit in the back. He does not see me but his face looks pale. I don't like what I am witnessing. Something is very wrong.

Seconds later the shop comes into view. A crowd of neighbours have gathered outside and are watching the police tape off the area around the shop.

Dashing towards the nearest officer I am aware that all eyes are on me.

'What's happened?' I ask the stony-looking man securing the perimeter. 'I'm her mother. Hope's mother. What's going on?' the panic in my voice stops him dead in his tracks.

'You will need to speak to the detective, ma'am.' His expression is grave and I fear the worst.

'Have you found her? Have you found Hope?'

'I will get the officer in charge to come and have a word. Please wait here.'

I am aware Mike has caught up and is standing beside me.

'What is it?' he asks.

'I don't know. They won't tell me anything yet. Someone is just coming to talk to me now.' My voice is shaky and my legs feel like jelly.

'I really think you should call Dan.' Mike encourages gently. 'He should be here with you.'

'Yes. You're right.' I fumble in my pocket for my mobile phone. 'Shit. I must have left it at home. Can you call him, please? Tell him to get over here as fast as he can.'

'OK, Lib. Will do.' Mike steps away to make the call as an officer steps out of the shop and approaches me.

'Mrs Bird?' The fat man in his fifties removes the blue latex gloves from his large hands.

'Yes.'

'I'm Dale Roth. I'm the crime scene manager.'

'What's going on?'

'We were called here this morning after the refuse collection reported making a discovery.'

'What does that mean?' I hold my breath not knowing if I want him to answer my question.

'A child's shoe was discovered in a bin belonging to this shop. The shoe is a pink plimsoll that matches the description of the shoes your daughter was last seen wearing.'

'What does that mean?' I stand there with my arms folded across my chest. My words are shaky.

'The shoe will go to the lab for testing.'

'Then what?'

'Well,' Dale peers over his glasses at me. 'We need to confirm whether or not the shoe belongs to Hope.'

'I understand that.' I am trying to remain calm. 'But then what? Have you found anything else?' I feel the colour drain from my face.

'We are doing a thorough search of the property. We will know more soon.'

'And what about Amit?' Danny appears and interrupts.

'He has been arrested. You will need to speak to the officer in charge.' Dale's face was sympathetic but he wasn't being much help.

'This is a waste of fucking time.' I grab Danny's arm. 'Let's go to the station.'

Danny nods and we leave Dale standing there, watching us walk away from the busy crime scene.

'I'm sorry about last night.' I say, as we are almost halfway home.

'I know. Just don't fall apart, Lib. I need you, too. We all do.'

'I know. I'm sorry.'

We walk at such a quick pace that we both break out in a sweat. I feel it dripping down my neck from my hairline. The muggy summer weather is only half responsible for this. Fear and worry are the real cause.

As we let ourselves back into our house I make a dash for the kitchen. I'm parched and have an urge to splash cold water on my face.

'I'll call Mum and let her know what's going on.' Danny picks up the house phone and starts to dial as I lean into the gush of cold water pouring from the tap and let my face get drenched. Today is not going the way I hoped it would. No day since she disappeared has been right. Everything feels wrong and now, since the discovery of her shoe, things feel suddenly worse. I am doing my best to ignore the fact that it was found in a bin. The thought makes me want to curl up and die. Nothing that belongs to her should ever be left in a bin. She loves those shoes. I bought them for her in the spring. We went shopping together in Cambridge. Then I took her to pizza express. She ate the largest slice of chocolate cake I'd ever seen. It was a fun day we spent, just the two of us.

If her shoe was in a bin it must be bad news. I want to ignore that but I can't. And not just any bin. It's Amit's bin. Amit, the man who has a record for sexually abusing girls.

I don't hear because I'm not listening to the conversation Danny is having with his mum. I know if I listen that I will hear his pain, and hers, translated through his voice. It's bad enough managing my own horror. I'm not sure I can spread myself that thin.

After drinking a pint of water quickly, I dash upstairs to my bedroom to change out of the clothes I was wearing yesterday. A clean but wrinkled pile of clothes sits piled on a faded blue velvet chair. Tipping it over in a hurry I scrabble through looking for something cool.

'Come on Lib, let's go!' Danny calls up the stairs as I pull a green cotton maxi dress over my head.

'Coming!' I bundle my dirty clothes into the overflowing laundry basket and rush out of the room, not giving a seconds thought to the mess I leave behind. Matters such as keeping a tidy house have gone out the window since Hope disappeared. She is the only thing I can focus on.

'Right.' Danny has the car keys in his hands and I follow him out of the house leaving my stomach upstairs in our bedroom.

When we arrive at the police station we are greeted by a whirlwind of press all eager to know what is happening.

Pushing our way through the crowd, refusing to answer any of the morbid questions being shouted at us, we make it into the reception area. Immediately my eyes fall on Kerry, who is standing there as if she has been expecting us.

'This way,' she beckons, leading us down one of the corridors and into a family room.

'I want to know what's happening.' Danny remains standing as I perch on the edge of a scratchy fabric seat.

'Mr Chadrad has been arrested for the abduction of Hope. Inspector King is questioning him as we speak. We'll know more soon.'

'What about his shop? Have they found anything else?'

'As far as I know,' Kerry comes and sits down next to me and rests her hand on top of mine, 'the shoe is the only thing so far. It's been sent to the lab. We should have the results back shortly.'

'Can you tell me,' my voice is quivering, 'what state the shoe was in?'

Kerry removes her hand from mine and straightens her back.

'There was no blood on the shoe.'

I look up at my husband wanting to share the relief I feel but he looks destroyed and close to tears.

'Why would he have her shoe? He must know where she is. He must have taken her.' Danny wipes his eyes and compiles himself. 'If he is here then she is out there somewhere on her own. We need to find her. You need to search his house and shop.'

'The scene of crime officers are doing everything they can. If anything else shows up, you will be the first to know. If Mr Chadrad has taken Hope I think it is highly unlikely he is keeping her near his shop. There are houses right next door and of course he has a wife and young baby. The inspector is doing everything in his power to get to the bottom of this. I know this is hard but for the moment you just have to keep calm and remain patient.'

'We've been doing that for the last eleven days. Where has that got us? You had him and you let him out. Fuck knows what he's done to her now!' Danny is shaking all over as I get up and go to him, wrapping my arms around his tense body and trying to soothe him.

'Don't freak out. Please. I need you to be strong right now. We'll find her. I'm sure of it. I'd know if...' my words trail off.

Kerry stands up and excuses herself, leaving us alone in the room with nothing but dark thoughts.

SEPTEMBER 2013

Libby

It has been a long and painful thirty-six hours since the discovery of the shoe in the shop wheelie bin. Kerry, who has been at home with us for most of the day, receives a call confirming the plimsoll belongs to Hope. When she breaks the news to us she cannot hide her concern.

'The shoe will now go for a chemical treatment in the hope that it shows up some print markers.' Kerry's professionalism never wavers. 'If we can link the shoe to Mr Chadrad then he will be charged. The officers have already been given an extension to hold him for longer.'

'I think I am going to be sick.' I stumble out of the sitting room and into the kitchen to hang my head over the sink. I close my eyes to try and stop the world from spinning. A moment later I feel a warm hand on my back, gently rubbing it.

'Take some deep breaths, Libby.' Kerry's voice is calming.

I stay hanging over the sink for a while before I'm sure the nausea has passed, then sink to the tiled kitchen floor in a heap.

'I've been so sure she is OK. All this time I believed we were going to find her. But I've lost that feeling now. It's gone. And I don't know what to do.'

Kerry hunches down onto her heels so we are on the same level.

'You don't know anything yet. Keep on being positive. It is so important that you don't stop believing.'

Just then Danny appears in the doorway. Kerry does the honourable thing and leaves us alone to digest the troubling news.

'Why only one shoe? Where is the other?' Danny comes and sits on the floor next to me.

'I don't know, Lib.' He closes his eyes and rests his head against the cupboard. 'I don't know what to think now.'

'I know we sent her away but I wish Gracie was here. I just want to give her a hug. I feel like I've lost both of my children.'

'Don't speak like that!' Danny jumps to his feet. 'You were the one who sent her away. You didn't stop to think what I wanted. This isn't about you, for fuck's sake.'

'No, you're right! It's not!' I feel my own temperature rising. 'It's about our daughter who has been missing for nearly two weeks, and no one seems to have a clue where she is or what has happened to her!' My anger and the tears that come seconds later make me feel dizzy. 'This can't be happening to us.' I begin to sob. 'I just want her back where she belongs.'

'Me too.' Danny softens. 'I just feel so bloody hopeless. I can't stand all this waiting around.'

'OK.' I wipe the tears from my cheeks and start to formulate a plan. 'Let's go and pay Simran a visit. If Amit took Hope she must know something. Maybe she knows where he's taken her. She's his wife. She's got to know something. I've had enough hanging around. Let's go and find our daughter.'

I stand up, take Danny 's hand and we slip out of the front door before Kerry has returned from her latest telephone call in the spare room.

'Come on.' Danny takes my hand as we step out into the muggy summer weather. Above us low dark clouds linger, threatening rain.

We walk in silence along the road that leads to the shop. My mind is whirling. I don't know what we are going to ask her, or if Simran will even agree to see us but we have to try.

'Let me do the talking,' I tell my husband firmly. 'She is more likely to be receptive to another woman. Besides, you might scare her.'

'I'm not going to scare her,' Danny scoffs.

'Not deliberately, but you might. You're angry and it shows.'

'And you're not?' He spits his words.

'Of course I am! But just let me do the talking, woman to woman. I don't think you should even come in.'

'We don't even know if she will agree to talk to you.'

'No we don't. But we are going to try.'

The last few hundred yards I can't get the image of Hope's shoe out of my head. I keep picturing it lying in amongst the garbage. Questions keep swirling around and around; *why only one shoe? Where is the other? Where is she?*

As we approach the shop we see that a few journalists have gathered, waiting for their pound of flesh. Determined not to be distracted, we walk right past them and towards the wooden side gate to the left of the shop front. I'm surprised to discover it is unlocked and we let ourselves in, forcing the gate shut behind us to keep out the looming press.

Neither of us has ever been into the place this way. We've never seen Amit and Simran's garden before. We have no idea what the flat above the shop looks like inside and it feels strange walking into their private home without an invitation.

'Right,' my breathing is quick, 'you stay here.' Danny and I are standing on a concrete patio at the back of the shop. Weeds and grass have pushed their way up through the slabs making the space look shabby and uncared for.

Danny nods as I go to the back door and knock. I wait for a moment, holding my breath, hoping for an answer. There is no sound or movement from inside so I knock again. Still nothing.

'Simran,' I take a step backwards and call up, 'it's Libby. Please let me in. I just want to talk to you.' Upstairs I see the net curtain twitch and realise she is at home. 'Please Simran, just a few minutes. I'm not here to cause trouble. I just want to talk to you.'

The curtain doesn't move again, and I stand there wondering if she is going to respond.

A minute later the back door opens an inch and I see Simran through the crack.

'I don't want any trouble. My baby is sleeping.'

'Hello, Simran.' I step forward slowly keeping my voice low. 'I just want five minutes of your time.'

'I don't know anything about what is happening. I am scared for myself and my child.'

'I know. So am I. My little girl has been missing for a week. I just want her home safely. Please talk to me. I just want to ask you some questions.'

'But I speak to police already. I don't know where she is. I am so ashamed that my family is being under investigation. We are good people.'

'I know you are, Simran. I know you would never do anything to hurt a child. You're a mother; you must understand how desperate I am. Just five minutes and then I'll leave. I promise.'

Simran opens the door a fraction more and peers out at Danny.

'Just me. Danny is going to wait out here.'

'OK.' Simran takes a weary step back and lets me pass before slamming the door shut and dashing up the stairs to check on her sleeping child.

I can't explain why, but a burst of adrenaline starts to flood around my body. Looking down at my hands I can see they are shaking and I follow her upstairs to the flat.

Once up there I see that the police have ransacked everything. Her life has been literally turned upside down and for a second I am glad. Now she knows how I feel. Then I stop myself and remember she is not responsible for Hope's disappearance.

Simran returns from what I presume is her daughter's bedroom and gives a nod of satisfaction. The child is still asleep.

'I promise I won't be long and I'm not here to cause any trouble.'

'I don't know what you want me to say. I can't believe that Amit would do anything to hurt your little girl. He is so good with children. He's a decent man. I would know if he wasn't.'

'But what about the shoe?'

'Anyone could have put that there.'

'OK. That's a fair point, but what about his past?'

Simran fixes me with her dark brown eyes. She is a very attractive woman and the red bindi on her forehead suits her.

'His criminal record. You can't ignore that.'

'I am not going to. That is our private business.'

'Simran,' I move over to the sofa and perch beside her. 'Did you know about it before?'

'It is private. I don't want to talk about it with you.'

'I need to know. Anything that might help us find Hope. Surely if he's innocent you want to help find the person who is really responsible. Anything you know could help. Please.'

'Amit is not a pervert. That is all I am going to say.'

'Simran, my little girl is missing. I don't know if she is dead or alive. Your husband has been taken to the police station and arrested. This is not going to disappear. Why won't you help me?'

Simran adjusts her turquoise sari and looks down at her hands.

'I was that girl.'

'Pardon? Sorry, I don't understand.'

'I was the young girl Amit was accused of raping.'

'He raped you?' I sit back, speechless.

'No. Never. He is a good man. I was fifteen when I met him and he was thirty-two. We were in love. My parents didn't approve. They wanted me to marry someone from a better family, so when they discovered us they reported us to the police.'

Suddenly everything I thought I understood crumbles in front of me.

'He was not going to prison but they put his name on that list. Then when I was eighteen we left London and moved to Luton where we were married. I do not talk to my family since I left home. I chose Amit.' Her Indian accent is warm.

'Did you tell the police?'

'Yes, but then they find the shoe,' she shrugs, 'and now they don't want to listen to us.'

From the other room comes the sound of the baby waking up.

'I have told you all that I know. Amit would not hurt your little girl. I have my own daughter to think of. I am sorry for the pain you are feeling but I have my own family to worry about.'

'I understand.' Getting up from the sofa I extend my hand. She shakes it awkwardly. 'I'm sorry for dragging up the past. I just need to find Hope.'

Simran looks at me with pity. 'I hope you find your girl.' From her expression it is clear she thinks this will end badly. 'You and your family will be in my prayers.'

As I turn to leave a thought occurs to me.

'If Amit is innocent, then he will be released.'

'He will.' Simran says softly as she goes to attend to her baby daughter.

When I go back into the garden I find Danny pacing backwards and forwards like a caged tiger.

'Well?' He darts over to me hoping I might hold the answers to the nightmare.

'She didn't say much that was any help.'

'God damn it, Lib. Maybe I should have a go,' he starts towards the door but I grab his arm.

'Leave it. Let's go home. I'll explain everything there.'

Hope

'If you could have anything in the world right now what would you want?' I talk into the darkness hoping that Zoe is awake and will talk back.

'A pet pig.' Zoe giggles.

'I'd like a great big stick of candyfloss. The pink one you get from the fair.'

'I've never been to a fair.' Zoe sounds sad. 'My mum never takes me.'

'Well when we get out of here you can come with us. My dad is really good at the shooting and he always wins a cuddly toy. He would get one for you, I bet.'

'I'd like that.'

'He'd have to have three goes though because Gracie would be sad if she didn't get one as well. Then we could all have candyfloss. It's so yummy in my tummy.'

'I don't think I've tried it.'

'It's really fun watching them make it in the big silver bowl thing. It's like pink cotton that spins round and round and then when you tear a bit off it gets all sticky on your fingers and you have to lick them.'

I can almost taste it I am thinking about it so much. Zoe has gone silent again. I prefer it when she speaks so that I know she is there and I don't feel so scared.

'Are you there Zoe?'

'Yes.' Her voice sounds quiet and far away.

'Where are you going?'

'Nowhere. I'm stuck here with you.' She begins to sob.

'Don't cry. It will be OK.' I don't know if that's true anymore but I don't want her to be frightened and I have to be the big girl and look after her, like I do with Gracie.

'I just want to go home.'

'I know. Me too.'

I don't know what to say to make either of us feel better. Then I realise that if we can hold hands that might be good.

'Zoe, try and follow my voice. Come as close as you can and hold your arms out.'

'But I can't see anything.'

'I know but feel around for me and I'll try and find you. Keep talking and we will find each other, OK?'

'OK.' There is a little bit of light in her voice and it makes me feel better.

Fumbling in the utter darkness it's hard to tell what I am touching. It feels like wood and I follow the edge round.

'Keep talking Zoe.'

'OK.' Her voice sounds closer and I start to think this might work.

'Do you know your left and right?'

'Only if I can see my hands.' Her voice sounds closer still.

'I think you're really close now.' For the first time in ages I start to feel excited. 'Keep your hands out in front of you.'

'I am.'

Beneath my fingertips all I can feel is the smooth wood then suddenly I come across something new that feels like fabric.

Zoe screams out, a real shriek that hurts my ears.

'It's me!' I think I might burst with happiness. 'It's OK, it's just me.'

Zoe starts crying again. 'I thought it was a monster.'

'Here feel for my hand.' I stay still because I don't want to lose her again and keep my hands grabbing on to the fabric of what I think is the back of her top. 'Turn around.' I feel the fabric being pulled away from me and panic starts to set in. 'Don't let go!'

Then a small, cold hand grabs me by the wrist and I know we are finally facing each other. We pull each other close and hug for a long time.

'I'm so glad I found you.' I tell Zoe, wanting to cry. It's difficult being brave all the time. 'Let's sit down together and not let go, OK?'

'OK.'

Gripping her hand in mine we lower ourselves back down again and sit in silence wondering what to do next.

'I was thinking you could come and live with me when we get out of here. I'm sure my mum wouldn't mind. You could sleep in the bedroom with Gracie and me. It would be fun. You could be our sister.'

'I'd like that.' Zoe squeezes my hand tightly.

'Then you could have a proper dad too.'

'But we need to get out of here first.'

'I know. Can you remember how you got here?'

'No, nothing.'

'But if we got in then we must be able to get out. There has to be a door somewhere.'

'But we can't see.'

'Then we will just have to feel our way like we did to find each other.'

'I'm tired.'

'And me.' I let out a sigh. 'OK, well, let's rest for a little bit and then we'll look for a door.'

'I really want to go to sleep.'

'So do I but we mustn't let go of holding hands.'

'I won't.'

'Neither will I.' It feels so good to have a person close to me who I can touch, even if I can't see her face and I don't know what she looks like. 'Well, we can have a rest and then we'll start looking.' The relief of having Zoe near makes me feel so exhausted my eyelids are really heavy.

'I've got a ribbon in my hair.' Zoe tells me. 'We could tie our hands together, like a dog lead.'

'That's a really good idea.' I'm impressed. 'Take it out and I'll tie it around our wrists.'

'Good, because I'm not very good at doing knots.'

'That's OK. I'm really good at them. I can tie my own shoe laces.'

'Even in the dark?'

'Well, I haven't tried before but doing a knot in the dark is probably OK. Let me try.'

I feel the silky ribbon between my fingers and wonder what colour it is as I wrap and fasten it around my wrist.

'It's not very long but I think there is enough to tie us together. Give me your hand.' She does and I fumble about securing it. 'Now give it a tug and see if it comes undone.' We both pull at the same time and the ribbon holds firm. 'There.' It's the first time I've felt satisfied since I ended up in this place. 'Right, now let's go to sleep.'

'OK. Good night.' Zoe giggles.

'Sweet dreams. See you in the morning.' I laugh. 'That's what my mum always says.' And all over again I start to feel sad.

Libby

'I'm afraid they have had to let him go.' Kerry can't meet my eye. 'There was no physical evidence that tied him to the shoe. I'm sorry.'

'So we're back to square one.' I put my head in my hands.

'Not exactly. We have the shoe.' Kerry is good at sounding positive even in the direst of situations.

'But you said the shoe can't prove anything.' Danny's voice is hoarse. He is so exhausted.

'It proves that someone put the shoe in that bin. Those bins are taken once a week and the shoe was discovered on top of the rest of the rubbish,'

'Meaning someone put it there recently,' I interrupt, looking up.

'Exactly.' She smiles. 'If Mr Chadrad was not responsible for placing the shoe in the bin then it must be someone else who is local.'

'Maybe someone tried to frame him.' I look over a Danny who is staring out of the living room window at the rain.

'That is a possibility.'

'So the person who took Hope is trying to throw us off the scent?'

'Anything is possible.'

'But now we're back to just sitting on our arses waiting for any more news.'

'I know how difficult this must be.' Kerry turns to Danny.

'Do you? Do you have children, Kerry? Do you know what this is actually like?'

Kerry blushes and shakes her head. She looks ashamed.

'Well then, please don't pretend you understand because you don't.' He is finding it increasingly difficult to control his reactions, particularly his temper.

'We're all just so tired.' I try to explain my husband's behaviour. 'The longer this goes on the harder it is to keep believing that she is going to be all right.' Danny glares at me before walking out of the room.

'Shall I make us a cup of tea?' Kerry offers, trying to busy herself.

'I don't want any, thanks. I've had enough tea to last me a lifetime.' I do my best to smile at her. She is only trying to help. 'Make yourself one, though.' I wave her off into the kitchen and sit back, alone with my thoughts.

When Kerry returns, holding a mug of steaming tea, I decide I want to know more about the woman who is so involved in our lives.

'How long have you worked for the police?' I ask her as she sits down and wraps her hands around the mug.

'Six years as a family liaison officer but I was a sergeant before that.'

'Do you like your job?' I can't imagine doing what she does, day in and day out.

'I do.' She looks at me thoughtfully. 'It's not always easy but I know that I have an important role to play. Relatives need a friendly face to turn to in times of stress. I like to think I am easy to talk to.'

'You are.' I smile at her.

'Thank you.' She sips the tea.

'Have you been on a case like this before?'

'There was one a few years back that was similar. A child abduction.' She straightens in her chair and I can see that she would rather not talk about it, but I press her anyway.

'What happened?' I lean forward.

'A young boy disappeared from his home. His mother called in, frantic and worried sick. His rucksack was missing, as were some of his things. The mother was worried he had run away to visit his father, who'd left the family six months earlier. We sent a car round to interview the father but he wasn't there. Turns out a neighbour had seen the man with his son getting into a car with a lot of luggage. The father was originally from Turkey, you see. So we contacted the airports and put out a description of the boy and his father.'

'Then what happened?'

'We were too late. The father had boarded a plane with the child at Stansted Airport and they were on their way to Ankara.'

'Could he do that?'

'Legally, he should have consulted the mother but practically, as you can see, it was hard to stop him. The mother was beside herself, as you can imagine.'

'Did she get her son back?'

'The case was passed on to Interpol and a legal battle started.'

Sitting back in my chair I wonder what became of that child. 'It's very different to what we are going through. Have you never had a case like this before?'

'No I haven't. It is not a common occurrence for children to be taken by strangers.'

'But what if it isn't a stranger? Like Amit. What if it is someone she knew?'

'That is possible, but until we have any evidence to back that up we are working under the assumption that the abductor is a stranger.'

'But you must be looking into people we know?'

'I can't share that information with you.' She shifts awkwardly before taking another sip to buy herself some time. 'There are a few avenues that are being explored.'

'Like what?' This is news to me. She knows something but isn't saying. 'What do you know?'

'We are examining the possibility that this case might be linked to another abduction.' The words hit me like a bombshell.

'You mean another child has been taken?' I feel as if I might pass out.

'Not exactly. There is a cold case we are looking into.'

'I have a right to know what is going on.'

'Until my inspector has confirmed anything I am not at liberty to say.' Kerry speaks in a half whisper; clearly worried that Danny will storm into the room demanding answers. 'I promise the moment I hear anything you will be the first to know.'

OCTOBER 2013

Libby

'Fine.' I hang up the phone.

'They won't give the shoe back no matter what I say.' I turn to Danny who is sitting on the sofa with his head in his hands.

It only takes a second for him to pick up a small vase that was a wedding present and hurl it at the wall.

'What was that for?' My eyes scan over the pieces of smashed porcelain that litter the floor.

'I just feel so fucking useless.'

Out of the corner of my eye I catch sight of a cobweb high up in the corner of the room.

I know the eight-legged freaks are waiting for me in their webs hoping to ensnare me. I've feared them ever since I was a small child. There is something unnatural about the way they move and the fact that they suck the blood out of their prey. What sort of creature keeps its victim alive for so long while slowly eating it?

The police have been keeping a close eye on Amit for weeks now. All our friends and neighbours have been investigated. But nothing showed up. It is as if she has just disappeared into thin air.

Kerry and Inspector King had – after much stalling – sat Danny and me down and confirmed that they were looking into another case from last year, involving a little girl who disappeared from her home. We were told that there were some similarities and at the time of the other child's disappearance there had been no suspect.

As the weeks passed the police investigation tailed off. The number of officers on the case was whittled down and Kerry was reassigned. It was as if life for everyone else went back to normal. But we're in limbo, lost without our little girl.

Gracie returned home and Danny and I did our best to remain buoyant for her sake. Still she asked daily where her big sister was. We decided to tell her that Hope had gone on holiday but she would be back soon. It was the best we could come up with.

At the nursery I received pitying looks from the other mothers when I dropped Gracie off. They stopped talking to me and avoided my company. I didn't blame them. They didn't know what to say to me. I felt like a leper shut out of normal society.

'Will you be having a birthday party for Grace?' One of the mothers asked me three days ago.

'We are going to keep it a small family affair.' I felt myself blushing, knowing I was depriving my youngest daughter. 'It's a difficult time for us at the moment.'

Hayley, an attractive woman with long blonde hair who was always neatly turned out, offered me an understanding look.

'Bless.' The word annoyed me but I didn't have time to react because she had already turned to go and talk to another mother who ran the PTA.

Danny became obsessed with his search for Hope. He could not focus on anything else. He spent hours on the phone and on his computer, trying to drum up interest to keep the case alive. He refused to give up.

So I did the only thing that I could and put all my energy into making sure Gracie was happy. I owed it to her to make sure her life wasn't ruined too.

As the autumn came round I began to gradually get used to life without Hope. I missed her desperately and I still wanted her back at home, but I stopped expecting to see her sleeping when I went into the bedroom. Despite that, she remained everywhere. Her toys and her clothes were a constant reminder that there was a huge piece of the puzzle missing from our lives.

I avoided going past Hope's school. I couldn't bear the idea that other kids were playing happily in the playground and learning new things when I didn't know where she was or what had happened to her.

Her friend's parents gave us a wide berth, which, although it initially hurt, actually it was a blessing in disguise. I had to be brave for Gracie.

After a while even the press lost interest in us. Half of me was grateful that they weren't around but Danny said it meant no one cared anymore and the idea of that was awful.

The strangest thing about that time was how life had to go on. The house still needed vacuuming, the shopping needed to be done, the ironing refused to be ignored, the bills still needed paying and we had to get out of bed. Daily tasks had to be performed – just like they always had – and the world kept on turning. But everything was different.

I learnt that the village had boycotted Amit's shop. People were still suspicious. The Chadrads were ostracised, having once been at the heart of the community. Kids spray-painted the word 'pervert' and 'paedo' on the walls and windows of the shop. Despite Amit's best efforts to clean it, faint red lettering still remained. He had been branded and nothing he could do would change that.

I couldn't decide how I felt about him. After speaking to Simran I started to doubt his connection but I couldn't shake the feeling that he was somehow involved. I understood it was ludicrous to think that the person who had taken Hope would be so careless as to dispose of her shoe in their own bin. Never the less, someone had put it there and perhaps that someone was counting on the refuse collection guys not noticing it.

The silly thing was that I wanted the shoe back. It was part of Hope and I wanted to be able to hold it but the police refused to pass it over. It was bagged as evidence and shoved into a box somewhere. The thought of that nearly killed me. How could something so precious be locked away?

On that Friday morning I went into the office to wake Danny, who had fallen asleep at the desk having worked too late and drunk too much whisky.

'Just go up to bed for a bit.' I placed the coffee down beside him. 'I'm going to take Gracie to the swings for a while. Get some sleep. This will help you to sober up.'

'I'm not drunk.' He wiped his mouth with the back of his hand and took a large gulp of coffee. 'Stop giving me a hard time.'

'You're like a bear with a sore head. Just go to bed. I'll see you later.' As I left the room I heard him cursing under his breath.

In the sitting room Gracie was watching cartoons and shoving a banana into her mouth.

'Finish your breakfast and then we'll go to the playground.'

'Yes!' Gracie squeaked with her mouth full. I smiled at my youngest child and tried not to wish it were Hope who was smiling back at me.

'Mummy's going to have her coffee and then we'll get ready, OK?'

'OK, Mama.' Gracie's eyes are back glued to bright flashing images on the TV.

Once in the kitchen I go over to the calendar and picked up a black marker pen. I put a large cross over the day's date. It had been exactly twelve weeks since we last saw Hope. In some ways those weeks had gone by painfully slowly; in others they had passed in a flash.

I couldn't believe I had missed twelve weeks of her life already. How much had she grown? Had she changed in other ways? Perhaps she'd lost another tooth. The thought of not knowing was unbearable.

Walking over to the doorframe I stroked the spot on the wood where we had marked her last measurement with a pencil. It seemed as if she was still here but she wasn't. Choking back the tears I sat down at the kitchen table. I felt utterly alone. I'd lost Hope and now I was losing Danny.

We stopped communicating some time ago. We merely co-existed in the same space. He was a stranger to me when he drank and his drinking had become a real problem. In some ways it was worse for him. He blamed himself for not protecting her the way a father should.

I didn't blame him, but that made no difference to how he felt. As the man of the house he'd seen it as his duty to look after us all and he believed he'd failed. Danny couldn't get over the idea that he might have been sitting in the pub having a beer with a friend when Hope was taken. The irony was that in order to escape that guilt he dived into a bottle looking for answers.

Luckily Gracie was still young enough not to really understand what was happening when her father was drunk but she became wary of him when he stumbled out of the office to help himself to another beer or a whisky.

Dr Vogler came and visited Danny at my request. I ushered him into the living room and offered him a cup of tea. He sat with a stiff back and politely declined.

'Please tell me what I can do, Libby.' His kind hazel eyes peered through his glasses.

'I'm at my wits end. He's drunk all the time. It's scaring Gracie.'

The doctor sat back and rubbed his chin for a moment.

'What would you like me to do?'

'I don't know. Talk to him. I think he needs help.'

'You cannot force an addict to accept help if they don't want it.'

'I know, but maybe,' I let out a long sigh, 'maybe he needs some medication.'

'To stop the drinking?'

'No, to help him deal with what's happening. Something to help him sleep so he doesn't have to get quite so drunk. And he's depressed. I mean, of course he is. He blames himself.'

Marcus nodded and leant forward. 'And how are you?'

'I don't know.' I shrugged, not knowing how to answer the question. 'I'm alive. That's all I can tell you.'

'I cannot imagine what you and your husband must be going through.' Marcus' eyes brimmed with tears. 'It is the worst thing that could ever happen to a family. I am so, so sorry for you all.'

'It's not knowing.' Looking down at the cuff of my blue jumper I picked at a small hole. Marcus nodded and composed himself.

'Right. I will have a word with Danny. I'm sure we can give him something to help in the short term.' He got up from the sofa and straightened his brown trousers. 'I would also suggest that you consider taking a low dose of an antidepressant. Just to get you through day to day.'

'If you think it will help.' I got up and faced him.

'I think you all need as much help as you can get at the moment.'

I managed a small smile and took his hand, shaking it. 'Thank you.'

'I'll have a prescription waiting for you this afternoon. In the meantime, get Danny to make an appointment.'

'I'll do my best.'

NOVEMBER 2013

Libby

There is a buzz about Christmas in the air. In the shops and on the television, it seems to be the only thing people think about; it's not like that for me. We have to face our first Christmas without Hope. I don't want to celebrate. I dread the idea of not watching her open her stocking on Christmas morning. But we have to keep going for Gracie. She shouldn't have to suffer any more than she already has. Every time I am reminded of the impending festivities I do my best to find a distraction. Christmas very quickly becomes a dirty word in our house.

After talking to Dr Vogler, Danny decided to tackle his growing issue with drink. We sat down and talked it through and came to the conclusion that he needed some time away to get his head in order. So at the beginning of November Danny packed a bag and went to stay with his friend in Scotland for a week.

Simon Perry, who had been best man at our wedding, lives in Edinburgh with his girlfriend. He's a stage actor who writes plays to subsidise his income. He was at school with Danny and the pair have been great friends ever since. They don't see each other as much as they would like – living at opposite ends of the UK doesn't help – but they get together when they can and each knows they can rely on the other.

I used to be slightly envious of their friendship. I don't have any old friends from my childhood. Most of my friendships fizzled out since I'm not very good at keeping in touch or making the effort. There are a few people from my past I wish I still had in my life but too much time has gone by.

Life is funny like that. People who you think you will remain friends with sometimes just fall by the wayside. Your lives take different directions, someone gets married to a person you don't particularly like, careers take off and suddenly you realise you don't have anything in common any more. I could have done with more friends around me especially since my family were no real use.

Thankfully Danny's parents are wonderful. They come up once a week and take Gracie out for the day. I think it helps them to be near us. They were understandably nervous that they might be left out of any developments and I think they had decided that helping gave them more of a role, as if they needed one, and therefore more control.

Apart from family members, people have stopped mentioning Hope. Everyone knows that the case has all but been closed and there is no news. Everything has changed for us but for everyone on the outside, their lives have remained the same. Apart from Amit and Simran, who have been forced to close the shop after it was boycotted by the locals, everybody else seems to go about their normal business as if nothing has changed. I suppose for them it hasn't. A little girl has gone missing, nothing more.

One day it was news but now, months later, it is a distant memory. No one likes the fact the case remained unsolved and it probably scares them to think that the person responsible is still wandering around. If it makes them feel uncomfortable, you can imagine how I feel.

Every day is like living a bad dream. At some point – it happened gradually, I think – the bad dream stopped seeming so foreign and became typical. The ache in the pit of my stomach is always there and has become a part of me. It guides my decisions and influences the way I live my life.

The moment Gracie is out of sight I become a nervous wreck. In the end, after much deliberation, I decided I couldn't stand sending her to nursery any more so pulled her out. Not wanting her to miss out on the important social interactions I have found groups that we could go to together in Cambridge. There are weekly mother and child exercise classes, which I hate, but Gracie enjoys.

It is good being away from the village. It had started to feel claustrophobic, being there surrounded by familiar faces who all know the ins and outs of our plight. In Cambridge we can blend into the background. I didn't know any of the mothers in the groups and they didn't know me. I even used a different name when I joined, just to avoid any awkward questions.

Our pictures and Hope's were everywhere, so it's likely we are recognised but because they don't know for sure, people feel less entitled to approach us and ask. No one with an ounce of common sense would approach a stranger and ask 'Are you the mother of that missing girl?'

Occasionally I'm aware of looks from other parents. Some are filled with pity, others curiosity.

But on that cold wet Thursday morning I realised I wasn't hidden at all.

Danny, an avid newspaper reader even before Hope was taken, always had the newspaper delivered to our house in the morning. Since she had disappeared he made sure he got a copy of every paper delivered to the house. He would retrieve the post, make himself some toast and coffee and then go into the office, with the paper, to comb through the pages looking for any mention of her.

That week was different. He wasn't there to collect his papers. On that morning I picked the papers from the doormat and glanced at the front page of the tabloid on the top of the pile. To my horror, there was a picture of Danny walking along a street, with his arm around another woman.

DESPERATE DAN LEAVES LIB IN THE LURCH

Cursing and dropping the paper I dash up the stairs past Gracie, who is munching on an apple while rolling out some Play-Doh, to get my mobile.

Shaking slightly, I ring Danny.

'Hello.' He sounds groggy and I realise it is well before eight o'clock.

'What the fuck do you think you're playing at?'

'Lib?' I can hear the sleep in his voice.

'Have you seen the papers this morning?'

'No. I've just woken up. What's wrong?'

'You. You're what's wrong.'

'Look. Calm the fuck down and tell me what's going on.' He is not happy to have been woken up like this.

'*The Mirror.* There's a picture of you on the front page.'

'Doing what?'

'With your arm around bloody Lara!'

'What?' he sounds more awake now.

'They are making out you're having an affair. Suggesting you've left me.'

'But I haven't.'

'I know that!' I yell down the phone. 'But they don't.'

'Who cares what they think. It's libel. We can get them to retract the story. They'll have to apologise.' I can hear the cogs in his mind turning.

'That's not the point,' I growl.

'I'm sorry, Lib, but I don't know why you're quite so upset about this. It's just a bullshit tabloid story.'

'But it makes us look as if we don't care about her any more. If people think we've given up looking–' I crumple onto the bed, unable to continue.

'Lib?'

'Yes.'

'I'm coming home. Enough is enough.'

Hope

'Zoe, are you awake?' I shake her arm gently because I don't like the silence but she doesn't answer. 'Zoe? Come on.'

I hear a long sigh and feel so relieved. For a moment I thought maybe she was dead and the thought of being trapped in the dark with a dead person really scared me.

'Hope.' She speaks in a half whisper and I worry that she isn't very well.

'It's OK. I'm here.' I try to soothe her the way my mum would if she was here.

'I can't stay here anymore.' Zoe's voice is faint.

'We have to. Just a little while longer and then someone will find us and get us out.'

'I don't think anyone is coming.' She sounds too sad to even cry.

'They will. I know they will.' I have to believe that. I have to. 'Someone will find us. You'll see.'

We sit in the pitch-black silence for a while lost in our own thoughts. I know Zoe is not very happy at the moment and I try really hard not to let it rub off on me. We need to stay happy. That's what mum would say. And I'm trying, I really am but it just feels like we have been in here for so long. Because we can't see anything it's hard to tell what the world is like outside. I don't know if it's summer or winter. There is no time in this place. We might have been here for a few days or a few years. I can't tell and that is what

117

scares me the most. We are so hidden, wherever we are, that maybe Zoe is right and we will never be found.

I remember once sneaking onto the landing when Mum and Dad were watching a film about a man who had been buried alive. It was naughty because I should have been in bed asleep but it was hot so I crept out to see what my parents were doing. I watched the film without them knowing. It was really bad. This man was buried in a coffin, in the desert, with only a lighter and a mobile phone. He kept trying to get help but no one knew where to find him. A bit like Zoe and me.

Then I start to wonder where we are again. Since I can't see anything it's hard to tell. There is a smell in here and I keep trying to work out what it is but I can't put my finger on it. It smells a bit like mushrooms. I hate mushrooms.

I remember going for a walk in the woods near our house, with mum and dad and Gracie, and in the woods an old tree had fallen over and on it was this large mushroom thingy. It looked like a bit like an alien. It was sort of grey-brown and fat like a football with curly edges. Dad and me went near to it to smell it. It smells like rotten wood and mud and Dad said that's because that's what it grows from. And that gets me thinking that maybe we are in the mud somewhere. A bit like that man in that film, stuck underground. I don't like thinking about it but if I can work out where I am then maybe I can get us out of this place.

'Zoe?' I whisper her name in case she is asleep. She doesn't respond so I unhook my arm from hers and turn in the darkness, with my arm outstretched, trying to find the edge of our prison. Then my hand meets a damp rough surface and I want to move away but I know I have to be brave.

I feel the wall, or whatever it is, for a while trying to find a space I can get my fingers into so that I can dig. When I watched that film I remember thinking he should have dug himself out and I decide that maybe I can do that now. All I need to do is find a gap to get started. I think about waking Zoe up to get her to help but she sounds poorly so I think I should let her sleep. She's giving up and I must not let that happen to me, so I will have to do this by myself.

I don't know how long I feel around the edge of this place. My fingers search the surface trying to find gap in it. I don't even know what the surface is made of but I start to think maybe it is damp wood because I keep thinking about that tree with the big mushroom fungus thing growing on it. And I know that if it is damp wood then I might be able to get through it somehow if I can just find a crumbly piece or a crack.

That is what I am going to concentrate on from now on. I'm not going to sit on the floor and wait any more. I'm going to keep going until I get us out of this place. I'm going to be brave like Princess Leia in *Star Wars*. She's really cool. She doesn't get frightened and always helps save everyone. So that's who I'm going to be and Zoe can be R2D2 if she wants.

It would be helpful if I had the force, like Luke, but it doesn't matter. I'm Princess Leia and I am smart and pretty and brave and we will beat the bad guy and get out of this dark, damp hole.

DECEMBER 2013

Libby

Danny has been back at home for over a week now. As he predicted the stupid story in the paper melted away from the spotlight. We became old news and it was a relief. Except that I wanted us and Hope to remain in the limelight. If people forget about her then the search will fizzle out. If it means Danny and I have to be smeared by the tabloid press, then so be it. I would do anything to find her and I will put up with any abuse that comes my way.

Since returning from Edinburgh Danny has been unusually quiet. He is not a loud man by any means but he seems distant and distracted, as if his mind is elsewhere. It crossed my mind, only for a second, that perhaps there had been something between him and Simon's girlfriend. But I'd met Lara, a nice woman who is a vet, and I knew that was very unlikely. None the less, something is preying on his mind. I probe him a few times, trying to get him to open up but it is useless. His shutters have come down and I am left alone on the outside.

Bothered by his change of mood I do the only thing I can, which is to shut up until he is ready to talk. No amount of bugging him will get me anywhere. He is a stubborn man and the harder I press the more likely he is to retreat into his shell. It frustrates me beyond belief but I have no choice in the matter.

As before, I throw myself into focusing on Gracie. She is wetting the bed almost every night, something she's not done since she was two. It is obvious that the atmosphere in the house is taking its toll on her. Poor little thing doesn't understand why Mummy and Daddy are so stressed and sad. She's stopped mentioning Hope's name, having come to the conclusion that whenever she did it upset someone. I know she longs to have her big sister back and she can't understand why Hope isn't there. She'd ask us a lot in the early days when Hope was coming home but Danny and I couldn't answer her. We didn't know how to respond. We didn't have any answers.

This Thursday morning is no different to any other. Danny has made his coffee and toast and silently retreated to the office to work on the computer. I sit at the kitchen table with Gracie, trying in vain to get her to eat her Marmite on toast.

'Come on, girlie, you asked for it. Just eat some.' I lean across the table holding a piece of cold soggy toast out.

'No. I not hungry.' She folds her little arms and looks at me defiantly.

'Gracie, please. Just this one piece, then you can get down from the table.'

I can see her thinking about getting down and walking away – but she decides to stay seated.

'No, Mummy. I'm really full.'

'But you've only had one bite. Come on, we are going to Tumble Tots later and you will need some energy. You'll be too tired if you don't eat anything.'

She eyeballs the quarter slice of toast I am offering before shaking her head and turning away.

'Fine.' I let out a long huff. I am too tired to argue.

My nights are frequently interrupted by nightmares. I dream I can hear Hope calling me but I can't find her. In the dream, every time I think I am making progress her voice grows further and further away. Sometimes the dream is different. I see Hope on the other side of a glass wall and I bang my fists, shouting for her to come back. But she can't see or hear me and I have to watch as she gets into a strange car and is driven away. It is always one of those two dreams. The same nightmares over and over, night after night. Often I wake up in the middle of the night, dripping in sweat with tears streaming down my face. After that it is difficult to get back to sleep so I lie there in my damp sheets willing my mind to take a break and let me rest.

Gracie smiles triumphantly before hopping down off her chair and rushing into the sitting room to play on the iPad.

I clear the table, wiping the crumbs onto the floor with the palm of my hand, before loading the dishwasher. When I turn to leave the room I find Danny standing there, in the doorframe, watching me.

'You startled me.' I take a step back.

'Sorry.'

'Everything OK?'

He has that strange look again. 'Yes. I've been thinking.'

I don't know why but I don't think I am going to like what he has to say.

'I really think you should take Gracie and go and visit your parents. It would do you the world of good to get away for a few days. Gracie would love to see them.'

'You know I can't leave this house.' I fold my arms across my chest. I am terrified by the thought of not being at home if there is any news.

'But I'll be here. I'll stay here. Just go, please? For a little while. Just a few nights? I think it would really be good for you to take a step back. That time I spent with Simon did me the world of good. It really helped me to order my thoughts. I feel much better for it. You should do the same.'

'It might be good, I suppose.'

'That's the spirit. I've been looking at the train. It's really not that expensive and it will beat being stuck in the car with Gracie for six hours.'

'No. I'm sorry but I'd want the car. If something happened and I needed to get home quickly I wouldn't want to have to wait for a train. If I'm going, I'll drive. Gracie will be OK. I'll stop every few hours and remember to take that fucking nursery rhymes CD.'

'OK. If that's what you want. You should call your folks and arrange when you are going to go down there.'

'If only they weren't in bloody Cornwall. It's such a long way.'

'It could be worse. They could live in Australia.'

'That's true.' I run my hands through my hair, brushing out the tangles. 'I'll call mum in a bit.'

'Try and see if you can go soon. No point delaying it.'

'Why do I feel like you are trying to get rid of me?' I'm half joking because really I get the feeling something is going on.

'Don't be silly.' Danny comes over and gives me a hug. 'I'll miss you both.' He kisses the top of my head. 'Just get away for a while. Let the wind from the Cornish coast blow some of those cobwebs away.'

'You're right. Thank you. I love you, you silly sod.'

'I love you too, Lib.'

'Right,' I release myself from his tight grip. 'Where's the phone?'

'That's the spirit, old girl.'

'Less of the "old" please.' I hit him on the arm gently as I pass. 'It will be great for Gracie. She'll love the beach, even if it is bloody freezing.'

'Bracing British weather.'

'I'm sick of it. I'm sick of it all.'

Before he has a chance to respond I leave to find the phone. Danny is right: the sooner I get away the better. This place is suffocating me and I feel pushed to the limits. I am sick of praying to an entity I am pretty sure doesn't exist.

Our front door is a portal to the past and every time I look at it I see Hope leaving for the last time. If only I'd stopped her, or made her wait for me to go with her. If only.

I find the phone, stuck between the cushions on the sofa and dial my parent's number.

'Hello.' My dad answers.

'Dad. Hi. How are you?'

'Can't complain Libby, can't complain. And yourself?' He speaks to me the way you might talk to a check out girl in a supermarket. It occurs to me that a normal dad, a proper dad, would assume I was calling with some news about his missing granddaughter.

'We're coping. Is Mum there?'

'No, she's out at the minute.'

'Oh. Well, I was thinking maybe Gracie and I could come and stay for a few days.' Silence greets me down the line. 'You know, we haven't seen you for a while and it would be good to get away.'

'You'd better speak to your mother about this.'

'Well I can't because she's not there, so I'm talking to you.'

'Erm, well, when did you want to come?'

'As soon as possible,' I say, wondering if that is even true.

'You'll have to share a room with Gracie. Alex is here.'

'That's fine. I'm looking forward to seeing him.'

'How are you going to get here?'

'I'll drive.'

'It's a long drive. Are you sure it's worth it just for a few days?'

'Maybe we'll stay a week. I don't know, Dad, I just need to get away.'

'Well if you're sure. I'll tell your mother to make up the spare room.'

'Thank you. We'll set off tomorrow morning.'

'Then we'll expect you for dinner?'

'If that isn't too much trouble.'

'Your mother won't be pleased. You know she likes to have notice about this sort of thing.'

'Perhaps you could remind her that I am her daughter and my child is missing and I need to be around my family.' Silence again. 'Well?'

'Of course.' Now he sounds like a brisk office worker. Did this man really father me?

'Thank you. Tell Mum not to worry about supper. I'll stop and get fish and chips on the way.'

'Good thinking.' His relief is tangible. All he ever worries about is Mum.

'See you tomorrow then.'

'See you then.' The line goes dead. Why am I going there? Did I think my parents had suddenly undergone a personality change because Hope was missing? The disappointment tried to get its grip on me but I wasn't going to let it. I did need a change of scene and it would be good for Gracie to see her other grandparents and there was always Alex. Seeing him would do me the world of good. I needed to let off some steam and catching up with my brother would be just the ticket.

'All set then?' Danny appears behind me.

'Yes. That was Dad. Charming as ever. Didn't even mention Hope.' I feel a flurry of rage bubbling up inside.

'Don't get cross. They just aren't very good at expressing themselves. They love you.'

'Do they?' I turn to look at Gracie who is playing with a doll and attempting to brush its hair. 'We are going to see Grandpop and GG. That will be nice won't it?'

Gracie shrugs and returns to playing her game.

'It'll do you good.' Danny puts his hand on my shoulder and gives an encouraging squeeze.

'I don't know why I'm going.' I feel miserable again.

'Because you need a break, Lib.' Danny puts his arms around me and pulls me close to him.

'They are so stunted. I'm not sure that being around emotionally retarded people is the answer.'

'Alex isn't like that, though, and I think you'd like to see him, wouldn't you?'

'True.' I rest my forehead on Danny's chest and realise just how exhausted I am. 'I don't know how much more I can take of this.'

'That's exactly why you need to go.' His persistence is beginning to bother me.

'Why are you so keen that I go and spend time with my parents? You don't even like them.'

'Don't start this.' He sighs and takes a step back. 'Just go. For Gracie's sake if not your own. We can't keep leaning on my parents.'

'You're right. I'm sorry.'

Libby

By the next morning we are packed and ready to go. Despite it being a long drive I only plan to stay for three or four nights. Any longer than that and I will likely kill my parents or myself.

My relationship with them has always been rocky. Despite doing OK at school and never getting into any very serious trouble, I always felt like a disappointment. What didn't help is that when I was born I was a twin. My sister was stillborn and it destroyed my mother, which meant she really struggled to bond with me. I was a constant reminder of her dead child.

As a teenager I didn't have much sympathy. I resented them for not loving me enough. When Alex was born that all changed. He came bounding into the world a happy little chap and both my parents instantly fell in love with him. He was their golden boy and I felt like the black sheep who sometimes wondered if it would have been better if I'd died as well as my twin.

It was strange growing up knowing that I shared a womb with a person who I would never meet. Sometimes at night, when I was young, I'd dream that I'd meet her and we would chat for hours. In my dream she was lovely and perfect and it was just the two of us. Then I'd wake up and feel lonely and sad.

The dreams stopped when I became a teenager. I miss not having my sister in my life any longer.

Birthdays were the worst. What should have been time spent laughing and opening presents was all swept under the carpet. They didn't abuse me, or anything like that but they just couldn't celebrate. I didn't have parties like other children because it would have been too difficult for my parents. I grew up knowing that, but it didn't stop me wishing I could be like the other kids. Then of course Alex arrived and there was a transformation in the way my folks behaved. We celebrated his birthday and they were natural parents to him from the moment he was born.

Part of me wanted to hate him. Sometimes I did. But as I grew up I learnt that it was pointless blaming him. He didn't ask to be born. He didn't want our sister to die and he was not responsible for the way our parents behaved.

Then when I was old enough to leave and go to university things changed. I got away from the people who didn't want me and made me feel bad about myself. As an adult I came to understand how difficult it must have been for them. Only after I had my own children did I appreciate how painful losing a child might be. Then Hope disappeared and suddenly I was in their shoes, wishing to God that I wasn't.

But there was a difference. They had a grave to visit. They knew what had happened to my sister. I didn't have that luxury with my situation. My little family unit was stuck in limbo.

Suddenly, sitting on the bed looking at my packed bag, I have a strong desire to cancel the trip. It isn't because I am trying to avoid my parents but something feels wrong. Leaving the house and Danny by himself makes me feel uneasy. I should stay in case she comes home. What if she came home and discovered I'd gone on holiday to Cornwall with Gracie? How would that make her feel?

Just as I am about to go downstairs and tell Danny that I've changed my mind, he appears in the doorway holding a mug of coffee for me. 'Here you go.'

'Thanks.' I get up off the bed and accept the mug.

'All packed?'

'Yes, but–'

'No, Lib. No buts. Just go. Please.'

I want to stay. I want to share my doubts. I want to be near Hope's belongings. But I don't want to argue to with Danny so I nod meekly and sip the coffee.

'OK.'

'Good. Gracie is downstairs. She's packed herself some things in her Peppa Pig bag. I can only imagine what sort of stuff she's put in there.'

'Oh, it's fine. Let her take it. No real harm.'

Danny cocks his head slightly. 'Are you OK?'

'No. Not really and, honestly, I wonder if anything will ever be OK again.'

'Come here.' He opens his arms and comforts me. 'We'll get through this. I am going to make sure we get her back.'

'How? We're doing everything we can. It's hopeless.'

'No, it's not. Just leave it to me. We will find Hope. I promise you.'

I don't understand where his newfound belief has sprung from but I am too tired to press him on it. I have a long drive ahead of me. 'I suppose we'd better get going.'

'That's my girl.' Danny brushes the hair away from my face and plants a small kiss on my lips. It is the most intimate thing we have done since Hope was taken. Neither of us can bring ourselves to have sex.

'I'll see you in a few days then. Please call if—' I can't finish the sentence. 'You have the house number as well? And Alex's mobile number?'

'Yes, yes. Don't worry. Go and try to have a nice time.'

Danny stands in the driveway waving us off as the car pulls away and I watch our cottage get smaller in the rear view mirror. There is something that is bothering me. I have a knot in my stomach and the feeling that something isn't right. But, forcing myself to ignore my instincts, I put my foot on the accelerator and head out of the village making sure I keep my eyes on the road and don't let them glance in the direction of Amit and Simran's shop.

As we join the trail of morning traffic on the M11 I start to relax. Gracie is happily singing a song from Disney's *Frozen* to herself in the back while we crawl slowly through the low-lying grey fog that smothers the south Cambridgeshire countryside.

'Will they have snow where we are going, Mummy?'

'No sweetie. I don't think so.'

'But I want to make a snowman like Olaf.' She is genuinely disgruntled that she is not going to be building her own Disney character any time soon.

'Maybe it will snow soon. I don't know.'

'Well I want it to be like *Frozen*.'

'Come on, girlie, we are going to have a lovely time. Don't be cross.'

'But I want to be like Anna.'

'You are, Gracie. You're just like Anna.' I don't understand where all this is coming from.

'No I'm not. I don't have a sister anymore.'

Those seven words stop me in my tracks and for a moment I forget that I am driving a car through thick fog.

132

Just before we plough into the back of a lorry I come to my senses and get a grip of myself, remembering to brake just in time.

'Don't speak like that.' My heart is in my throat and I wish we weren't stuck on a motorway.

'But it's true. Hope has gone and she isn't going to come back now.'

'Gracie, please.' I don't know what to say to her. 'This isn't the time for that talk now. When we stop the car we'll have a talk about Hope, OK?'

In the mirror I see her nod in silent agreement and decide the only thing to do is turn the radio on to drown out the tension.

This is not how I thought my morning would go.

Danny

As I wave them off, a calm washes over me. Most of the morning I've been jittery but as I watch our car disappear into the distance, I know what I have to do.

I get my bag that I've left hidden in the cupboard under the stairs, and stand looking around our messy living room for a moment. The house is so quiet without Lib and Gracie. Putting the bag down on the floor I leap up the stairs to the landing before dashing into the kids' bedroom. I don't like to go in there very often. It is too difficult being surrounded by Hope's things, although I understand it is a comfort to Lib. Sitting down on Hope's bed I pick up her pillow and hold it for a moment. It still smells faintly of her.

Laying the pillow back down I smooth the case with my hand, not liking that the fabric feels cold.

'I'm going to bring you home, monkey. I promise.' Speaking to the empty room doesn't seem strange, more cathartic.

Then I leave the room, make my way back downstairs, haul my bag on to my shoulder and pull the front door closed behind me. Checking my phone I see that it is nearly 11am – time for me to go and catch the bus into Cambridge. Phase one of my plan is underway.

Hope

'Zoe please talk to me. Say something.' I can't find her anywhere and I am beginning to panic.

'I'm sorry I let go but I was trying to find a way out of here. Please say something. We can find each other again. We did it before.'

Nothing. Not a sound. Even if she was asleep she can't be now. I've been shouting loudly.

This space that we are trapped in feels as if it is getting smaller all the time. It smells so horrid. I try not to think about what I might be stepping or sitting in.

The thing about this place that I still don't understand is where the door is. It's like a nightmare game of hide and seek where I have to feel about in the blackness looking for my friend.

Once I saw a program on the TV that mum and dad were watching where this woman was put in a box with loads of worms and snakes and insects and she had to feel about looking for plastic stars so that her friends in the jungle could eat some food. And the cameras taped her. It feels a bit like doing that. But what I don't understand is that someone is making me do this. Someone put me in here when I didn't ask to be. The person on the TV walked into the box by herself. I remember thinking that was really weird.

But I don't want to think about that now because if I remember all the creepy crawlies I saw on the TV, I might start to imagine that they are in here and then I'd be too scared to move, even though I know I have to because I want to find Zoe.

By now I am pretty sure we have been here for a long time. Even though there is no sense of time I can tell that my hair has grown because I think it feels longer than it used to before when I was at home. And my toenails feel long too.

'Come on Zoe!' Suddenly I feel angry. I'm so sick of this place. All along I've been brave and trying to find a way out but Zoe has given up. She's not even talking now. 'Don't sulk. Just get up and help me.'

Silence.

Then I hear a screeching noise all around me. It makes my teeth ache and I put my hands up over my ears. I can feel it vibrating through the floor and I hug myself into a tight ball, worried that the walls of my prison might be about to fall down. Suddenly the shaking stops and I can't feel the sound any more so I take my hands away.

'Zoe,' I whisper frantically, 'did you hear it? Zoe?' Still not a sound from my friend.

'She's gone.' A scratchy voice echoes around the room. 'It's just you now.'

I'm so terrified I wet myself. The urine running down the inside of my leg is warm and stings my bottom.

'Please,' I sob, not knowing where to direct my words, 'please bring her back.'

'She's gone.' The voice sounds angry this time and I huddle, making myself as small as possible.

'It's just you now.' The voice is calmer and I realise I can't tell if it's a man or a woman.

'Please let me out. I want to see my family. Please, I won't tell anyone anything.'

A chuckle explodes around the space.

'You aren't going anywhere. You will be staying here for now.'

'But why have you let Zoe go?'

'It was time for her to leave.'

'I... I don't understand.'

'No, you don't. And until you do, you will remain here.'

Then without any warning the voice is gone.

I want to call out and scream and beg for the voice to come back but I don't, because I know it is useless. The voice has gone; Zoe has gone; and my courage has gone.

Danny

The bus journey seems to take forever. The large cumbersome vehicle plods through villages pulling in at every stop to collect kids on their way to the cinema or pensioners with plans to go shopping.

The windows have a coating of condensation on them that reappears within seconds of being wiped away. I give up trying to look out at the bleak countryside in the end.

An hour later and the bus stops on Hills Road in Cambridge. I nod to the disgruntled driver and jump down into a puddle, soaking the bottom of my trousers and my socks before setting off towards Newmarket Road that lies on the eastern side of the city.

Trudging through the drizzle my heart pounds in my chest. My mind is alive with ideas. This is something I've been planning for over a week and now it is all starting to come together.

As the rain starts to come down harder I can feel the bag on my back getting heavier with the water it has absorbed. The sound of the drops hitting the pavement play like a beat on the ground and helped to sooth my frantic brain. I can't lose it. I have to remain calm and in control.

By the time I arrive at the car rental place I am soaked through. The guy behind the desk chuckles to himself at my drenched state but I am not amused. The smirk on his face quickly dissolves when I eyeball him from across the counter.

'I'm here to pick up a van.'

'Name?'

'Bird.'

'Righto.' He taps away at his keyboard searching for the relevant information. 'For a week, yes?'

'That's right.'

'A Ford Transit. For one week?'

'Yep.'

'I need to see your license.'

Removing the soggy bag off my bag I remove my papers from a zip compartment and hand them over.

'So,' the guy runs an eye over them before handing them back, 'going anywhere nice or is it business?'

'Business, I suppose.' I wish this guy would stop talking.

'Right, well, if you can sign the papers here and here,' he points with his dirty finger, 'then I'll hand over the keys.'

Twenty minutes later I am behind the wheel and making my way out of the congested city. Christmas shoppers block the roads with their cars and I have to contain my frustration with the gridlock.

After crawling through the city in the damned rain, having hit every fucking red light, I'm relieved to see the back of Cambridge.

As the van joins the motorway my pulse quickens again. This is going to be the hardest part to pull off. Thinking about it starts to make me feel a bit sick and I slow down and open the window, taking in gulps of cold fresh air to quell the nausea.

Looking over at my large damp backpack helps to steady my nerves. Everything I am going to need is in that bag. I've planned this carefully and as long as I stick to the plan then nothing will go wrong. Despite telling myself this over and over I am still nervous about the next phase. I'm just an ordinary bloke. This stuff should be reserved for the fucking SAS, but desperate times…

I know exactly what has to be done as I pull off the motorway and head through Duxford on my way home.

I need to find a suitable place to park, somewhere hidden from sight. Then I have to sit tight and stay calm. That is the most important thing, to stay calm. If I panic it could all go horribly wrong.

It makes sense for me to take the long way back to the village, so that I approach it from the other side where I will need to wait.

Winding through a quiet country lane on the outskirts of Duxford, I pass a stream where I used to take Hope to play. Although I know it's pointless I stop the van on the side of the road and get out. I want to go back to a time when we were all happy and I think that if I can spend a minute in a place where that was the case, it might give me the strength I need to continue.

Walking a few steps along the road the trees on my right hand side part and there is a clearing where the stream slopes gently down. I remember watching Hope paddle there, splashing and laughing in her turquoise swimming costume, while I splashed her and her mum sat in the shade cradling a newborn Gracie. That had been a good day; a happy day. The sun shone and after playing in the water we picnicked on the bank. I flash back to a vision of Hope eating strawberries and the red juice dripping down her chin. For some reason the thought makes me shiver, as if someone has walked over my grave.

The memory of that day should make me feel happy but it doesn't because it was so long ago and I can't think of a time in the last few months when any of us have been happy like that.

Bending down I pick up a small smooth stone and rub my thumb over it. It's icy cold, like a corpse. With sudden anger I hurl the pebble through the air watching it splash into the trickling water and sink.

'I'm coming to get you.' I look up at the grey clouds threatening yet more rain. 'I'm going to make this right.'

Getting back into the van I realise I am shaking but it's not as a result of the cold. Before starting the engine I sit staring at the bag lying on the passenger seat. The bag represents my future and now appears smaller than before.

As the van roars into life I put my foot down on the accelerator and speed away from the place that harbours those special memories. There's no point getting sentimental. I just have to get on and get the job done.

Arriving in Ickleton, via Brookhampton Street, I slow down to a crawl, searching for the ideal spot to stop and decide to park on the pavement next to the churchyard. In this position I am fairly well hidden. I leave the battery on so that I can listen to the radio. I need something to do. I could be waiting for a while.

Then I reach over and grab the bag, unfastening the straps that keep everything in place. As I unzip the top a few items come bursting out onto the passenger seat. Spotting what I was looking for I grab the baseball cap and put it on my head, pulling it low over my eyes so it shadows my face. I shove some of the other bits back into the bag, leaving only the small glass bottle and syringe on the seat.

When I turn the radio on I am greeted by Justin Bieber, singing a tuneless number. I hate that kid. Such a smug little git but I can understand why girls like him. He's clean-faced and doesn't look like much more than a boy himself. Fiddling with the dial I am determined not to let that song be what I listen to and thankfully find something altogether more tolerable on Radio One.

My phone buzzes in my pocket, alerting me to the fact that I've received a text. It's from Libby.

Just stuffing our face with McDonalds in the services on the outskirts of Bristol. Will call when we arrive at Chez Hardy xxx

I smile at myself at the thought of Gracie's little mouth covered in ketchup.

Hope she's not car sick! Have a great time and don't worry about me. Love you xxx

I need to eat and the banana in my pocket sits heavy but I just don't have an appetite. The last thing I am thinking about is food but reluctantly I remove the fruit and peel the skin. The flesh is brown, bruised and unappealing but it's the only thing I brought with me so it'll have to do. If I'm going to pull this off I am going to need to remain focused on the task at hand and not be distracted by a rumbling stomach.

After sitting in the van for nearly two hours I begin to get bored. Adrenaline kept me going to begin with, but that has long gone. I just sit there, staring out of the windscreen at the same bloody view, listening to average pop on the radio. The one positive is that it is beginning to get dark now. The darkness will help cloak what I am about to do. Glancing at my clock I see it's three-thirty. It can't be much longer now.

Fidgeting in my seat, I wish I could get out and stretch my legs but I can't just in case I miss my opportunity.

Then, a figure appears around the corner walking towards me. I have to really concentrate on the shape to be sure it is who I think it is. When the person has come ten yards closer I can clearly see who it is. I need to act quickly. Adrenaline reignites when I grab the small glass bottle off the passenger seat, turn it upside down and plunge the end of the needle into the foil cap, extracting some of the drug. Stay calm, stay calm; the mantra goes round and round in my head.

As casually as I can manage I get out of the van and walk around to the back to open the doors, then seconds later, as I am arranging the blanket on the floor, the figure appears in my peripheral vision and I leap towards the unsuspecting person, who wriggles in my grasp and ends up burning the palm of my hand with the cigarette they are smoking.

After putting the needle into their neck and releasing the drug it takes less than a minute for the body to stop fighting and start to go limp. Bearing the dead weight of the body, I manage to wrestle it into the back of the van. Panting heavily I then reach for the cable ties and bind the arms and feet together before gaffer tapping the mouth. Despite shaky hands I get this job done quickly before another person appears or a car drives past. Then I close the doors of the van, double-checking they are properly shut, before scooting round to the driver's side and getting back in. I check my side mirrors just to be sure that no one has seen us before starting the van and driving up to the house.

Leaving the engine running I dash indoors. I turn my mobile off and place it on the pillow in my bedroom, along with a letter to Lib. Then I lock the house, get back into the van and drive out of the village, heading back towards the motorway.

I feel like a criminal myself and try to push this thought out of my mind. It's a long drive up to Scotland and I can't afford to have any doubts. The easy bit is over. The rest will be the real challenge.

Libby

After a long drive I finally make it to my parents' house, on the edge of St Austell on the south coast of Cornwall. The sheets of rain come down at an angle, making it difficult to see on the narrow road that leads to my final destination.

Outside the sky is dark with night-time clouds. Coming to a stop I stare at the house, floodlit by my bright headlights. The windscreen wipers rush backwards and forwards, allowing me glimpses of the building, which hasn't changed much since I was last here.

In the back of the car Gracie sleeps soundly with her mouth wide open and her head slumped to one side.

It has been some time since I came back here and it takes me a while to pluck up the courage to go in. Something is telling me to turn around and head straight home and I've felt like that since I left this morning, but I put it down to guilt for leaving Danny, despite his insistence that I go. Finally, I step out of the car and into the harsh Cornish elements.

Pulling my coat up around my neck and mouth, I fumble about trying to unlock Gracie's seatbelt without waking her up, all the while being pelted in the face with icy rain. She does not stir as I remove her from her seat. Her head lolls immediately into a relaxed position on my shoulder.

The luggage can wait, I decide, closing the door. I turn towards the house and find Alex on the porch waiting to greet me.

'I saw your headlights,' he calls against the ripping wind.

'Hi,' I mouth, not wanting to disturb the child sleeping in my arms.

Alex, in a pair of old man slippers, shuffles towards us and takes Gracie out of my arms before planting a kiss on my cheek. For a twenty-five-year-old he has questionable taste in footwear.

'Good to see you, Sis.'

'And you,' I wipe raindrops off my forehead, 'let's get inside.'

As soon as we step into the warmth I am hit by a familiar smell; the scent of my mum's cooking mixed with the air freshener she always uses. The food smells good. The air freshener does not.

Following Alex into the sitting room I see my father sitting in his armchair flicking through the papers. He gets up and comes to give me a stilted hug. He's never been good at physical affection.

'Hi, Dad.'

'All right, girl.' He peers at me over his reading glasses. 'You made it then.'

'Looks like it.'

Alex carefully manoeuvres Gracie out of his arms and into position on the sofa before covering her with a blanket.

'Hasn't she grown?' Dad remarks. I have to bite my tongue to stop myself saying that if they bothered to see her more often it wouldn't come as such a shock.

Alex, feeling me tense, quickly defuses the situation.

'Fancy a drink, Sis?'

'Yes please. A large one.'

He winks and heads off into the kitchen where I can hear Mum crashing about.

'How are you, girl?'

'Shit. To be honest.'

My father scratches the back of his neck and looks at the floor. 'Awful business,' he mutters.

'How are you, Dad?' My only option is to change the subject. I cannot do this with him right now.

'Can't complain. My knee is playing up, bloody thing. Don't know why they won't just give me a new one and be done with it.' Easing himself back into his armchair he winces. 'Your mum's cooking up a storm.'

'Great. I'm starving.' My mother always hides in the kitchen busying herself cooking rather than face the music. It's her way of being nice to me without having to talk to me. I've come to accept it. 'What's on the menu?'

'Some pie or other I think.' Dad has returned to looking at his paper already.

'I was happy to go and pick up fish and chips.'

'Your mum wouldn't have it.'

Alex arrives just in time brandishing a large glass of white wine.

'Get your chops round that.' He says, tucking into his pint of beer.

On the sofa, Gracie begins to stir.

'Thanks, Al. I'm just going to call Danny and let him know we've arrived safely.' I say stepping back out into the hallway and removing my mobile from my pocket.

Holding the phone to my ear I take a long sip of the wine. The sweetness is unexpected and I remember my mother has no taste. The phone rings and rings until going to answerphone.

'This is Dan's phone. I can't answer right now but leave a message and I'll call you back. Cheers.' Beep.

'Where are you? Anyway, just letting you know we've arrived. Dad has already insulted me and I'm drinking a glass of really nasty white wine. Other than that everything's fine. Call me back. Love you.'

As I hang up I can't help but notice that the uneasy feeling has returned to the pit of my stomach.

Entering the sitting room again I see that Gracie is now sitting upright on the sofa rubbing her eyes, clearly discombobulated.

'We're at Grandpop's house.' I sit down next to her and rub her back.

'Do-do.'

'It's in the car. I'll get it a bit later.'

Do-do is her name for her dummy. As a baby she couldn't pronounce the word and that's how it came out. Despite being nearly four years old she still hasn't given it up and since Hope went missing I'm not inclined to try and make her. She's had enough taken away from her already.

'Hello, trouble.' Alex comes over from where he was sitting with his beer and greets his niece.

She looks at him like he's a threat and I remind her he is her uncle, who she speaks to regularly on Skype. Quickly her caution evaporates and she begins to interact with him.

'You're very big.' She examines her six foot three uncle.

'And you're very small.' He ruffles her hair.

'No I'm not. I'm a big girl,' Gracie corrects him.

'Not too big for this,' Alex sweeps her up over his head so that she is sitting on his shoulders. Gracie giggles with delight.

'I'm going to see if Mum needs a hand.' I leave the two of them to bond uninterrupted.

As I open the door to the kitchen my nostrils are flooded with the smell of meat cooking. My mother has her back to me and is standing over the stove, stirring something furiously in a pot.

'Hi Mum.'

She whips round to face me, her cheeks flushed red from the heat.

'You've arrived.' My mother was always one for stating the obvious.

'Safe and sound.'

'I'm just cooking us all a nice meal.' The front of her floral apron is dusted with a fine layer of flour.

'Do you need any help?'

'All under control.' She returns to stirring whatever is bubbling in the pot.

'So,' I'm desperate to try and fill the awkward silence, 'how've you been?'

'Busy. I'm taking a much more active role in the parish council. We're trying to raise money to fix the church roof. It's in an awful state.'

What neither of us mentions is the fact that my twin in buried in the graveyard of the church Mum is talking about. It was after she died that Mum found solace in religion. Her problem was that she put too much time and effort into the church and not enough into focusing on what she already had – me.

'I'm glad you've got a hobby.' My bitterness is not lost on her.

'How's Danny?' She continues stirring the pot while changing the subject.

'Couldn't be better.' I drink half the glass of wine in one go. 'We are all doing really well.'

'I'm pleased to hear it, love.'

Slamming the glass down on the kitchen surface makes mum jump, but gets her attention.

'What's the matter?' she rubs her hands on her apron looking genuinely confused.

'What's the matter?! Are you fucking kidding me?' She never likes it when I swear and glares at me. 'My daughter is gone. I don't know where she is, or who took her or if she's even alive. She has been missing for months now and my family is falling to pieces. You ask how Danny is. Really? Do you not know the answer to that question already?'

'Well, Libby, I knew you'd talk about it in your own time. I didn't want to pry.'

'She's your granddaughter for fuck's sake! And you haven't even said hello to Gracie yet. What the hell is wrong with you? I thought of all people you would understand what I am going through.'

My raised voice has meant that Alex has come into the room to investigate.

'What do you want me to say, Elizabeth?'

'I don't know. Something. Anything that tells me you actually give a shit.'

'Come on,' Alex tries to defuse the situation.

'No. I won't be hushed by you. I came here for some support but all I've got is an earful from Dad and disregard from Mum. I've only been here for five fucking minutes.'

Then the tears come. Alex puts his arm around my shoulder and ushers me into the hallway.

'How do you stand it, living here?'

'Dad's watching Gracie. It's OK. Take five minutes to yourself. You're in a state.'

'You don't say.' I manage a mumble through my sobs.

'I wish you'd told me you're not coping.'

'What good would that do? You can't change anything.'

'I should help out more. Come and visit.'

'No offence but I've got all the help I need. Danny's parents have been wonderful. I knew I couldn't rely on Mum and Dad to be of any use. I know you all live miles away and it's not as easy, but other people's parents would have moved heaven and earth to be of help. Hope is their first grandchild. I am their child. I know things have always been tricky but if ever there was a time for them to step up, surely it should be now.'

'You're right, Lib. I don't know what to say.'

'I think I'm going to go and check into a B&B for a couple of nights before going back to Cambridge. It was stupid to come here. I don't know what I was expecting. Danny kept pushing me to come.'

'Well I'm pleased to see you. I don't want you to go.'

'I can't stay here, Al. I just can't.'

'OK. I understand.' His dark blue eyes look sad.

'I'm going to go and say bye to Dad and get Gracie. Sorry, I didn't mean to come here and cause trouble.'

'I've missed you.' Alex hugs me and I start to forget my anger. 'I've got an idea, why don't we go to the pub, The King's Arms, in Luxulyan. They do decent food, better than

Mum's,' he adds in a whisper, 'and they have rooms. We can get some dinner and have a few drinks. What do you say?'

'Mum won't be happy.'

'Is she ever?' Alex chuckles.

Hope

I've not heard the voice for ages now. I keep looking up at where I think it came from but it's not there and neither is Zoe. She's gone for good. I know that now. I'm all alone in this place and I feel more scared now than I have done before because I know someone is watching me. Even though I don't hear them anymore I know they are there. Maybe they have been there the whole time.

If only I could remember how I got here. It's all blurry, a bit like when you wake up in the morning and for a minute you aren't sure where you are because you've been dreaming. Then you rub your eyes and look around and it takes a little while for you to get used to the world because you've been somewhere else, somewhere very different from the place you've woken up in. That's what it feels like all the time because I can't see.

For the first time since being put in the darkness I wonder if maybe I am blind and it's not that the world is black, it's that my eyes don't work anymore. Maybe someone hurt my eyes.

Slowly I raise my hands to my face and run my fingertips over the space where my eyes should be and without meaning to I end up touching my eyeball, which hurts a lot but I'm happy because it means that my eyes are working and it's just that it's too dark to see. And it gets me thinking about that voice. How can they see me in the dark? Maybe there is one of those tings that makes everything look green and can see in the dark. I remember seeing it on a programme about animals when they had to film at night because that's when the badgers come out.

I'm happy I have remembered the badgers because I like them. They look cute, a bit like dogs and it's a change to think about something nice and not be scared. But then it makes me think of something that I hadn't thought about before. Maybe I'm underground, like in a place where badgers live. And I think that if I am then it will be really hard for Mummy and Daddy to find me because I could be anywhere in the world but for some reason I think I am still in England. It smells like England in here.

My eye is still sore and I can feel it is streaming with water since I put my finger in it. Then I stop and realise actually I am crying because I've wet myself again and not only does it hurt but I know I am sitting in a puddle of my own wee.

Danny

'I've got him. Are you at the place?' I'm holding a pay-as-you-go mobile between my ear and my shoulder as I drive at a snail's pace down the small dirt track.

'Right. I should be there soon. I think I'm close now. See you in a bit.' I lift my head letting the phone drop into my lap and peer through the windscreen trying to make out a familiar landmark in the darkness. There are no street lamps in this part of the world. Only sheep live out here. Occasionally I meet one on the track who looks startled by the bright lights from the van and skips away.

It feels as if I've been crawling along this track forever and every time I drive over a pothole I am terrified that it is going to wake him up from his drug-induced slumber. I don't think I'd cope that well with an angry and probably scared man flailing about in the back. Luckily I remembered what Lara had told me about intravenously injecting him.

Just then I spot what must be the crumbling cottage because there is light coming from inside. My pulse quickens as I put my foot on the accelerator, eager to get there, although I know what's waiting for me.

I drive the van around the back of the decaying building and park it. Getting out I stretch my legs after the six-and-a-half-hour drive from Ickleton to this place in the middle of nowhere. I only stopped once for a pee and didn't allow myself any other breaks since I was nervous someone might discover that I have a man tied up in the back of the van.

It is bitterly cold and my breath frosts up into a cloud. Above, the night sky is thick with stars and I stop for a moment to absorb the beauty in the world before turning my back on it to face the ugly task I have begun.

The disused shepherd's cottage is situated between Cleish, which is about ten kilometres north of Dunfermline, and the Loch Glow Reservoir. It hasn't been used for decades, which is why it's the perfect place to bring my prisoner.

A warm yellow light is coming from inside and I peer in through the grubby window to make sure I'm not going to be greeted by an unexpected stranger. What I see is a chair placed in the middle of the room, a table with a bucket of water on it and a gas lamp sitting on a small table. On the far side of the room Simon is leaning against the wall chewing his fingernails. Rapping lightly on the glass I watch as he jumps and then frowns at me with disapproval before nodding in the direction of the entrance.

'You scared the shit out of me.' Simon scowls before hugging me. 'How did it go?'

'He's in the back of the van.' I shrug, not knowing what else to say.

'I guess that stuff Lara got you worked then.'

'He's out for the count. I shat myself when it came to putting the needle in but I did what she said and it seemed to work.'

'Benefits of having a vet for a girlfriend.'

'As it turns out. I really don't want any of this coming back to her. You know, if we get caught or something.' I grimace.

'Me either.' Simon sounds nervous. 'And no one saw you?'

'No. No one saw me. I ditched my phone too. I've seen enough on the box to know that those things have GPS tracking.'

'Good then. That's good I guess.'

'Is it?'

'You're having second thoughts?'

'What do you think?'

'I don't know. This is your show, mate. You decide what happens next.'

'Christ.' I bunch my fists and hit the wall splitting the skin on my knuckles. 'This isn't me.' Simon stares blankly back. 'I don't kidnap people. This is insane.'

'You can drive him back if you want. Drop him off somewhere near his shop. As long as he doesn't see your face, no harm done.'

I let out a long sigh and turn my attention to the chair that sits in the middle of the room.

'I have to. For Hope, for Lib and for Gracie. We need her back Si, or at least some answers. We deserve that much, don't we?'

'Course mate. I'll help, like I said I would. Just let me know if you want to do this or not.'

Looking at my old friend I wonder how on earth we ended up here. Simon and I used to go to Amsterdam to smoke pot. We went interrailing around Europe trying to get laid. We aren't violent people. But my desperation has led me to this point and I know that there is no going back.

'Let's get him out of the van.' I check my watch. 'He'll start to come round soon.'

'Yes Dan, all right. Let's do this.' Simon does a good job of faking confidence.

'I appreciate everything you've done so far but you don't have to do this. You can leave. Just walk out of here and pretend you never knew. This is my fight, not yours.'

'That little girl means the world to me too. I'm not going anywhere.' He leans across and pats my shoulder firmly with his hand. Simon was appointed her not official godfather, since we never had her christened.

Moved by his show of loyalty I nod silently, not wanting to crumble.

'Right,' I have to remain stoic, 'you take his legs and I'll hold his arms. Once we get him in here we'll tie him to the chair.'

'Got it.' Simon rubs his hands together in an attempt to battle the cold.

'He's got a bag over his head so even if he is awake he won't know who we are until we're ready.'

'I've made sure the place is prepped, just like we planned.'

'OK. Let's do this.'

The dilapidated shepherd's hut is hardly warm but stepping back out into the freezing December night I catch my breath. I suppose the gas light in the building was giving off some heat and the walls protected us from the angry wind that blows across the black hills.

'Ready?' Simon stands poised by the boot of the van.

'Ready as I'll ever be.' I remove the keys from my pocket and with a trembling hand fiddle to fit them into the lock. 'Even if he's awake it shouldn't be a problem. He's bound with cable ties.'

'This sounds like something out of a really bad B-movie.' Simon, the actor, pulls a face helping to ease the tension.

With a click the door pops open and we listen for any sounds of life. Silence. I open the door a few more inches and peer into the darkness. A lifeless figure lies static on the floor of the van.

'He's still out.' Simon whispers. 'That's good.'

'Let's get him inside.' Reaching into the van I grab his ankles and begin to pull the dead weight towards me.

'Fat fucker.' Simon puffs joining in.

Despite there being two of us to carry Amit, his body rolls out of the van and onto the cold hard ground with a thud.

'Shit!' I take a step back terrified that he is in fact dead.

'Feel for a pulse.' Simon says beginning to panic and following his instruction I bend down over the body and pull his jumper back to reveal his wrist.

'He's alive.' I breathe a sigh of relief and sit back, suddenly aware of the beads of sweat running down my neck. 'Come on, help me lift him.' I hook my hands under his armpits.

'OK, OK,' Simon's breathing is erratic.

'Take his legs. Ready, one, two, three.' Together we manage to heave the figure up off the ground and stumble back towards the building, struggling not to drop the heavy weight.

Once inside we lower Amit to the floor as carefully as we can before both falling back breathless.

'Now all we have to do is get him onto the chair.' Simon chuckles and I am so glad my friend is with me. I could not have done this alone.

'I thought I was fit.' Wiping the sweat from my forehead with my jacket sleeve I do my best to keep calm.

'Yes, mate, with all that tennis you play, you should be.'

'Haven't picked up my racket since Hope was taken.'

'Sorry. Should have thought.' Simon rubs the back of his neck and opens a bottle of water, draining a third of the contents before offering it to me. I thankfully accept the drink and relish the icy cold liquid running down my throat.

'Right,' I screw the lid as tightly as I can, trying to put off the inevitable. 'Let's do this.'

Libby

When I wake up in the small twin room of The King's Arms it takes me a moment to get my bearings. I'm supposed to be waking up in my parents' spare bedroom. Then I remember last night and the argument with Mum. Rolling over I bury my face in my pillow wishing I could go back to sleep. Then I realise Gracie is tucked up close to me, her face half covered by the duvet. She must have crawled in during the night.

Turning carefully so not to wake her, I reach out of bed for my mobile that is lying on the floor charging. The room is still cloaked in darkness and I squint at the screen hoping to see a message from Danny. Nothing.

The time on the phone reads eight-fifty. Where the hell is he? Why hasn't he called me back? I sent him a message late last night telling him I'd checked into the pub because of my falling-out with Mum. He's an early bird, never up later than eight so why hasn't he texted? Bringing the phone to my ear I try and call him again. I feel so far away from him. I want to hear his voice but again the phone goes straight to the answerphone. I can't be bothered to leave another message or and I don't want to risk waking Gracie, who is snoring lightly due to a slight cold.

The room is grey and tired, longing for some sunshine. A television from another century sits bulky on an orange pine chest of drawers that has seen better days. A fine layer of dust covers the TV's silver plastic top. This is not where I am meant to be.

I had a good evening catching up with Alex. I do love my brother. He's a good person, kind and witty. I wish we saw more of each other. He's great with Gracie, a natural, and will no doubt make a good father one day, if he ever settles down.

Doing my best not to replay in my mind the confrontation I had with Mum I decide to slide out of bed as carefully as possible and go for a wash. Shifting the cover away from my body the cold temperature of the air gives me a shock. I tuck the duvet tightly around Gracie and adjust her position slightly so that she won't fall out of bed. Then I make a dash towards the en suite and start to run a bath.

As a powerful gush of steaming water chokes its way out of the tap I dread the drive home. It's such a long way and Gracie doesn't sleep in the car as much as she used to, but I'm desperate to get home to Danny. Sitting on the edge of the bath watching the steam rise, fighting with the cold air, I decide we'll stop off for a night somewhere on the way home. I promised Gracie some fun and that is what she's going to get.

Tiptoeing back into the bedroom I take my phone off the floor and search the internet for a suitable place to stop. I find a lovely but expensive hotel in Bath that has a pool and decide to treat us to a night there. Gracie loves the water: she's a real water baby.

On holiday in Turkey one year, when she was two years old, her father and I watched her walk along a wooden jetty. Halfway along she decided, despite the fact she couldn't yet swim, that she should jump in. I've never moved so quickly in my life. Luckily she was wearing one of those swimming costumes with built-in floats. Seconds later I was dragging her out of the water. Initially she looked shocked but it only took a moment before a large grin spread across her face and she demanded to do it again. She's always been fearless.

Once the bath is hot and deep enough I drop my t-shirt and shorts onto the floor and climb into to the water, leaving the bathroom door open so that I see Gracie and she can come in if she wakes. It has been years since I could have a bath in peace, but it's what you get used to when you're a parent.

A memory of telling Hope to bugger off so I could enjoy a bath haunts me and I wish now I'd never said it. I should have let her get in with me that time. I was tired and grumpy and wanted some time to myself, now I wish I could take it back. But I can't and the worst thing of all is that I can't even tell her I'm sorry.

Silent tears start to fall as I rest my head on the edge of the tub, closing my wet eyes, aware that despite the fact my body is submerged in warm water my skin feels cold.

I already know I have a long day ahead and I've not even had a cup of coffee yet. The worry is exhausting. I feel tired all the time but I cannot give up. I have to keep going. We have to find Hope and I have to be a good mother to Gracie and a good wife to Danny. This is my role, whether I like it or not.

Letting my head sink under the water I lie there immersed in the warmth. My body feels weightless and small as if I might slip down the plughole when the water is drained. Holding my breath for as long as I can, I imagine what it might be like to drown at sea. The thought doesn't scare me like it should. My head is somewhere else, trying to find an escape from my situation. Death seems easy in comparison.

Rising up out of the water, I suck in a large gasping breath and find Gracie standing next to the bath watching me, with her thumb in her mouth and her other hand wiping the sleep from her eyes.

'Morning, monkey.'

She nods, not ready to speak yet.

'Did you have a good sleep?'

Again she nods.

'What did you dream about?'

She removes the wet thumb from her mouth, cocks her head to one side and thinks for a moment. 'Elephants eating cucumber.'

'Well that sounds like a nice dream.' I say, amused.

'Lots of cucumber.' She smiles showing her small white teeth.

'Do you want to get in the bath with Mummy?' I move my legs up to make room for her.

'Not now. After.'

'After what?'

'After breakfast.'

'Oh OK. Just give me a minute to get out the bath and get dry and then we'll go down and get something to eat.'

'Are we seeing Alex today?'

'No baby, sorry.'

Disappointment shadows her face.

'But,' I encourage, 'we are going to go to a hotel with a swimming pool in it. Would you like that?'

She stares a me for a moment deciding. 'Yes, but I haven't got rubber ring.'

'I'll buy you a nice new one,' I tell her, wondering where the fuck I am going to get hold of a rubber ring in England in the middle of December. I wrap a threadbare towel around myself. The tiles beneath my naked feet are freezing and I hop out of the bathroom and onto the navy carpet in the bedroom.

'Will Dada be there?' Gracie puts her thumb back in her mouth and crawls back onto the warm patch in the bed.

'No. He's at home.' I rub my hair roughly trying to warm my dripping wet skull. 'Let's put on the TV and see if we can find some cartoons,' I pick up the old-fashioned remote control and point it at the set, waiting for the screen to light up. After channel surfing for a little while I eventually find what I'm looking for. Gracie's blue eyes fix on the brightly coloured images as I turn my attention to getting dressed as quickly as possible. The room really is unbelievably cold and I decide I'm going to grumble about it to a member of staff when we go down for breakfast.

After hurriedly pulling on a pair of jeans and a green mohair jumper I check my phone again to see if Danny has been in touch. No messages. No missed calls. *What is he playing at?* I try and call again and again I'm taken straight to the answerphone.

'Please call me, OK. I haven't heard from you and I'm getting worried.'

I throw the phone down onto the bed with frustration. Gracie manages to tear herself away from the screen for a moment, long enough to frown at me.

'Why did you throw the phone?'

'Because it's annoying me.' I dig through the suitcase looking for something clean and warm to dress her in. 'Come on, little one, time to get dressed.' Gracie sticks out her bottom lip before pulling the duvet up over her head in an effort to hide. 'Come on, monkey. I'm tired. Please be a good girl. If you get dressed, then we can go and have some breakfast.'

'Not hungry.' The muffled words travel through the thick blanket.

'Fine,' I feel myself losing my temper, 'don't eat anything then but you still need to get dressed.' I stand with my hands on my hips waiting for an answer but there isn't one. 'Gracie?'

'Not hungry!'

'OK. No hotel and no swimming pool then.' I watch her legs through the fabric starting to kick and twist as she groans low screams. 'No use acting like a brat.' I tug the duvet realising she has a firm grip on it. 'Get out of bed now!' A tug of war commences and I try to remind myself not to pull too hard because she is little but my anger is rising with each defiant tug she makes. Then common sense kicks in and I let go of the duvet and straighten up.

'You have until the count of three to come out of there and start to get dressed. One,'

'Hmpf.' I watch her outline roll up into a ball.

'Two,'

'Nahhh.'

'Two and a half. I'm not joking Grace. If you don't come out now you will go and sit in the car in your pants and I'm telling you, it's freezing. Two and three-quarters...'

Slowly the duvet peels back revealing the top of her head and her wide eyes peering over.

Sitting down on the bed I separate a pair of folded pink child's socks.

'Sorry Mama,' she looks at me, knowing I mean business.

'That's OK. Now be a good girl and come here and get dressed. If we get a move on we can make it to the hotel before it gets dark.'

Gracie hugs me, knowing full well that I was never going to cancel our plans.

'Chop chop, monkey,' I pull the snug fitting jumper down over her head, 'or there will be no breakfast left!'

'Yoghurt. Rawberry.' Gracie grins like a clown.

'See, I knew you were hungry. They might not have it but if they don't we'll get you something else yummy instead.'

She offers a satisfied nod as she stretches out her legs for me to feed into her red corduroy trousers. They are hand-me-downs from Hope and my heart does a somersault remembering how I used to dress her when she was little. She was so different from Gracie when she was three. They are chalk and cheese and it never fails to amaze me how Danny and I have produced such opposite little girls.

Watching Hope grow had been such a pleasure and I keep hoping that it's not over, that somehow she will be returned to us so we can carry on being a family. I want to know what sort of woman she is going to become. I want to see her married with a family of her own. Her father should be able to give her way on her wedding day. We are meant to wave her off to big school and then university. That is how the story is meant to go. Not like this. Not like this.

Danny

We've been waiting for him to wake up for hours. My adrenaline was pumping when we got him into the building and tied him to the chair but now I feel exhausted. Sitting here waiting has killed my energy. Neither Simon nor I have slept or eaten anything. It's sodding cold and I'm really doubting my decision to go through with this.

Panic is setting in and I keep getting up to check his pulse. He is alive, I'm certain of that.

Most of the time Simon and I sit in silence. Neither of us have much to say, we are both brooding.

Frustrated by the lack of action I get up off the floor and pace around the small building.

Simon watches me go back and forth. 'All right, mate?'

'No. This is taking too long. Why won't he just wake up?' I approach the slumped figure in the chair and shake him by the shoulders.

'Careful,' Simon warns.

'We're not here to make friends.'

'I know. Just be careful. The bloke has been dosed up to his eyeballs.'

I flash Simon a look and it's clear he instantly regrets his decision to show pity.

Knowing my old friend is right I back away from Amit and return to pacing. 'The sooner he wakes up the sooner we can let him go.'

'Look, we're both tired and hungry. Give me the keys to the van. I'll go and get us some supplies. This isn't happening as quickly as we first thought. If he wakes up, talk to him. Don't DO anything without me.'

I nod, knowing that food will help quell my building frustration.

'Don't be long, yeah?'

'I won't.' Simon takes the keys and disappears out of the building pulling his hood up over his head.

I return to my position sitting on the floor in the corner of the room with my back against the cold, stone, wall. The rough hardness from the local stone can be felt through my thick jacket. Simon's right: eating something will help. We need to keep our energy up, especially since it's so damn cold.

Since Amit appears to be still unconscious I decide to talk a little walk around the outside of the building. The room is beginning to feel claustrophobic.

Pulling the rickety wooden door closed behind me I rub my hands together and look out at the view. The sky is white and thick with cloud. Looking out over the rolling green fields around Cleish and the Loch Glow Reservoir I admire how peaceful it is. It is much more beautiful than the flat arable countryside around Cambridge.

Taking a moment to breathe in some of the clear air I decide that what I need to do is make a fire. It's too cold to be stuck in a building without central heating and the last thing any of us needs is hypothermia – Amit included.

With a new-found determination I scour the area around the disintegrating building. It has clearly been used as a dump by the locals. Old tyres, bits of wood, metal and even a burnt-out car are scattered around the perimeter. Eventually I spot what looks like an old oil drum, which I roll towards the door. It will make a suitable fire pit. Then I set about collecting as many pieces of wood as I can to fill it.

By the time I'm done, I'm sweating and I see the van and Simon approaching in the distance. After persuading the awkward oil drum to pass through the small door way I push it to the centre of the room, about a metre and a half away from Amit, so that he, too, will benefit from its warmth. Then I begin to retrieve the wood I have collected and bring it inside and pile it up. Looking around I wonder what I can use for kindling. In my inside pocket I have a hip flask of whisky. A splash of that should help but I need paper or leaves to soak it in to get the fire going.

Simon appears in the doorway carrying a plastic bag full of food and drink.

'Still asleep?' He nods over to Amit whose head is flopped over to one side.

'I'm trying to make a fire. This place is fucking cold.'

'Let me help.' Simon drops the bags and comes over to peer into the empty metal barrel.

'We need something to get it going. I collected all that wood.' I point over at the stacked pile.

'This is proper Ray Mears shit.' Simon smiles boyishly.

'I've got a lighter and some whisky,' I show him the solid silver antique hip flask. It was a wedding present from my father.

'I know!' Simon returns to the shopping and rummages through the bag. He pulls out a packet of kitchen roll. 'I thought, you know, if we need a crap.'

'I'm sure we will, after eating all the grub you brought back with you.' I open a packet of Doritos and shove a large handful into my mouth. 'That should work to get the fire going,' I take the kitchen roll and rip the plastic off using my teeth.

'I nearly picked up a few beers but I didn't think it was a good idea. Looks like you've taken care of that front already.' Simon runs a disapproving eye over my hip flask.

'It's just a drop, mate. A bit of Dutch courage if we need it.'

'Fine. But we have to do this straight.'

'I know we do.' I start to ball up bits of kitchen roll and place them around the thinnest piece of wood I can find. 'That should do.' Stepping back I admire my handiwork before cautiously bringing the flame from the lighter to the doused paper.

Orange and blue flames lick their way around the inside of the drum searching for something to grab before settling around the piece of wood like witches around a cauldron.

I shove another handful of crisps into my mouth and settle in to watch the fire but just as I start to relax something in my peripheral vision catches my attention. My head darts towards the movement and I see Amit regaining consciousness.

'He's waking up,' Simon squeaks.

'Right.' I put my crisps down and wipe the crumbs from my short beard using the back of my hand. 'This is it. It's too late to pussy out now. You've still got time,' I turn to Simon, 'you can back out.'

'I'm staying.' He says puffing his chest out as grunts begin to come from the bagged head.

'Pass me the bottle of water.' Adrenaline is kicking in again and I feel ready to tackle this. 'He's going to want a drink.' Simon nods and hands me the bottle of Evian. I notice his hands, like mine, are shaking.

Libby

By the time we arrive in Bath it is almost dark. The journey was long and troublesome with horrendous amounts of traffic crawling slowly along the M5 due to an accident involving an overturned lorry. Inquisitive drivers slowed down to look at the carnage on the southbound side of the road causing the delay. Out of frustration I got off the motorway and decided to take the route past Glastonbury instead.

The gods were not on my side. Not only did I get stuck behind a huge piece of machinery that trundled along the road but then I got to a road closed sign and ended up getting lost after following what was meant to be a diversion. When we arrived at the hotel in the fading light, I had spent too long cooped up in the car with Gracie, who thought it a good idea to sing songs from *The Little Mermaid* at the top of her voice. I was in a foul mood.

'Come on, Grace,' I only called her that when I was cross, 'we've been in the car long enough. Out you get.' With a teddy tucked firmly under one arm and her thumb in her mouth she finally conceded. 'It's got a pool, remember, and if you are a good girl, after mummy has had some coffee, you can go for a swim. OK? Deal?'

She rolls her eyes but that is answer enough.

Our hotel is on the outskirts of the city. According to the website, it has seventy acres of garden and woodland and the Bath stone manor house has long views over the valley. It sounded like heaven when I read about it – but now, with night falling, and the rain and fog descending, it is not where I want to be at all.

I march over to the reception desk with Gracie in tow and announce our arrival. A woman in her late forties wearing enough makeup to sink the Bismarck, peers at her computer screen while typing unnaturally slowly. For a moment I imagine myself climbing over the desk and pushing her backwards off her chair.

'Bird. Yes. A twin room.' Her nasal voice is as irritating as her face.

'That's it.' I smile through gritted teeth knowing that this woman is not solely responsible for my anger but unable to feel anything other than cranky.

'Room 11.' She hands the key over and I wonder how her lashes can bear the weight of that much mascara. 'It you take the lift to the first floor the room is a few doors down on the left. Breakfast is served from seven-thirty until ten o'clock. Enjoy your stay at The Combe Grove Hotel.'

'Thanks.' I take the key and retrieve my small overnight bag from my feet before pulling Gracie away from a large variegated indoor plant that she has decided to tear leaves off.

A moment after the bell on the lift dings, and just before we are about to step inside, my mobile phone begins ringing in my handbag. Hopeful that Danny has finally decided to get back to me, I scrabble about looking for it in amongst the chaos of make-up, pens and other junk I deem important enough to lug about everywhere I go.

Finally, my hand finds the glass screen and I pull it out not bothering to check who is calling.

'Danny?' I answer.

'Is this Mrs Elizabeth Bird speaking?' My hopes are dashed when I realise it's not my husband.

'Yes,' I fight to keep hold of Gracie's hand as she pulls back in the direction of the helpless plant.

'It's Inspector King, Mrs Bird. Do you have a moment?' I let go of Gracie and without realising it bring my hand to my mouth. My heart feels as if has stopped and I cannot speak.

'Mrs Bird?' King prompts.

'Yes,' the word comes out in a half whisper.

'This is regarding your husband.' Time seems to stand still.

'What's happened? Is he OK?' I manage to choke the words out, not knowing if I'm relieved or horrified.

'We are trying to locate him. Do you know where he is?'

'Erm, at home, I think. Why? What's going on?' Dread grabs hold of my stomach.

'We need to speak to him regarding a matter. Can you please tell me when you last spoke to him?'

'Why are you asking me these questions? What's happened?'

'Please Mrs Bird; it would be very helpful if you would just cooperate.'

'I spoke to him yesterday. I was visiting family in Cornwall. I'm on my way back now. Is it something to do with Hope?'

'I can't divulge that information at this time but we are eager to speak to your husband regarding an urgent matter.'

'He's not answering his phone,' my voice quivers down the line.

'We have been trying to trace his calls but the last one picked up was made to you yesterday. Do you have any idea where he might be?'

'No, I don't. He's meant to be at home.'

'OK, Mrs Bird. Well thank you for your time. If you speak to your husband, would you please let me know his whereabouts?'

'Yes. But can't you just—'

'I'm not able to share any information with you at this time. I'm sorry.' King's interruption is unnecessarily abrupt.

'Fine.' I'm beginning to feel myself getting huffy.

'Please call us the moment you hear from him.' *If* I hear from him, I think to myself, realising that he has been ignoring my calls for a reason. 'Thank you for your time.' The line goes dead before I have a chance to ask any more questions.

The strange sickness I felt before leaving Ickleton returns to haunt me as I stare down at the mobile phone in my hand wondering what on earth just took place. From behind me a pair of large Americans barge their way out of the lift.

Looking up I see that Gracie has returned to tormenting the plant. I see what she is doing but I am unable to move to stop her because I am glued to the spot with fear. When I open my mouth to call her nothing comes out and quickly the world begins to spin. Putting my hand out against the clean wall I steady myself. *Don't let me lose Danny too, please*, I pray to any god that might be listening.

After a minute spent composing myself I realise I need to get home. Not wanting to disappoint Gracie yet again or break another promise I approach the reception desk.

'Can I help?' Mascara lady looks up at me.

'Yes. I won't need the room tonight after all. Something personal has come up but would it be OK if I took my daughter for a quick swim before we leave. I promised her she could go to the pool.'

The receptionist stares at me as if I just asked her to do a striptease.

'Look, I'm not asking for a refund for the room. Can I take my daughter for a swim?'

A bemused look spreads across her face and she frowns at Gracie who is still tormenting the plant.

'The pool is that way.'

'Thank you.'

'Come on, girlie.' I try to sound as normal as possible. 'Time for a swim.' She drops the shredded leaf she is playing with, claps her hands and charges across the stone floor shrieking like a banshee. 'Just a quick one, OK?' I lead the way towards the pool. 'Afterwards we need to go home.'

'OK, Mama.' She skips along beside me. Thankfully she couldn't care less that we aren't spending the night and I'm grateful for small mercies. I don't need her causing a scene.

Pushing open the heavy door for Gracie, I dread the thought of getting into the pool. It's the last thing I want to do but I'm determined to keep my promise, especially since our visit to Cornwall was such a disaster.

'Just a quick swim, OK?' We enter the changing room.

'Can I have treat after? Please, mama?' Who could resist that cheeky little face?

'Yes, if you get out of the pool without making a fuss.'

'Yay, yay.' She jumps up and down on the spot, her grubby pink shoes squeaking on the floor. Then I remember neither of us have our swimming costumes. Shit.

'Gracie,' I bend down and tuck a loose curl behind her ear, 'Mummy can't come in the pool because she doesn't have her swimsuit,' Gracie is immediately ready to kick off, 'but,' I interrupt just in time, 'You can swim in your pants for a bit and I'll sit on the side holding you.'

She offers a shrug of acceptance before bending down to undo the Velcro on her shoes.

I watch my daughter for a moment, so oblivious to the looming drama. Whatever is going on my job is simple; I have to look after Gracie. I let Hope down and I am not about to make the same mistake again.

Danny

Pulling off the cloth sack I'd placed over Amit's head, I watch as he squints and tightly shuts his eyes.

'Here, drink this,' I hold the bottle of water to his mouth.

Without bothering to look at me he opens his mouth, desperate for hydration. The water spills running down his chin as he gulps greedily. When I think he's had enough I take it away and screw the cap back on, watching him pant with relief. Simon stands back, a few feet behind him and Amit is unaware of his presence.

I go over to the makeshift table and put the water down before turning to him with my arms folded across my chest.

'What do you want?' His thick Indian accent fills the silence.

'I want to know what you did with my daughter.' I eyeball the man sat prisoner in front of me, feeling calmer than I presumed I would.

'I had nothing to do with that.' He shakes his head fervently.

'I don't believe you.' I tut, circling his chair and making him more nervous.

'Please, Mr. I am very sorry about your little girl but I did not touch her.'

'You've got a history of touching little girls, though, haven't you Amit?'

His brown cheeks turn a deep shade of pink and he hangs his head. 'My past is my private business.'

'Now it's my business too.' I come round to face him and shove my face up close to his.

'You cannot do this to me!' He lunges forward so that his forehead meets my nose and I fall back surprised by his sudden show of strength.

'Calm down.' Simon barks from behind him on the other side of the room. Amit twists in his chair trying to see the person the voice belongs to.

'I will not calm down. You have kidnapped me. This is an outrage.'

Crawling back to a standing position I dust off my trousers.

'The outrage is that you took my daughter.' Bunching my fists I step towards him as he cowers with nowhere to go.

'This is a mistake, a horrible mistake.' Amit pleads, his wide brown eyes searching my face for sympathy.

Standing there, towering over the snivelling pervert I start to slowly relish the fact that I am in control. Removing the bag that was over his head from my coat pocket I shake my head.

'No, Amit. Wrong answer.'

His eyes grow wider still when he realises he is going to be plunged back into darkness. 'Please, Mr, I can't breathe in there. Please!' he shakes his head from side to side violently, trying to escape the inevitable.

With one hand I grab the hair at the back of his head in my fist to hold him still. 'Night, night.' The fabric slides down over his face once more.

Turning to look at Simon, who is watching as if he is an outsider, I raise my finger to my lips telling him to remain quiet then take up my position again sitting in the corner of the room.

Amit's head flails about as he does his best to shake the sack off of his head. But it is useless. After five minutes of squealing and thrashing he stops moving and quietens down. Small sobs can be heard coming from beneath the fabric. I look over at Simon who shrugs, wanting instruction. I move my finger back up to my lips suggesting I think we could use silence as a tactic. He nods seeming to understand me and sits down, resting his head against the wall. He closes his eyes, trying to ignore the pathetic sounds that come from Amit.

I start to prepare myself for the long haul. In my head, before this begun, I thought it would be over quickly. I was wrong.

Libby

By the time we arrive home I am starving. Having not eaten anything notable since breakfast time I carry Gracie, who remains asleep after drifting off just as we were getting close to the house, up to her room and tuck her in. She needs to sleep and she can clean her teeth in the morning. I'm too exhausted to go through the rigmarole of the night time regime.

Danny is nowhere to be seen. The house is dark and quiet and feels unlived in. I've been away for less than forty-eight hours. How can so much have changed in that short space of time?

Turning the kitchen light on I rummage through the fridge looking for something to quell my appetite. Removing an aging Brie from the fridge I go in search of oatcakes, which I know are hiding somewhere in one of the disorganised cupboards.

After putting a plate, a knife and butter dish on the table I pick up an open bottle of red wine and pour myself a large glass. Before sitting down to enjoy my meal I am overcome with emotion and burst into tears. I have never felt so alone in my life. How is it possible for two members of my family to disappear into thin air?

I am crying uncontrollably, with snot running down my face. My eyes ache. I rest my tired head on the table, wishing that I had someone else's life, just for a minute. I know self-pity doesn't get me anywhere but I don't have the energy to stay strong.

When the tears dry I gulp down half the glass of wine and spread some gooey cheese, which is far past its sell-by date, on a cracker. I take a large messy bite. The food and drink hitting my stomach feels good and I start to regain my composure.

Three cheese biscuits and a glass and a half of wine later my mood does a flip. I no longer feel sad and alone, instead I feel angry. Angry that Danny has disappeared, angry that we still have no news on Hope, angry that my mother is such a disappointment and angry that Inspector fucking King ruined what was meant to be a deserved break from reality.

Tidying up the mess of crumbs and putting my plate into the sink I decide I am going to call King in the morning and demand some answers. My husband is missing, the police are looking for him and I don't have a clue what the fuck is going on. I will not be condemned to the role of gibbering wreck – I'm better than that – and tomorrow, after a good night sleep, I'm going to sort this mess out.

I flick the light in the kitchen off, pick up my luggage and take myself upstairs to bed. Slowly pushing open my bedroom door, which creaks, I stare at the silhouette of the bed in the darkness and for a moment imagine Danny lying on it fast asleep as I have seen him so many time over the years. But he isn't there.

Sighing I throw my bag down onto the floor with a thump and feel for the bedside light switch. A low creamy light fills the room, bringing it to life. I glance over at the pillow and see an envelope with my name on it written in Danny's handwriting.

With trepidation I remove a folded sheet of crisp white paper.

Lib,

I've not been the husband I wanted to be. Since Hope disappeared everything is wrong.

It is my role to protect this family and I have failed.

Please know that everything I do, I do it for us. I knew if I'd told you what I was planning to do, you would have tried to talk me out of it. I'm sorry I but I had to keep it to myself.

I have to do something. We deserve to know where she is. We deserve some peace.

All being well, we will have the answers we crave when this is over.

Don't think badly of me. Remember I love you and Gracie very much.

Dan xxx

I read the words over and over again trying to make sense of what Danny is trying to tell me. I don't understand. What has he done? What is he planning to do?

My head throbs as I lay back on the pillow holding the letter out so that I can read it one last time. This isn't a suicide note. It can't be. He wouldn't do that to us, would he?

Folding the letter and slipping it back into the envelope I chastise myself for going to Cornwall. I should have listened to my instincts. I knew something was wrong. Why did I let him persuade me to go? And then it clicks into place and I realise he planned it all along. He implemented the trip by suggesting it in the first place. It was his plan to get me out of the way. But why? For what reason?

Too tired and too emotionally drained to think straight, I curl up into a ball, pull the duvet up over my clothed body and decide to tackle whatever this is in the morning.

Danny

Pointing my head in the direction of the door I signal to Simon that I want us to step outside. He nods and we both get up and leave Amit sitting alone. Once outside in the early morning gloom I go over to the van, reach into the glove compartment and remove a brand new packet of cigarettes.

'Want one?' I hold the packet out to Simon.

'Thought you gave up?' He takes the packet and starts to unwrap the cellophane.

'I did.'

We both puff away in silence for a while, watching the cloud of smoke surround us in the stillness of the morning.

'Do you have Spotify on your phone, Si?' I ask breaking the quiet.

'Er, yes. Why?' He looks at me as if I've completely lost it.

'I remember seeing on the box once, in a film or documentary or something, that they played really loud music to a terror suspect in order to wear them down and get information. The silence isn't getting us anywhere so I was thinking that might work.' Throwing the cigarette butt down on the cold frozen ground I stamp it out with my boot. 'Just thinking.'

'Nah mate, it sounds like a good idea. Not sure my phone will be loud enough though.'

'It will, if we Sellotape it to his fucking head.' The appalled look on Simon's face takes me back. 'What? This isn't a game. I need to break this fucker somehow.'

'Yeah I know, Dan. I just didn't think it wasn't going to be this hard. I thought that once you got him here he'd be so shit scared he'd just open up. But he hasn't.'

'No, he hasn't so we have to do something.'

Simon nods and kicks the hard ground with the toe of his shoes.

'What do you have in mind?'

'I don't know maybe some heavy metal or something like that. I'd confess to anything if you played that stuff to me long enough.'

'Exactly.' Simon throws his hands up in the air. 'You want a genuine confession.'

'I didn't mean that. It's worth a go.'

'But we can't leave him alone in there so that means we have to listen to that shite too.' It's a good point, one that I hadn't considered.

'We'll sit in the van. He's not going anywhere.' I hold my hand out wanting Simon to give me his phone.

'If you think it will work.' Simon hands his Samsung over to me begrudgingly.

'An hour tops.' A strange excitement floods over me. 'Go sit in the van,' I call over my shoulder heading back into the building, 'I'll be with you in a minute. Gaffer tape is on the table, right?'

Libby

'I really think you owe me an explanation.' I hold the phone between my ear and shoulder while buttering Gracie's toast.

'I cannot comment at this time, Mrs Bird.' Inspector King will not give an inch.

'My husband is missing. This is my business. Why won't you tell me what's going on?'

'It's an on-going investigation.'

'What is?'

'When I have something to tell you I will be in touch.'

'That's not good enough.'

'Look, this is a very fragile situation. Until we have more information I cannot discuss it with you.'

'I'm worried, Inspector. I found a letter from Danny.'

'Oh?' That has piqued his interest.

'I'm really worried.'

'I need to see the letter. I'm coming over.'

'You aren't seeing anything unless you tell me what's happening.'

'I'll be with you shortly.' King hangs up, leaving me fuming.

I hand Gracie her breakfast and then I dial Danny's parents. They have a right to know he is missing.

'Hello?' Clare answers the phone.

'Clare, it's Libby,' I don't know what I'm going to say.

'Hello darling. How are you?'

'Not great, to be honest.' A lump forms in my throat. 'It's Danny.'

There is a long silence before she responds.

'What is it?' Her tone is grave.

'He's, well, he's disappeared.'

'What?'

'I don't know what's going on. I went to see my parents in Cornwall. He suggested I go and then on my way back I got a call from the police asking me if I knew where he was. I came straight home and when I got here I found a letter. He's left his mobile phone, too. I don't know where he is. Did he say anything to you?'

'Not a word. What did the letter say?'

'I can't make sense of it.'

'Do you think,' she swallows, 'he's hurt himself?'

'I don't know.' The tears begin to well.

'We're coming down. I'm going to speak to Paul. We'll be there by the afternoon.'

'Thanks Clare,' I didn't realise until that moment that I'd actually called

her for support, 'I'll make up the spare room.'

Just as I am about to go and change the bedding there is a loud thump at the door. I rush to it hoping, but knowing it's unlikely, that it's Danny.

The woman standing on the other side of the door is the last person I was expecting.

'Simran.' In her arms she cradles her baby.

'What have you done with my husband?' Her eyes are red and swollen and she looks exhausted.

'Excuse me?'

'Where is Amit? Where have you taken him?'

The world begins to spin as all the pieces start to fall into place.

'Danny is missing,' I hear the words come out of my mouth but feel like someone else has spoken them.

'So is my Amit. He didn't come home two nights ago. I've been worried sick.' The baby in her arms begins to cry, sensing her mother's despair.

'Have you spoken to the police?' We remain standing in the cold on the doorstep.

'Yes. They are looking for him. He would not walk out on us. Something has happened to him.'

'What makes you think Danny is involved?' I feel myself growing defensive.

'I am not a fool.' She looks me in the eye and I feel awkward.

'Look, I don't know what's going on. If I speak to Danny, you'll be the first to know.'

'I want my husband at home.' She looks down at the crying child in her arms. 'These months have taken their toll on us.'

'My daughter is still missing,' I remind her.

'I know and I am sorry about that but it has nothing to do with my husband.' She turns on her heels, her beautiful turquoise sari blowing in the chilly wind, and walks away with her head held high.

Danny

We've been sat in silence for some time. Simon is looking out of his window, brooding, smoking like a man possessed. His bottom lip is stuck out and he looks like the petulant teenager I remember travelling around Europe with.

My right leg won't stop moving. I can tell it's annoying him but I can't help it. I have too much pent up energy.

'That's probably long enough, don't you think?' I turn to Simon who remains scowling.

'I dunno. Probably.' He crosses his arms across his chest.

'I'm going to go and check. You coming?'

'Nah. I'll stay here for now.' Despite the heater, sitting in the van is not comfortable. The windows can't decide whether to steam up or freeze.

'Fine. Suit yourself.' I get out of the van, slam the door and crunch across the ground towards the door, stopping to peer through the grubby window just to double-check that he is still tied to the chair and hasn't wormed his way free.

The sight before my eyes is pathetic. He sits hunched over. The bag is still over his head, tightly bandaged with the gaffer tape, the phone still clinging to his ear.

Amit's body language suggests he's given up and I have a spring in my step as I make my way around the outside of the building to the door. Swinging it open, triumphantly, I let my arrival be known.

'Enjoying the music?' I call over the noise. He doesn't bother to move and I wonder if he might be dead. Has it given him a heart attack, or a stroke?

'Amit!' I spit as I bend down over his slumped body. His head moves slightly, enough to tell me he is still alive. 'Right,' I try to pull the phone away but the gaffer tape is stronger than I give it credit for. His skull is yanked to one side as I tug at the Samsung. Amit grunts.

Putting him in a headlock I manage to get enough traction to tug it away from the bag over his head. His neck makes a crunching sound and then bounces back into an upright position.

I've only been in the room for a few seconds but already I've had enough of the music. The screaming, so-called singing, sounds like how I imagine hell.

'You can't keep me here like this.' Amit's voice is hoarse and it sounds as if he needs water.

I tear the bag off of his head, throwing it to the floor. He squints, the dull winter light too much for his eyes. I wait for his sight to adjust. I then pick up a bottle of water and standing a few feet in front of him slowly open it. His eyes bulge with longing, as if he's watching porn, while I take a long sip before letting out a satisfied breath.

'Ahhh,' I hold the bottle out admiring the glint of the water, 'that's better.' Taking my time to screw the cap back on, I watch as the hope fades from his deep brown eyes.

'This can all end. It's up to you Amit. All you have to do is tell me what you did with her.'

Amit lets his head drop down onto his chest again and shakes his head.

'What is that? I can't hear you!' I shout.

He remains still and silent, which only ignites my anger.

'You stupid fucking prick.' I shove my face into his, having a sudden urge to bite his nose off. 'You will tell me or you will suffer.'

'My conscience is clear.' A large tear forms and streams down one cheek. Furious I stand up and slap him hard across the face using the back of my hand. A drop of blood forms on his bottom lip and travels down his chin.

'Why do you do this? You are a good man. This is not right. What about your wife? Does she approve of your treatment of me?'

'My wife is none of your fucking business. This is on your head. You are making me do this.'

'I am not responsible for your actions.'

'Yes you are. The moment you took my little girl from me, you put yourself in this position. You are a father.' The idea disgusts me. 'You must understand that I will do anything within my power to get Hope back.'

'If I had her I would give her to you,' Amit pleads.

'Wrong answer,' I sigh, getting hold of the bag and placing it back over his head.

'Not the music, please,' he blubbers.

'No Amit, not the music.' Leaning down I retrieve the water bottle from the floor and take the lid off. Then I walk around so that I am standing behind Amit, I put one arm around his throat and tip his head back before pouring the water over the fabric covering his mouth.

He spits and chokes, wriggling in my grasp. I take the water away, wait a second, before doing it again. At that moment I hear a noise and spin round to see Simon watching horrified.

'What are you doing?'

I let go of Amit who continues to cough and wheeze, desperate for breath.

'I'm trying to get some answers!' I really don't appreciate the way Simon is looking at me.

'Come on Dan, this is going too far.'

'I've told you, if you don't like it you can leave.'

'No, please, don't leave me with this madman,' Amit splutters.

'You nearly killed him.' Simon rushes over to him and removes the bag from his head. Amit's eyes are red and swollen.

'He's fine.' I take a sip of the water, finishing the bottle before crunching it up and hurling it over into a corner of the room.

Simon stumbles backward putting distance between himself and Amit.

'I can't do this, man.' He looks at me shaking his head. 'I want to find Hope but not like this.' Ever the drama queen.

'What did you think we were going to do? Have a nice chat?'

'I'm sorry. I'm going. Don't worry I won't tell anyone where you are but I can't be a part of this.' Before I've had a chance to respond, or defend myself, he's left the building.

Shaking with rage I pace backwards and forwards.

'Just tell me where she fucking is!' I scream at Amit.

'I cannot.' His eyes fill with tears again as I bring my fist hard into his nose, which cracks, sending a spray of blood across his face.

Hope

I speak to the voice hoping to get an answer but no one responds. Why are they just watching me? Why won't they speak?

I miss Zoe so much. I don't understand why she's gone or where she's been taken. She was my friend. It was nice having a friend in this place. It's scary when you're on your own.

My arms and legs hurt. Everything hurts at the moment, like I'm broken or something. I wonder if I get out of here if the doctor will be able to fix me.

Then I start to think that maybe Zoe escaped. Maybe she found a way out. But then I remember the voice and I know that isn't possible. There is no way out.

Libby

By two o'clock Clare and Paul have arrived. Both look similar to the way they did when they discovered Hope had been taken. We are all reliving that horror again.

'Darling,' Clare gives me a big hug, sniffing away the tears that had fallen during their drive from Tunbridge Wells. 'Any news?'

'No.' I decide not to mention that Amit is missing. There is no point worrying them until something – anything – has been confirmed.

Paul, whose brow is furrowed, bends down and scoops Gracie up into his arms.

'Let me get you both some tea.' I lead them into the living room and leave Paul and Gracie to play while Clare slips into the kitchen with me.

'What is going on, Libby?' She wants all the details and she knows I'm hiding something.

'I don't really understand, Clare. It's all such a mess.'

'What is? Where is he?' She stands with her arms folded across her chest, fixing me with her bright eyes.

'I think he's done something really stupid.' Sitting down on a chair I bury my face in my hands. 'Amit is missing.'

'Amit? The shopkeeper?' She pulls up a chair next to me.

'Yes. His wife came knocking on the door this morning. She thinks Danny has taken him. I think the police do too.'

'Taken him? Why?' The penny hasn't dropped with her yet.

'Because he's convinced that Amit knows what happened to Hope.'

'No. Danny would never harm anyone. This must be a mistake.' Her head shakes from side to side as she does her best to convince herself that this isn't happening.

'He left me this note.' I take it out of my pocket and slide it across the table to her. 'It's a lot to take in.' Resting my hand on her arm I gently squeeze.

Clare removes a pair of reading glasses from her handbag and carefully unfolds the paper. I watch as her eyes scan the words, finish reading it and then start again.

'Dear God.' She sits back in her chair and removes her glasses. 'We have to find him.'

'I know.'

'Come on Libby, think. Where might he have gone?'

'I don't know. I've been racking my brains all morning trying to work it out.'

'He'll be arrested. He'll go to prison for this. We have to find him before the police do.'

I hadn't got that far. Prison. Jesus. 'You're right. But I don't know where to begin.' My exasperation echoes around the room.

'Have you tried his friends? Someone must know something.'

'Simon!' Eureka. 'I'll call Simon. Danny went to stay with him recently. He might have said something to Si.'

'Good. I'm going to make some sandwiches. We all need to keep our strength up.' She approaches the kettle and puts it on, something that I failed to do.

I excuse myself, leaving Paul and Gracie mucking about in the living room and dash upstairs to make the call.

'Hi.' Simon answers.

'Simon. Good. Do you know where Danny is?'

A long silence.

'Simon. Did you hear? I'm trying to find Dan. It's really important. Have you spoken to him in the last two days?'

Silence again.

'Simon, I really need your help. If you know something, please...'

'Libby, I...' he lets out a long sigh.

'Where is he?'

'It wasn't meant to be like this.'

'What wasn't? You knew? You knew he was planning this and you didn't try to stop him?'

'He's in bits, Lib. He thinks he's let you all down. All he wants is to find Hope.'

'For fuck's sake, Simon, you think I don't?!'

'No, sorry, of course. He's my best friend. He asked for my help and–'

'Tell me where he is.'

'This is all getting way out of control.'

'What do you mean? Simon, please help me. I need to speak to Danny before he ends up getting arrested.'

'I promised I wouldn't tell.' Simon sounds like a scolded child.

'This isn't a game.'

'I know that. I shouldn't have left them alone. Dan was so angry.'

'You were with them? He's in Scotland?' I can't hide my disgust. 'You were involved in this?'

'We were just meant to frighten him a bit.'

'Oh Christ. What have you done?'

'Nothing! Nothing!' Simon starts to panic. 'I didn't lay a finger on him I swear.'

My entire body is shaking with fear. After taking a few deep breaths I manage to speak calmly.

'Simon, I am going to come to Edinburgh. When I get there you are going to take me to Dan.'

'I'm not sure.'

'That's what's happening.' I interrupt. 'If you don't help me, I will call the police and tell them you are an accomplice in this.'

'OK, OK.' Simon was always weak.

'Do not call Dan and let him know you've spoken to me. He clearly isn't thinking straight and I don't want to spook him.'

'OK. I promise.'

I don't point out that Simon also made a promise to Danny.

'Stay put and I'll be there as soon as I can. If the police call you don't mention anything. You've not seen him, OK?'

'Sure, Lib.'

'Good. You're a bloody fool Simon. I could slap you, I'm so cross.'

'Sorry. I just wanted to help my friend. He was so convinced it would work.'

'He doesn't know if he's coming or going,' I say, realising that I am the strongest person in our marriage. 'How could you be so stupid?'

Simon doesn't answer. There is nothing he can say.

'Just stay put. I'll see you soon.' I hang up the phone and throw it down onto the bed. It bounces off before tumbling to the floor. 'Shit, shit, shit.'

At that moment Clare comes bursting into the room.

'What's all the commotion? I heard you shouting?'

'Danny has taken Amit to Scotland. He's trying to get him to confess to taking Hope.' My voice sounds foreign to my ears.

'You are not serious.' Clare stands with her mouth half open.

'I'm going there now to try and persuade him to come home.' Standing up I grab a jumper and a pair of knickers out of my chest of drawers and throw them into an overnight bag. 'I'm sure it will be fine.' I wonder who I am trying to convince.

'We are coming with you.' Clare turns to leave the room.

'No. You have to stay here and look after Gracie. I'll talk him down.'

'I'm sorry Libby, but that isn't good enough.' Clare stops with her hands on her hips. 'He is our son and I think in this instance he needs his father. He will listen to him.'

'It will make things worse. You know how stubborn he is.'

'We are coming with you and that's final.' She closes the door gently, leaving me standing there like a child.

I go over to my bedside table and remove a bottle of pills from the drawer before popping two into my mouth and swallowing them dry. It has been a while since I needed the mild sedatives that Dr Vogler prescribed when Hope went missing, but I want them now.

'He what?' I hear Pauls booming voice travel up the stairs. Great, I think, just what we need, another irate man to contend with.

Danny

Sitting on the floor tucking into a chocolate bar I watch as Amit's lips begin to turn blue. I filled a bucket with cold water and have plunged his naked feet into it. At three o'clock it is beginning to get dark already and despite the fire burning in the oil drum the room is beginning to freeze. The glass in the windows has frozen and the air appears in a while cloud everything I exhale.

Despite his best efforts to knock it over he has failed. His legs are securely fastened to the chair and he cannot move his feet. His face is a bloody mess; his eyes are nearly swollen shut as a result of the broken nose. Blood has collected in a huge crimson scab on his top lip.

'Please, I am so cold,' his teeth chatter uncontrollably.

'Where is she?' I take another bite of my chocolate bar enjoying the sweetness.

'I tell you, I don't know.'

'Fine,' I get up dusting off my trousers, 'then you can go back into the dark until you're ready to talk.'

'No. I cannot feel my feet. Please I am going to die.'

'Don't be so melodramatic.' I'm finding it increasingly difficult to have any sympathy for him but as I get closer to him I see that he has pissed himself. I recoil with disgust. 'Don't you have any self-respect?' the smell of urine fills my nostrils.

'You would have let me go to the toilet?' He cannot hide the sarcasm in his question.

'Don't get cocky, dickhead.' I decide not to bag him after all. With one foot I push the bucket of icy water away from him. He lets out a yelp as if the sudden change in temperature causes him further pain.

'Let's try another tactic shall we?' I turn the bucket upside down, letting the water pool all over the floor before perching on it a few feet away from him. 'I want you to look at this,' I put my hand into my pocket, remove my battered leather wallet and take out a small picture of Hope I keep in one of the sleeves. Kissing the photo I then hold it out for him to see.

'This is what I want. This beautiful little girl who you took from me in August.' A lump forms in my throat. 'You are going to tell me where she is right now.'

Amit drops his head again and lets out a long low groan.

'Is she alive?' I can barely contain my emotion when the question comes bursting out of me. Amit shakes his head.

'You've killed her, haven't you?' I leap to my feet sending the bucket rolling away and dropping the photograph and wrap my hands around his neck. His already swollen eyes bulge even more as I squeeze the life out of him.

'No,' he gargles, gasping from breath, 'I have not hurt her.'

Instantly I let go.

'So where is she?' Could I have finally broken him?

'I tell you I don't know. I do not hurt your daughter.' His words come out with rasping breaths.

Overcome by the disappointment I begin to sob. Sitting in the puddle of cold water on the floor I cry and I cry and I cry until there are no more tears left.

When I finally look up I see him watching me with pity.

'You don't get to feel sorry for me,' Getting up I wipe the snot away with my hand and move over to the fire to restock it before it dies out.

'I cannot think what you are going through. If anything happened to my daughter my life would be over; but you must believe me that I did not harm your girl.'

'Explain the shoe then.' I have my back to him and stand over the oil drum warming my hands.

'I cannot.'

'That isn't good enough.'

'Maybe someone framed me!'

'You really are grasping at straws, aren't you? Don't patronise me.'

'If I had taken your daughter I would not be so stupid to leave a shoe in my bin.'

'OK, you have a point I suppose but you are on the list, Amit. You are a paedophile. Maybe you made a mistake, panicked, I don't know.' Spotting the picture of Hope floating in a puddle of water on the floor, I rush over to retrieve it. The water has already warped the photograph. Trying desperately to salvage it I rub it on my jacket as if that will absorb some of the water.

'You are wrong about me. It is a mistake I am on that list. My wife, she will tell you.'

'I've spoken to your wife already, months ago.' Amit looks over at me as if this is news to him. 'She didn't mention it?'

As he shakes his head, I smile.

'You see, that's what I mean. People keep secrets.'

Libby

The drive up to Scotland was awful. There was an atmosphere in the car. Clare and Paul had a huge argument about how best to handle Danny. Even Gracie has been as quiet as a mouse and that's unheard of.

Paul drove most of the way, speeding along the motorways and gripping the steering wheel like a man possessed. Clare sat in the front passenger seat of their large blue Audi, her arms crossed, staring out of the window not speaking.

Since they have known Simon longer than I have, plus the fact they are older, I encouraged them to take the lead once we got into the house. Paul had no problem with that and knocked on the door with the authority of a bailiff.

I sit on the sofa in Simon's small apartment sandwiched between Clare and Paul who are still not talking, while Gracie sits on my lap twiddling my hair. Simon perches awkwardly in an armchair opposite us. He looks uncomfortable.

'So where is he?' Paul leans forward and rests his elbows on his knees. No time for niceties.

'It wasn't meant to get out of hand.' Simon looks at the floor and scuffs the carpet with his shoe. His dark hair is dishevelled and he needs to shave.

'We need to know, Simon. You're not schoolboys any more. This isn't a game.' Paul's words are cutting but fair.

'There was this old abandoned place up in the hills that I once did some filming in. It's really quiet and he remembered me mentioning it a while back. He asked if he could use it.'

'You're a bloody fool.' Paul stands up and storms out of the room, slamming the front door on his way out, leaving Clare looking embarrassed.

'Where is it, Simon?' I move Gracie over onto the sofa between Clare and me.

'In the hills the other side of Dunfermline, near Cleish. It a forty-five-minute drive.'

'Thank you.' I stand up not wanting to waste a second more. 'Let's go.' I turn to Clare who is looking at Simon strangely.

'I wouldn't just barge in if I were you. He's not behaving like himself. Let me come with you. You won't find it by yourselves. Maybe I can talk some sense into him.' Simon is doing his best to make up for his stupidity.

'What do you mean "he's not himself"?' Clare asks.

'Just weird. Like it's a different person. He kind of scared me to be honest, which is why I left.'

Clare and I share a look. We both know that Danny has a temper.

'Let's go then.'

'Follow my car.' Simon says picking up his keys out of a neglected-looking fruit bowl on his dining room table. 'Because of its position he'll be able to see us coming if we have our lights on. I don't want to spook him. When we get close I'll call you. I think it would be better if we park the car and walk some of the way.'

'You're acting as if we are trying to catch a criminal.' Clare says.

Simon doesn't respond.

'I think Simon's right, Clare. Look, it's pitch black already. It's nearly nine o'clock. Why don't you stay here with Gracie and I'll go with Paul and Simon? She shouldn't be witness to this.'

Clare nods with what I interpret as relief.

'There's some food in the fridge and in the cupboard by the sink I always keep a stash of chocolate and crisps.' Simon points towards the kitchenette after pulling on his coat.

'Chocolate!' Gracie's eyes light up.

'Do whatever you have to do to keep her happy.' I kiss Gracie on the top of the head before following Simon out of the door, leaving Clare looking bereft.

Danny

Amit's mouth is dry and cracked. The blood from his broken nose has dried on his top lip like a dirty brown moustache. He sits shivering in the chair, his eyelids heavy from exhaustion.

'Here.' I approach him grab his face in my hand and tip a small amount of water into his mouth. He winces from the cold for a second before licking it up like a dog. His big pink tongue comes out of and searches for any stray drop he might have missed.

'Thank you.'

I sneer and turn away. I don't need his thanks and no amount of politeness is going to stop me from doing what needs to be done.

'You are lucky Simon took his phone with him, otherwise you'd be listening to that shit again.'

'You cannot force me to tell you something I do not know.'

His determined resistance pushes a button and I grab a piece of burning wood out of the oil drum, thrusting it against the bare skin on his foot. Amit lets out a high-pitched scream that sounds more animal than human.

'Stop fucking with me. You will talk or I will keep on hurting you!'

He whimpers and looks down at the red, blistered skin on his foot. Little pieces of glowing charcoal are splintered around his feet in a halo. He tries to move his swollen foot away but the restraints on his ankle prevent him from doing so.

Opening yet another bottle of water I throw some down towards his foot, extinguishing the glowing coals and making the blisters on his foot even angrier.

'I will pay you.' He says suddenly, clenching his teeth because of the pain. 'I have money. Name your price.'

'I don't want your money.' I look at him with a newfound level of disgust.

'Please. Simran will get you money. Her father is rich. You can use money to find your daughter.' His pleading is pathetic.

'Nice try.' I turn my back on him and walk towards the door.

'No, don't leave. I need a doctor. Please!' His begging falls on deaf ears as I pull the door closed behind me and go out into the black night.

I need fresh air. In the bitter cold I walk around the perimeter of the building, trying to think of a way to make him talk. Nothing I do is working.

Until recently I felt convinced Hope was alive but since coming to this place that feeling has abandoned me. It's as if I've lost her somehow and there is more distance between us than ever before. Perhaps Amit's refusal to cooperate is fuelling my suspicions that he has killed her.

Overcome with a mixture of sadness and violent anger I turn and punch the stone wall as hard as I can. The sound of my knuckle breaking echoes in my ears as I collapse to the ground holding my hand. Instantly I regret my decision to hit the wall. That was stupid. The last thing I need is an injury.

Cradling my bad hand I return indoors grateful for the heat coming from the waning fire.

In the light I examine my bloody hand. The knuckles are swollen and split. The pain is excruciating.

'Shit,' I mutter pouring water over the wound to clean it before searching for something I can use as a bandage. Amit looks over at me and I feel his pity.

'Don't fucking look at me.' I roar and he quickly turns his head the other way. It dawns on me for the first time that he is actually frightened of me and it is a surprise to discover I relish it. I do have the upper hand, even if he hasn't broken down yet. Realising this gives me renewed hope and as I wrap a wad of kitchen roll around my knuckles I watch as the white paper soaks up the blood, turning crimson. Watching the blood seep in reminds me of a rose unfolding. It is hypnotic and almost beautiful.

I am calmer now and I realise that I am in control. I sit on the floor near the fire and face Amit.

'Let me tell you a bit about my daughter.' My voice is calm and measured. 'Hope was born on July 21st in 2006. She weighed six pounds one ounce. She was tiny. It took her mother twenty-eight hours to give birth to her. But after doctors, nurses, gas and air, and a troublesome lumbar puncture, Libby brought Hope into the world. She did not cry. She came out quietly and looked around. I cut the umbilical cord. My hands were shaking I was so overcome with emotion. It is one of the few times in my life that I have cried. She was so small and perfect I thought I might break her when the nurse handed her to me to hold for the first time.' The memory is as clear now as it was then. I remember everything. 'She was our firstborn. There is something special about that, something that can never be relived.' Looking down at my left hand, the one that isn't bandaged, I find myself staring at my wedding ring. 'Hope coming into the world changed my life forever.' I swallow down a wave of emotion. 'She became the focus of my world, my reason for getting up in the morning, for working a shit job. It was all for her and her mother.' I get up off the floor, compelled to pace once again. My hand is beginning to throb and I don't want to focus on the pain.

'She was the happiest little soul and such a good baby. She didn't really grumble and she wasn't demanding. Although, at first it was exhausting, her mother and I found parenting her a breeze. Waking up to her face in the morning was a real pleasure. She was smiley and content.' A vision of her sitting on the duvet of our bed, aged one, comes flooding back to me. 'She was always giggling.'

'When she was ten months old her mother and I got married. That was one of the happiest days of my life. I had a beautiful wife and a gorgeous daughter. What more could I ask for?'

'Hope was carried down the aisle by a friend. She wore a little cream dress that cost her mother a fortune. I often look back at photographs from that day. She was the star of the show, everyone gravitated towards her. Libby and I were proud as punch. The fact that she was there for our wedding made it even more special.'

Looking over at Amit I see that he has closed his eyes. He doesn't want to hear this.

'Is it hard listening to this?'

He doesn't respond.

'She took her time to develop. She was in no rush to walk or talk. Hope was...' I pause. '*Is* a cautious kid. She refuses to do anything until she is entirely convinced by it. She was not going to walk before she was sure she could do it without falling over. On her second birthday she finally took her first steps unaided and she never fell once. I remember that day so clearly. It was sunny and we had a barbecue in our garden. My mum and dad came. Libby made a cake in the shape of a caterpillar. It took her hours. We'd blown up a paddling pool and Hope was sitting in it splashing water at Mum and Dad's old dog, who thought it was great fun trying to catch the drops in his mouth. In the afternoon she simply let go of holding the chair and walked across our patio. That was such a good day.'

'When she went to nursery she was slow to talk. All the other kids were chatting away, mostly nonsense, but Hope wouldn't say a word. Then when she was nearly three she began to speak using whole sentences that made sense. Up until then her mother and I had been worried but she proved, once again, that she would do everything in her own time.

'The thing about being a father to a girl is that you want to protect her. The idea of anyone ever hurting her, well… you have a daughter. You must know how it feels.

'My job is to bring her up, to teach her how to be strong and independent. I'm meant to walk her down the aisle and be a grandfather to her children. That's all I ever wanted, to be a good dad. But no. Thanks to you, I let her down. But I will find her, Amit. Believe me when I tell you that I will find her – and you are going to help me. We can do this the easy way or the hard way. It's up to you.'

I make the mistake of leaning on my hand to prop myself up, I wince and get up. My arse is cold from sitting on the ground. I retrieve a piece of broken glass from the floor by the window. It is clear some kids have been spending time up here with their BB-guns. Small perfectly circular holes are scattered across some of the panes. One of the pieces of glass hangs onto its frame, sharp and glinting in the firelight.

It catches my eye and I watch the prism of colours disappear as my shadow looms in front of it.

'You always seemed like such a non-entity. Nice smiling Amit, who sits behind his till taking payment for bread and milk. So very nice. How many years have you been at the shop now? It seems like a long time. Were you there when Hope was a baby? Did you peer into her pram when she was tiny, looking forward to the day you could snatch her from her family and molest her?' It seems as though someone else is talking through me. I can hardly bear to listen to the words coming out of my own mouth. 'Have there been others? Your own daughter, perhaps? Is she the new focus of your attention?'

I hold the blade of broken glass in my hand and turn it round slowly, examining it from every angle.

'You do not say those things about me!' Amit begins to buck in his chair backwards and forwards shaking it with a ferociousness I've not seen from him before.

'Struck a nerve, have I?' I hold the glass up to my chin and let the cold edge rest against my skin while he continues to rock in his chair. The sound of the wooden feet against the floor is horrid, like nails down a board.

'Sit still, you fucker!' I begin to feel less sure of my position. He is really angry. I thought I was in charge. 'I said sit still, or I'll fucking cut you!' The words leave my mouth before I've had a chance to even think them but nothing I say has any effect.

As if in slow motion I watch the chair tip back and the man strapped to it falling towards the floor. With lightening quick reactions I catch him using my bad hand and stop his skull from cracking onto the ground. Letting out an almighty scream I manage to push him back into an upright position using all my strength.

Collapsing into a ball I cradle my limp hand wondering if I am going to die. Small white dots fog my vision as I vomit up a puddle on the floor. The bitter taste of bile brings me back to reality.

Amit sits in his chair, a horrified look plastered on his swollen bloody face and stares at me. 'You are mad.' He speaks in a half whisper. 'You are actually mad.'

I hardly hear what he says as I straighten myself up.

Lying on the ground, a few feet away, is the piece of glass I was holding. Without thinking I pick it up and move towards my prisoner.

Libby

'What the hell was that?' I whisper in the darkness, looking towards the small lit building in the distance.

'It didn't sound good.' Simon sounds scared.

'Nearly there.' Paul leads the way, like a poacher out hunting. Either he didn't hear the blood curdling scream or he is trying not to think about what it might mean.

'Stop! Stop!' I call out louder than I intended.

'What is it?' Paul's figure turns in the darkness. Above us the sky is full of beautiful white stars.

'This isn't right. We can't just walk in there. What if...' my words fade like my hope.

'Fine. You stay here then but I'm going to talk some sense into him.' Paul is as stubborn as his son.

'Didn't you hear that?' Simon stands by my side and I welcome the warmth from his body. Paul doesn't answer.

'What if it's Danny in trouble?' I turn to Simon petrified of what we might find in the cottage high up on the hill.

No one speaks. We stand there, frozen by both the cold and our fears, beneath the universe that circles above us, its weight on our shoulders.

'If I go up there and call out he's less likely to freak.' Simon is finally showing he has common sense. 'He wouldn't be surprised if I turned up.'

Shivering in the freezing cold I check the time on my mobile.

'It's nearly two in the morning.' I wish I had brought gloves. It's fucking Scotland in December for Christ sake. 'Maybe this is a bad idea.'

'You heard that noise.' Paul's gruffness cuts through the night. 'We can't wait.'

Then in the distance we hear the hum of car engines. Peering out into the black countryside I try to identify the direction it is coming from. My head swivels left and right trying to determine the source.

'What the fuck is that?' I am feeling really spooked.

'Sounds like cars.' Paul removes his mobile phone from his coat pocket, turns the torch app on and shines it around trying to see where the sound is coming from.

None of us can see anything but the noise is getting louder.

Danny

'I told you, you little fucker, that I would get answers,' the broken edge of the piece of glass tears through the skin on the back of his neck revealing bright pink wet flesh, which contrasts with his brown worn skin. Blood floods out of the wound and spills down his back.

Amit squeals like a pig as I move away from him.

'You're a stinking mess,' I take my hand up to my nose trying to avoid the stench of faeces that wafts up into my nostrils. 'Jesus Christ.' My eyes start to water and I feel the vomit rising once again in my throat.

'Animal,' I spit a mouthful of saliva onto the floor.

'Would you have let me go toilet if I had said?' Amit doesn't even try to hide his sarcasm and I am shocked he has time for it still.

'Shut the fuck up, pig.' It is unbelievable that he still hasn't talked, even when I sliced his skin. He is a harder nut to crack than I gave him credit for.

'I think it is you who is the animal.' Amit talks through chattering teeth. Clearly the pain and the cold are having more of an effect than he is letting on and my faith is restored. But I do wonder how much more I am going to have to do to break him. How much more violent are things going to get? How much am I capable of?

Tired by the throbbing ache of my broken hand I go and rest against the far wall facing him. The stone is cold and hard but supports my weary frame. Slumping to the floor I let my hand rest in my lap.

Amit and I look at each other for what feels like a long time. Neither of us is prepared to look away first. We play the game like experts, never blinking. When he finally hangs his head, wincing from the gash across the back of his neck I smile inwardly. One nil.

'So when Hope was nearly four Libby announced she was expecting our second child. We'd been trying for a while but it didn't happen as quickly as we'd hoped it would. I remember sitting down with Lib and telling Hope that she was going to have a little brother or sister in a few months. She dealt with the news the way she dealt with everything, quietly absorbing it before responding. She said she hoped she'd have a sister. Her mother and I laughed and said we couldn't promise if the baby would be a boy or a girl but we were sure she'd love and enjoy the child whatever sex it was.

'As the months passed and Libby's stomach swelled, I'd often see Hope resting her head on the belly trying to hear the baby. She was convinced it would start talking to her and give away whether it was a boy or girl.'

Amit groans.

'You rude motherfucker,' I hurl a loose stone towards his head but miss by a few inches, luckily for him. His head springs up and the shock on his face reassures me he will be listening without making another sound from now on.

'When Gracie was born I was almost relieved she wasn't a boy. Don't get me wrong, I'd love to have had a son to kick a ball with, teach how to shave, that sort of thing but I was used to girls. I knew what to expect from Gracie. Having a son would have been like stepping into the unknown.

'She was a funny looking thing with pixie ears that curled slightly at the top and stuck out of the side of her head. Just like her mother's used to, I'm told, before the surgery.

'It was sod's law: the birth was easy but when we got her home we discovered that Hope had come down with chicken pox. It was a nightmare. She was burning up and the first few chicken pox were beginning to appear. My mum, who'd been looking after her while we were at the hospital, insisted on taking Hope home with her for a few days. None of us wanted to put fragile, newborn Gracie at risk. But sending Hope away when we'd just brought a new baby home did not go down well. I offered to go with Mum but she insisted I stayed and bonded with my youngest. She was right – but the guilt I felt was miserable.

'Before Mum scooped her off back to Tunbridge Wells we let her get a good look at her little sister. Hope examined her sibling for the first time as if she were an alien made of china. Lib and I really wanted to let her hold Grace but we knew it was a bad idea.

'Lib told Hope that she was getting to go on a special holiday with Nana so she didn't have to listen to her little sister crying all night. We promised her there would be presents waiting when she got back. That softened the blow a bit.' I can't help but smile at the memory of my two children together in the same room for the first time. I had been waiting for that moment for months.

'When Gracie was born both Lib and I knew instinctively that our family was complete. We wouldn't have more children. We already had our chalk and cheese.' The smile from my face disappears. 'But then you took her away and now there is a part of our family missing.'

Getting up off the ground using my good hand to balance I stomp towards Amit who has been doing a sterling job of paying attention. Hocking up a large ball of phlegm I spit it into his face. It hits his forehead and slowly works its way down his face like a slug.

'Don't kill me,' Amit's eyes fill with horror and tears.

'Why not?' I have no intention of ending his life.

'Because I will tell you what you want to know if you let me live.'

Libby

'How did you find us?' I hiss at Inspector King who stands there looking bloody pompous. He smiles smugly but refuses to answer.

This situation is getting graver by the minute. Damn Danny for being such a fool.

Paul, Simon and I all peer at each other in the dark wondering if we are also in trouble.

'This is a police matter.' King clears his throat.

'He's my husband.'

'What are you going to do?' Simon asks sheepishly.

'Well we could arrest you for aiding and abetting a kidnapping.' King flashes his small torch in Simon's eyes and holds it there for a moment, 'but we have a hostage situation to deal with currently. I need you all to move aside and let us do our job.'

Through the blackness I start to make out more and more figures buzzing around us. We are surrounded by police.

'Just let me go and talk to him and I'm sure this can all be resolved amicably.' Paul steps up, talking with authority.

'I cannot let you go in there, sir.'

'I'll bloody well just walk in right now. I don't need your permission.' Paul swings around and begins to go towards the building but King catches his arm in a tight grip.

'You are interfering with a police matter. If you jeopardise this I will have no choice but to arrest you.' King will not take no for an answer.

Paul slumps and for the first time in a long time his frail figure shows his age.

'Paul,' I reach out and put my hand around his shoulder, 'let's do as he says.' There is no point in fighting.

'We are going to cordon off the area. We need you back there, behind the line.' King flashes his torch at a junior officer, instructing him to take us away.

'What are you going to do?' I feel the bitter cold biting my nose.

'Firstly we will initiate contact. A hostage negotiator is on the way. Until then we sit tight.' King turns to the officer again. 'Get them out of here.'

'I thought you were on our side.' My voice fills with tears.

'Mrs Bird, I cannot condone what your husband has done. It is against the law to abduct someone, no matter what the circumstances.'

'If that's the case why the fuck is Chadrad walking around freely?' I feel a rush of blood hit my head and quickly find that I am shaking with rage.

'We found no evidence to suggest–'

'Like hell you did. The shoe. Have you forgotten that minor detail? You're spending your time, and taxpayers' money, out here trying to get my husband when there is a child abductor on the loose.'

'Lib.' Simon puts himself between the inspector and me.

'I have every right to be upset!'

'Please stop shouting.' King barks. I do as he says only because I don't want to spook Danny and land him in even more trouble.

'Let's go and sit in the car and let the police get on with it.' I realise Simon is being rational now but it's too late as far as I am concerned.

'Shame you didn't think of that before helping Danny make the biggest mistake of his life.' I shrug his hand off my shoulder and stomp away from the conversation.

As I get closer to the convoy of police cars that have gathered a hundred yards from the hut, the seriousness of the situation becomes clear. There are policemen with guns and more panda cars that I have ever seen. It makes me even more angry that they are spending so much effort on this and not on finding Hope.

Kerry spots me and comes rushing over.

'Are you all right, Libby?'

'What do you think?' I've no time to be polite.

'Of course.' She shrinks back into herself and adjusts her coat so that the collar is up around her face.

'You traced my mobile, didn't you?' It finally dawns on me. She doesn't speak but her expression says it all. 'That's how you got here so bloody quickly.'

'I have to ask you, do you know if Danny is armed?'

'What?!' The idea is laughable. 'Is that what you all think? Danny wouldn't know where to get a gun. He's not some lowlife criminal. He's just desperate. He's trying to find our daughter which is something you haven't been able to do.' My accusation cuts through the bitter air and the expression on her face is tragic. I immediately regret my words. 'Look, Kerry, I'm sorry. I'm stressed. I can't believe this is happening. As if things aren't bad enough...' My words trail off in a cloud of icy fog.

'Come and sit in the car and warm up. It's too cold to be standing around out here. I've got some tea in a Thermos.' Her voice is calm and soothing.

'Thank you for being kind to me.' I see a small smile form at the edge of her mouth as she opens up the rear passenger door and signals for me to get inside.

'I need to go and talk to my inspector. Just wait here. I'll be back in a moment.' She closes the door quietly leaving me sitting in silence alone, with fear as my only company.

Danny

'Speak then!' My face is so close to his we are almost touching noses and I can smell the blood, piss and shit very clearly.

'I... I...' he stutters, his Indian accent sounding like a caricature, 'I will talk if you go and sit over there.' He nods his head towards the wall on the far side of the room.'

'You need to get a couple of things straight here. I don't have time for games and you are not in charge.' I stand up tall, with my chest out, trying to ignore the pain in my hand. He is winding me up and I can picture myself making a fist with my good hand and bringing into his face over and over again until he no longer appears human.

Trying to remain cool and collected I go back over to the fire that spits in the oil drum and stand looking into the flames for a while.

This is it, I tell myself. *This is the moment you have been waiting for. He is going to confess.*

Libby

I've been sitting in the car watching police swarm around the dark countryside with their torches and radios for nearly an hour now. So far no one has made a move to approach the building or tried to make contact with Danny. I wonder if he knows we are out here and if he does what he plans to do about it.

Never in my life have I felt as far away from him as I do now. I knew something was wrong; but then of course it was. Hope has been missing for months. We are about to face our first Christmas without her and still don't know where she is or what happened to her.

This never-ending nightmare just keeps pulling us down deeper and deeper into despair. Danny would never have dreamed of hurting someone when I first met him. Sure, he has a temper and he's been known to swing the odd punch when some idiot stepped out of line but that's fairly normal. He's not a kidnapper or a criminal. Or a killer.

If he loses it, though, and feels backed into a corner, I can't be sure what he will do. We have both been so altered by events I don't know who either of us is any more. Our marriage has suffered and now I doubt that we will ever be the same again. Every time we look at each other we are reminded of what is missing. But we need one another to get through this. We were always so strong before – Mr and Mrs Invincible.

No one knows what they are really made of until the worst happens. Some people run and others stay and fight. I guess Danny is a fighter. But what does that make me?

As I sit here, clinging to a now tepid Thermos, I wonder if I have the strength to see this through and to be there for Danny when he needs me most.

I'm startled when there is a sudden rap on the window. King is peering down at me through the glass. I open the door and get out.

'So?'

'So we have secured the area. Nothing is coming in or out without my say-so.'

'I bet the local sheep are quaking in their boots.' I know it's not necessary to be sarcastic but something about his manner is asking for it.

'I understand that this must be a worrying time for you, Mrs Bird.' He refuses to rise to the bait. 'But I need you to answer some questions for me. Can you do that?'

I look up at the man who I was counting on to bring my daughter's kidnapper to justice and all I feel is bitter disappointment.

'All I want is for this to be over.'

'Good.' He senses my discontentment and looks away. We both know he failed with Hope. Maybe he can get it right with Danny.

'I'll answer any questions you have if you promise me this,' I move so that I am back in his eye-line, 'you will not do anything to harm my husband.'

King stands there for a moment contemplating his answer. 'There is no reason for us to think we need to use any force at the moment.'

'That's not exactly an answer.'

'It is the only one I have for now. Perhaps if you answer my questions, then I will be in a position to respond properly.'

'Fine. Where do you want to talk? We're not exactly spoilt for choice.'

'We have a major scene vehicle parked at the end of the lane. If you wouldn't mind accompanying me.' He politely puts his hand out so I can go past.

'Why is nothing happening? What's everyone standing around for?'

'We are waiting for the NCA negotiator to arrive. They should be here soon.'

'NCA?'

'National Crime Agency,' the inspector walks with his hands behind his back, taking large strides over the muddy track.

'That sounds serious.'

'It is, Mrs Bird. This is very serious indeed. Your husband has abducted a man and is holding him prisoner in a building in the middle of nowhere.'

'How do you know that? I mean, have you asked Danny to let Amit go? They might just be having a chat.' The words sound foolish even to my own ears.

'That is what the negotiator is for.'

Moments later we are standing looking at a police van. It looms over us like a large white Winnebago.

King approaches the door and opens it.

'In here,' he instructs, as I step up into the unknown.

Inside there are a row of computers and machines. Officers sit tapping away furiously and barely acknowledge my arrival.

'Do you want some tea?' King pours himself some into a polystyrene cup and blows on the steaming contents.

'No thanks. I've had enough tea already.' He shrugs, taking a sip.

'Can you tell me, were you aware of your husbands' intentions?' His beady eyes fix mine.

'Don't beat around the bush, will you.' I'm tired of his games. 'No. I had no idea at all. He didn't tell me. He convinced me to go and see my parents in Cornwall, I suppose so he could put this hare-brained scheme into action. I can't believe I was so gullible. He hates my parents. I should have smelled a rat.'

'I've spoken to Mrs Chadrad. She has told me that you and your husband went to her house and talked to her. She says she felt threatened.'

'For fuck's sake!' First he offers me tea then he grills me. 'It wasn't like that.'

'But you admit you and your husband approached her?'

'That was months ago. Look, do you think I would be here hoping to persuade Danny to let Amit go if I was in on it? Really?'

'Mrs Bird, I am simply trying to establish what led to this.'

'Hope being taken. That is what led to this.'

'But your husband has no history of violence, no record.'

'Yes, of course it is out of character. You don't need to have a badge to work that out, Inspector. He's desperate.' A lump forms in my throat making it difficult to continue.

One of the officers who has been glued to the phone turns to us. 'Sir, the negotiator will be here in five minutes.'

Things are about to get even more serious.

Danny

'Speak or I will cut you again.' Amit looks up at me like a scolded dog.

'You promise not to hurt me if I tell you?'

'Yes.' If my hand wasn't so busted up, I'd cross my fingers and cement the lie.

'OK. Your little girl did come to my shop.'

My heart is beating hard in my chest and I can't tell if I am breathing or not.

'She wanted magazine. So I watch her flick through them all.'

I start to feel sick.

'Then she decides she wants one with toy hairbrush so she comes to the counter and gives it to me.' He goes quiet and looks down at the ground.

'Then what?' I cannot bear the wait. 'Tell me!'

'She puts her hand in her pocket to take out money but she drops it on the floor.' Amit's dark eyes are looking around the room, anywhere except at me.

'She bang her head on the counter when she stands up. So I go round to see if she is alright and I put my hand on her shoulder.'

The thought of this grotesque man putting his hands on my little girl is too much for me to take. Without a second's hesitation I kick him hard in the chest so that the chair falls back. His hands, which are tied to the back of the chair take most of the weight and I hear a crunching noise as Amit lets out a loud yelp.

'You say you would not hurt me.' His voice is filled with despair.

Breathing heavily, as a result of my sudden burst of energy, I shrug before kicking him hard, once again, in the ribs.

Amit coughs and out of his mouth comes a spray of blood. The shock in his eyes mirrors my own. Then he starts to choke.

Part of me wants to do the decent thing and lift him up off the ground but I am enjoying watching him suffer. He is panicking now and coughing repeatedly. Blood and saliva trickle out the side of his mouth and worm their way down his face. Feeling detached from the situation I watch him as if I am viewing a film.

'I cannot breathe properly,' he splutters.

I do not move.

'Please, I will tell.'

'Where is she?' I feel nothing for the man lying on the ground dying in front of me.

Libby

'Sir!' An officer holding a large gun bursts into the van. 'We just heard screaming coming from the property.' His grey eyes are wide and the cold has turned his nose red.

King throws me a look that I cannot interpret before dashing outside to talk to the armed policeman. I follow, feeling giddy on my feet as I step out of the van. My legs are like jelly and the world feels as if it is spinning.

'I want you all in position. Try and get a clear view of the suspect. The negotiator is on his way: we just need to wait a few minutes.'

'Yes sir.' The officer turns and walks away, talking into a radio that is strapped to his navy bulletproof vest.

King ignores me and sets off to talk to a group of senior-looking officers who are gathered a few yards away.

Standing alone in the freezing cold I look around desperately trying to see Simon and Paul. In the distance I see a haze of cigarette smoke floating up into the black night and know that Simon is responsible for it. Hurrying along the dried mud track, trying not to fall over in my heeled boots, I make my way towards him.

I cannot get the image of that large metal gun out of my mind.

'Simon, Paul, something's happened!'

'What?' Paul barks.

'I'm not sure.' I'm breathless due to the cold. 'There was screaming coming from the building. Did you know that there are armed police here?'

'I saw them earlier.' Simon drops his roll-up and stubs it out with his shoe.

'King told me they have a negotiator coming here but he told the armed officers to surround the building and look for a clear view of Danny!'

Simon and Paul look at each other for what feels like a long time.

I break the silence. 'What are we going to do?'

'They won't shoot him.' Paul is trying to sound confident but failing miserably. 'It might not have been Amit screaming.' All three of us know that is highly unlikely. 'They are bound to wait for this negotiator to show up before doing anything drastic.'

'I'm so cold,' rubbing my hands together I realise my teeth are chattering again.

'I can't stand this,' says Simon closing his eyes and putting his hands over his face. 'This is a waste of time. One of us should go in there and talk to him.'

'I agree.' Paul nods.

'But they won't let any of us in,' I remind the men.

'Maybe if we get close enough we can shout out and warn Dan.' Simon is thinking on his feet.

'But he might panic and do something rash.' This situation is spiralling out of control with each passing minute.

'We can't just do nothing.' Simon begins to roll himself another cigarette.

'Give me one.' I put my trembling hand out having a sudden need to smoke again.

'Go on then,' Paul chips in causing me to raise an eyebrow. 'Stopped twenty years ago.'

I can't believe I never knew that about him. It seems that he's the second man in my life who is full of surprises today. Silently I hope there won't be any more.

Danny

'I will sit here and watch you choke on your own blood if you don't give me an answer right now.'

Crouching down on my heels, still cradling my broken hand, I cock my head to one side so that I can get a closer look at Amit. His eyes are large and bulging. It strikes me suddenly that he looks like a mad bull. The whites of his eyes have almost disappeared and his pupils look like deep black wells.

Amit continues to spit and splutter as I get back up and move towards the oil drum, hoping the warmth from the fire might sooth the cutting pain in my swollen hand.

From the corner of my eye I see a flash of light pass outside through the window and immediately duck down. There is someone out there walking around with a torch.

As panic wraps its arms around my chest I look back over at Amit and realise I cannot let him die. If someone is going to find me here I cannot be sitting with a dead body.

Scrabbling across the floor on my knees I lift Amit so that he is back in an upright position. Being so close to him I can hear the wheezing in his chest. I think I must have broken one of his ribs when I kicked him. Things have gotten out of control and now someone is creeping about outside. For a second I wonder if Simon has come back – but he'd come straight up to the door and announce his arrival, not creep around with a torch.

I am thankful that Amit did not notice the torchlight; otherwise he might try to call out.

Thinking on my feet I reach for the roll of tape and tear a strip off, slapping it onto his mouth so that he cannot speak. He flinches as the sticky plastic makes contact with his wounds.

'Don't fucking move or make a sound.'

Amit gives an exaggerated nod that opens the cut across the back of his neck, which starts seeping blood again.

My eyes are fixed on the small window where I saw the torchlight. The night has returned to inky black again and I can see nothing else. But I know what I saw. Someone is out there.

Then the entire cottage floods with light. All around the outside of the building there are bright lights shining on us. I freeze with fear.

'Daniel Bird,' a booming voice calls out through a megaphone. 'My name is Dave Hardy. I am a negotiator working with the police. I'm here to talk to you and to try and find a peaceful way out of this situation.'

There is a pause and I realise my heart is beating at a thousand miles an hour.

'I need you to confirm that you are there, Dan. Is it all right if I call you "Dan"?'

I freeze, not knowing how to respond. They know I'm here. Shit.

'Dan, can you hear me?' the man's voice is rough around the edges but his tone is calm and collected.

'Yes.' I call out in response, my voice cracking.

'OK. Good. Dan, is it OK if I call you "Dan"?'

'Fine.' As if it makes any difference what he calls me.

'Can you please tell me if Amit Chadrad is with you?'

Then I realise I am surrounded. Everyone out there knows Amit is here but I am not ready to admit the severity of the situation to myself yet.

'Is Amit there, Dan?'

'Yes.'

'Good. OK. Is he hurt, Dan?'

I wish the fucking man would stop using my name. I know what he's doing. I'm not stupid but I don't know how to answer the question.

'Dan, is Amit hurt?' The voice booms again.

'He's fine,' I lie.

'OK. That's good.'

None of this is good, I think.

'I need to know if you are armed, Dan. You need to be honest with me if we are going to get through this.'

Armed? I'm not some nutter with a gun. 'No. I don't have a gun,' I call out realising how dangerous they think I must be.

'Do you have any weapons?' Dave calls back. Again, I'm not sure how to answer the question.

'No.' It's half the truth.

'OK, Dan. I am going to treat you with the dignity you deserve. You can trust me. But you need to move away from Amit. Can you do that?'

'No. I won't.' They are not getting me to back down that easily after everything I've done. 'He confessed! I got him to admit he took Hope.' I wrap my good arm around his throat and hold him in a headlock so that they can all see I mean business.

There is silence for a while as they plan their next move.

'OK, Dan. We are going to work together to make sure everyone gets out of this safely. No one needs to get hurt.' *Hope has been hurt*, I think, tightening my grip on Amit who squirms and bucks on the chair.

'I'm sorry, but I am not letting him go until he gives me all the information I'm after.'

'It would be much better if you left it to us.'

'It's been months and the police have done nothing! This paedophile has been walking about free. You had your chance. Now we do this my way.'

'This is the first time I have met you. You seem like a reasonable man. I understand you are desperate but this is not the answer. This is not your fault but I can't help you unless you cooperate with me. Can you do that, Dan?'

'Not until he tells me where she is.'

'You are an intelligent man. You are not an idiot. You understand that you need to let Amit go. You have a wife and a daughter who need you.'

'I'm doing it for them.'

'Libby doesn't want you to hurt Amit, Dan. She wants you to let him go and come out unharmed. That's what we all want.'

'Is Lib with you?' I feel my resolve beginning to wane.

'Yes, Dan. She's worried about you. She loves you.'

Those three words pull my heart stings but don't stop me feeling like an animal backed into a corner with nowhere to go.

'And I love her.' I yell. 'This is why I'm doing this. We deserve to know what happened to our little girl.'

'This is not the way.'

'If you don't all leave me alone I am going to fucking kill him!' Amit begins wriggling again. 'I'm serious! Back off.'

'We can't do that, Dan.' Dave remains calm. 'We will not let you hurt him.'

'You can't stop me.' I sink my teeth into the top of Amit's sweaty skull and bite down hard. Through the gaffer tape he whines like a stuck pig.

'Dan, you need to understand that we have the building surrounded and there are armed police on the scene. No one wants this to end badly.'

Armed police? Oh fuck.

I realise with the amount of artificial light being flooded into the room through the window I am exposed. Dragging Amit on his chair across the room, the wooden legs scrapping on the stone floor, I try to reposition myself so that those police officers with their guns cannot see me.

'All I want is to be able to talk to Amit. Then I'll let him go. But you have to give me five minutes to get the answers I want; otherwise this is going to get ugly really quickly.' I hear myself say the words but don't recognise the person speaking. This is not me.

'Why don't you let me come in, Dan? We'll have a chat, face to face.'

'Why?'

'Because I am here to help you. Let me help you, Dan.'

'How can you possibly help me?'

'Let me see that Amit is OK, then, together you and I can talk to him.'

'No.'

I don't want that man in the room. I don't think I could look him in the eye.

Libby

'Let me try. Please let me talk to him. I think it might help.' I cling onto Dave's coat pulling at the sleeve like a child but he keeps his steely eyes fixed on the building waiting for Danny to speak again. When he doesn't Dave turns to me, flicking off the megaphone so our conversation won't be heard by anyone else.

'OK. It is important that you remain calm. Talk to him about your life together and your daughter. Don't engage with him in any discussion about Mr Chadrad. He thinks he is doing this for you and he could twist anything you say to fit his plans. Tell him you want him to come home and that you don't want this.'

I nod, accepting the megaphone he holds out.

'If the conversation starts to aggravate him, I will put an end to it. We all want this to end well.'

As I turn the megaphone back on with my shaking hands, Dave takes a step backwards. The stage is mine now and I have to get this right.

'Danny?' my voice sounds strange and distorted. 'It's me. It's Lib.' There is silence and I am terrified that he won't talk to me. I have to get through to him. 'Danny, please talk to me.' I wait again for a response.

'Lib,' his voice sounds distant and weak.

'Come home. I miss you. You don't have to do this. Come home and let's put this behind us.'

'He's admitted it Lib! He confessed. We are so close to getting the answers. Just let me have five more minutes then I promise this will all be over.'

'No Danny, it has to stop now. You got the confession and that's great but let the police take it from here. You've done enough. Now it's time to walk away.'

The silent response that greets me makes me want to cry. Standing in the cold, surrounded by the elements, I have never felt so alone.

'Hope wouldn't want this,' I cry out. I'm grabbing at straws.

Still he doesn't speak.

I feel a hand on my shoulder and turn to see Dave standing there.

'You did your best.' He takes the megaphone out of my hands and returns to the spot he had been standing in to talk to King about their next move.

'He must be so scared.' I wipe my snotty nose on my coat sleeve as Simon comes and puts his arms around me. The smell of tobacco on his coat reminds me of my grandfather.

'He'll see the light, Lib. I'm sure it will be fine.'

'If he wants to talk to Amit, why doesn't he? Just ask the monster the questions then walk out of there. I don't understand.'

'He feels trapped and he's panicking.'

'I know. That's how I feel too.' I look over at Dave and King who are in intense discussion. 'I've got a bad feeling about this.'

Danny

'Right, you piece of shit, everyone knows you're here. You've got a large audience now, buddy. It's time to sing like a canary. I'm going to remove the gaffer tape and you are going to tell me exactly what you did to my daughter. If you don't, then we are in for the long haul. It's up to you now. Talk and you walk out of here alive. Don't and, well, it won't be pleasant.'

Amit slowly nods his head.

Before removing the tape I take a long look into his terrified face. I want him to know I am serious.

His tired eyes are red and puffy and tears gather in the corners. He is no longer recognisable as the man I brought into the building twenty-four hours ago.

Tearing the tape off with no attempt at being gentle I watch as he gulps in large breaths of air. The rattling noise coming from his chest grows louder with each breath he takes. I start to wonder if I've killed him already.

'Talk.' I say as Amit looks around the room hoping he might find help from somewhere.

'I… I…' his voice is hoarse and the words come out raspy as he stutters.

'Speak up man!' Spittle flies out of my mouth as I speak.

'Well, she had hurt her head.' He keeps trying to turn to face the window but the restraints hold him firmly to the chair.

'Then?'

'Then I say I take her upstairs to put ice on her head. She comes with me. I don't hurt her, I promise.' Amit's eyes dart around the floodlit room searching for a possible exit. I can read his thoughts.

'This doesn't make sense. How does Hope go from banging her head in your shop to disappearing? Explain that to me.' My patience is growing thin.

'Well, I... she... I mean when we go up to the flat she has the ice on her head for a while. Then she just fall asleep at the table. I try to wake her up, I really try, but she does not move.'

He is telling me she died and that it was an accident. I sink to the floor and cradle my head in my hands before letting out a long scream.

Libby

'What the fuck was that?' I look up at Simon whose expression mirrors my own. Sheer panic envelops his face.

'I don't know.' He looks over to King and Dave who have both turned their attention back to the building.

Dave steps forward and brings the megaphone up to his mouth.

'Dan, is everything all right in there?' We all wait with bated breath for a response that does not come.

'Dan, you need to talk to me. I need to know you and Amit are all right.' King shakes his head and walks away from Dave, talking into his police radio.

I watch as armed police move in closer to the cottage, their guns held up. It all seems to happen in slow motion.

'Dan, you need to talk to me.' Dave's voice has lost its control and his desperation echoes over the dark hills. 'Dan?'

'He said it was an accident!' Danny wails, his words cutting through the still cold air. 'He says she's dead. My baby. She's dead!'

Danny

'Where is she?' I get up off the ground. My legs feel like jelly as I approach the man who is responsible for my daughter's death. I have been waiting for months to find out what happened to her. Now that I know, I almost wish I didn't. In a matter of seconds everything has changed. Until then, part of me continued to believe she was alive and that I would see her again.

'What did you do with her? Where is her body?' I can hardly bring myself to believe that there is a body. The tears fall freely and, strangely, I've forgotten about the pain in my hand. Some things hurt more.

'If you let me go, I tell you.' Amit will not look at me. His head is hung low.

'No. You will tell me now.'

Before I've had a chance to think I react and wrap my hands around his throat. His neck is fat and soft and I squeeze as hard as I can. His eyes bulge and his mouth falls opening trying desperately to let some air in. I continue to tighten my grip, not feeling any pain in my broken hand, not hearing the calls from the police outside as his face starts to turn puce. I can feel the blood in the veins in his neck trying to pump its way up to his head. His pulse ticks against my palms.

Then I notice the blood vessels in his eyes getting redder and his tongue makes its way out of his mouth, flailing around like a living piece of steak. His breath smells like blood and his body twitches violently trying to escape. I hear a faint popping from somewhere inside his throat. Then the familiar scent of shit hits me and I realise he has defecated again. Still I grip harder until his body starts to go limp and the light in his open eyes begins to fade. A trickle of blood runs out of the corner of his mouth and down his chin but I cannot let go. I will not let go. Not even when the police burst into the room and point their guns at me. Not even when I hear them load their weapons. Not even when the first shot is fired.

Libby

Everyone else seems to rush towards the cottage. Figures pass in a flurry, making their way towards the drama. But I can't move. I stand perfectly still, not hearing the shouts from various directions. I see people's mouths moving but don't hear what they are saying.

As if I am a ghost I seem to float up out of my body and I watch the pandemonium unfold, feeling completely detached from it all. Paul marches towards the building, which is now alive with police, forensics investigators and a couple of paramedics.

My legs don't move. They remain frozen to the hard ground beneath my feet. Simon remains by my side and we both look on in silence.

When King finally emerges from the scene I watch him coming towards me. With each long stride he takes I am filled with fear. The blur of officers around us seem to melt away when he finally reaches me.

'I am sorry. We did not have a choice.' King stands tall, his hands folded in front of him. Simon puts his hand over his mouth and walks away leaving the two of us looking at each other in silence.

'He was killing him.' Then from behind King I see two black body bags being wheeled out of the cottage. How long have I been standing here?

'They are dead.' I watch the ambulance doors being thrown open and the bags being loaded onto them.

'I'm afraid so.' King takes a step towards me looking as if he is ready to catch me. But I don't fall. I still can't move. My eyes are glued to the black body bags. From here I can't tell who is in which bag. They both look the same. How strange that I cannot recognise the body of my husband. It seems wrong not knowing which bag he is in.

Not listening to King, who is still talking at me, I start to go towards the bagged corpses. I don't remember walking but somehow my body knows to put one foot in front of the other. When I am just a few yards away from the ambulances with their flashing lights I stop and stare, still unable to determine which of them is Danny. The outlines of the bags give nothing away – just bodies that could belong to anyone.

'Where is Danny?' A female paramedic turns to look at me. She knows who I am without asking my name. From a medical bag that is tucked under a chair in the ambulance she retrieves something before coming over.

'Come and sit down, love,' She removes a foil blanket from its cellophane wrapping and pulls it across my shoulders. The foil crunches as I am led towards the ambulance.

'I need to know where he is.'

'You are suffering from shock. I don't think it'd be wise fer you to see the body at the moment.' Her Scottish accent is soft and rolling like the hills that surround us.

'He's Danny.' I cannot think of him as a body.

'Of course.' She guides me into a sitting position.

'It will be easier fer you to see him when he's bin cleaned up.'

'But which one is he?' My whole body starts to shake as if there is an earthquake taking place below us. But she is not shaking and I realise it is just me.

'Yer husband'll be taken to the hospital.'

'I want to go with him.'

'I'm afraid that will nay be possible.'

'You can't just take him away from me. I'm his wife.' Then the tears come and I start choking because I feel a wave of violent nausea.

'Deep breaths.' The kind paramedic strokes my back as I vomit all over the cold ground.

Bent over, looking down at the meagre contents of my stomach on the floor a pair of men's brown shoes come into view. Without looking up I know they belong to Paul. 'I can't breathe.' Panic starts to set in and I feel as if I am drowning.

Paul bends down, so he is level with me. His face is red and puffy. His blue eyes still blurry with tears.

'He's gone.' Paul's voice breaks and I wonder which one of us he is talking to.

'No.' I stutter and collapse onto the ground hugging my knees and burying my face. 'I can't lose anyone else. Not Danny. Not like this.'

I feel the paramedic back away, leaving us together to absorb the enormity of what has happened.

'He is with Hope now,' Paul says, sniffing before standing up and walking away. We cannot bring ourselves to look at each other for a moment longer.

JANUARY 2014

Libby

The day of the funeral has arrived. After the initial shock of Danny's death, twinned with the horror of finding out that Hope had been killed had sunk in, I was catatonic for a few days. I don't really remember what happened. There were police and questions and press. It remains like a mysterious dream that happened to someone else.

To begin with, Paul and Clare wanted to be close to us. They wanted to spend time with their remaining granddaughter and the only thing left that was a link to their son. But I couldn't deal with my pain as well as theirs. I had so much to process in those early days.

Alex, my wonderful brother, came to the rescue. He gently suggested that they go home and grieve for a while so that Gracie wasn't subjected to so many different people's misery. He was right of course, and finally Paul and Clare agreed to return to Tunbridge Wells. I think the arrival of the press on my doorstep, once again, helped to persuade them. They didn't want their pictures plastered across the tabloids any more than I did.

One freezing morning, when I was collecting the milk from my doorstep, I happened to come face to face with Tom Daler. The weasel shoved a Dictaphone into my face and asked me if I'd ever suspected I was married to a murderer. Battling against a mixture of emotions I tore the foil lid off the top of the milk and threw the contents in his face. I don't know which of us was the most surprised. I didn't wait to find out and slammed the door shut behind me. I was still shaking with rage nearly half an hour later.

Dr Vogler paid me visits on a few occasions and explained that I was living with the after-effects of shock. He warned me that I might experience flashbacks, amnesia, detachment and anxiety. He wasn't wrong.

The flashbacks and the nightmares were the worst. My head played games with me and sometimes placed me inside the building just as the trigger was being pulled. In those nightmares I'd call out to Danny, begging him to walk away from Amit but he wouldn't hear me. No one could hear me. I would scream in silence. Then moments later I'd wake up dripping with sweat and shivering.

I found it so difficult getting into bed alone and since Gracie was so disturbed by the loss of her father, I let her sleep in bed with me every night. Waking up after having a nightmare meant I had to stay very quiet and still so as not to disturb Gracie, who tossed and turned beside me, sometimes crying in her sleep.

It had, naturally, never occurred to me to be prepared to deal with a grieving child. It wasn't something you ever think you will need to do. Sure, people lose their grandparents and that can be very traumatic but little girls aren't meant to lose their big sisters or their daddies – especially in the way that she had. It is like a bad film and we are stuck in the middle of it but there is no director shouting 'Cut'.

After many hours spent worrying about how to handle the funeral, Alex finally helped me to decide. The issue was that Danny's name was now mud. Despite the fact people tried to understand how desperate he was, no one could get past the issue that he had taken another man's life. I still don't know how I feel about it. We had the answers we wanted about what happened to our girl, but his actions didn't bring Hope back and they left Gracie and me without him. Strangely, though, there was no peace in that. Until Amit confessed we were able to cling to some belief that she might still be alive and returned to us. When Danny died so did that wishful thinking, which had kept us going during those horrific months.

The biggest issue I faced, regarding the funeral, was that people from all over the area wanted to come and pay their respects to Hope, but they were less willing to shed a tear for Danny. Despite the fact we never discovered where Amit put Hope's body, it was decided that we should have a funeral for her anyway. It would allow us to lay her to rest at last. But I wanted her to be with her father. So after an agonising decision Danny was cremated at a small service near Cambridge in those quiet days between Christmas and New Year.

Today, the first working day of 2014, there would be a separate memorial for Hope.

The local community had been so invested in the case. Men and woman from all walks of life had helped with the search in the early days. Strangers had posted fliers around asking for information. The support was phenomenal.

Strangely enough the vicar from the village church, St Mary Magdalene, began to pop in and pay me visits. He was a skinny man and not very tall. His greying hair produced an absurd amount of dandruff that sat like a fine covering of snow on his shoulders.

The Reverend Robert Waller had been at the church since before we came here. He was often seen strolling about the village, his hands behind his back, his head bowed low.

Dan and I had never really spoken to him, since I wasn't a church goer or a believer but I had visited the church once.

Ickleton had been home to a Benedictine nunnery in the Middle Ages and in 1979, before I was born, there had been a fire at the church after an arson attack. What the fire revealed was a number of beautiful and rare paintings on the church walls beneath the whitewash, which dated back to the twelfth century.

I don't care much for religion but art is another matter and soon after moving to the village, Danny and I went into the church to see the famous paintings that depict the lives of some of the saints and a few biblical stories. The artwork appeared in dusky pink and sandy brown shades all over the walls. After picking up a leaflet in the church we discovered they were not only unique to England but also the only surviving example of their kind.

Standing in the church that day, with our heads craned up to the ceiling we could feel the history of the place. Despite the smell of old books and dust, the building had a welcoming feel to it. It was then I understood what appealed to people in the village who showed up for the services.

The church was a big part of the community and at last I realised why.

Danny and I had never really gotten involved with village life. We lived in our small cottage on the outskirts and had always been content to nod at people from time to time. We weren't rude, I hope, but we just weren't looking to make friends. English village life can be claustrophobic if you get too involved. But since Hope's abduction it was as if our life belonged to everyone. They all felt it was their business to know what was happening and who we were.

When the vicar showed up at my door, wearing his dog collar, which immediately put me off, I was taken aback.

'Hello.' I didn't open the door fully, wary of any lurking press.

'I am Robert Waller.' He spoke with a nasal voice. 'I've come to express my condolences.' The stranger stood there in the cold, looking uncomfortable.

'Well, thank you. I'm Libby.' What else could I say?

'I was wondering if I might come in for a moment.' He removed a large cotton handkerchief from his coat pocket and dabbed his nose.

Not wanting to be rude, and somewhat intimidated by any man of the cloth, I moved aside and let him in.

'I won't stay long.' He folded the hanky and put it back in his pocket, 'I just wanted to introduce myself properly.'

'I appreciate you taking the time to pay me a visit, reverend, but I must warn you I am not a believer.'

The grey man did not bat an eyelid. 'One does not have to have faith to know suffering.'

'I can't argue with that.'

'We have been praying for you and your family.'

That put my back up. 'That's very kind of you.'

'The lord teaches us about forgiveness,' Robert continued, 'and in order to find comfort you must let forgiveness into your heart.'

'Who is it you want me to forgive?'

'The man who hurt your daughter.'

'Why do you care?'

'"And when you stand praying, if you hold anything against anyone, forgive them, so that your Father in heaven may forgive you your sins." Mark, chapter eleven, verse twenty-five.'

I stood there gobsmacked, not knowing how to respond.

'But I don't pray.'

'We pray for you, Libby.'

'And can you please tell me, has everyone forgiven my husband for his sin?' I spit the last word out as it if tastes vile. 'I am meant to forgive the man who murdered my child, but can you please tell me that you are asking your congregation to forgive my husband?'

'Perhaps you need to forgive them both.'

'Perhaps I do. Or perhaps it is not your business.'

'I thought you might need to talk about what happened. This is a tragic case and it has been brought to my attention that you are suffering.'

'Of course I am. But I am not suffering as much as my child did.' My hands begin to shake.

'If you do not wish to talk to me, perhaps you have friends and family you can confide in. Or the police.'

'Why would I need to talk to the police? They shot my husband.'

Robert sighed and dabbed his running nose again.

'I'm sorry, I just don't understand what it is you want from me.'

'I wanted to encourage you to forgive your child's abductor. For your own sake.'

'Thank you for thinking of me but I will deal with this in my own way.' Then I showed him out.

After everything that had happened, all I wanted was to be left alone to work through it. But the world was watching and talking about what Danny had done. It was almost as if Amit's crime had been forgotten and replaced by something even more sensational.

In the weeks after the events in Scotland, I learnt all about the final show-down between my husband, Amit and the police.

It seems that Amit claimed killing Hope was an accident. We will never know if that is the truth but the general feeling is that he was lying, especially given his criminal history. The argument was that if it were an accident why didn't he call for help? Why hide her body? None of it made much sense to me. I was told that after he admitted to being involved in her death that Danny lost it and strangled him in a fit of rage.

I also learnt that during the hours Danny kept Amit hostage he did, in fact, torture him. That is something I will never understand. Sure, Danny had a temper, like a lot of men, but he was fundamentally not a violent person. He had been pushed to it.

A week or so after his death I remember turning on the television to see a psychologist being questioned about his interpretation of the events leading up to the shoot-out. The doctor was a stuffy-looking man, with a head of thick grey hair. He peered at the interviewer as if he were giving a lecture and said that what had happened could be explained if we studied The Stanford Prison Experiment, which took place in the United States in 1971. A psychology professor used students to study the effect of becoming a prisoner or guard. The students were split into those groups and put into a mock prison. What unfolded astounded everyone involved. The students, given the roles as guards, became violent and authoritarian, having never shown signs of this behaviour before. This, the doctor said, mirrored what happened with Danny and Amit. The conclusion of that experiment was that the situation was responsible for shaping the actions of those involved, rather than individual personalities.

'We see a very clear correlation between this study and the inhuman treatment Mr Bird inflicted on Mr Chadrad,' the doctor concluded on the morning news show.

After his interview the channel received an unprecedented number of callers, all eager to share their opinions. When one woman called in and said that Danny was 'just evil' I switched the television off. I'd had enough speculation and bullshit. No amount of examining what happened would ever really explain why Danny did what he did. And what angered me is that none of the press looked into what Amit did or why. Amit became a victim and his crime went by unnoticed. Focus remained on Hope and the tragedy of her young life being cut short but how she died and the reason, were brushed under the carpet.

How I survived for those weeks I'll never know. I must have fed Gracie and changed her. Life went on somehow, although it was all a blur.

When Danny's funeral arrived I was a wreck. Vast amounts of Valium helped me to make it through. Gracie, who had always been a petite child, got more and more skinny. Her skin was so pale that the bags under her eyes looked as if they covered her cheeks. She became very quiet and withdrawn.

When I sat her down and explained to her that her Daddy was gone, her thumb went into her mouth and she went silent. Her thumb has been in her mouth ever since and she will not leave my side for even a second. She comes with me when I go to the loo. It is as if she is terrified that I am going to disappear, too.

This morning, as I lie in bed waiting for her to wake up, I try to prepare myself for the day ahead. The press will be back again, no doubt, spoiling our quiet little village.

When I was with the undertaker planning Danny's funeral the kind gentleman asked if I wanted them to produce a coffin for Hope. It took me aback because I hadn't thought about it. It seemed strange to have a coffin when we didn't have a body. He explained that it helped some people who were grieving to have a tangible focus for their grief, even if the box would be empty. It would be symbolic, he said. But I couldn't abide the idea. No empty box would help me come to terms with my loss. The thought of a hollow coffin only reminded me that we didn't have her small body to bury. I politely declined his suggestion and after talking it through with Alex settled that Hope's name would be added to the stone that was going to be laid in the gardens at the crematorium.

The memorial was to be held in the hall at Hope's school. The head teacher, Mrs Fenton, agreed it would be a fitting place for the service and the entire school was invited to attend, along with friends and family. Mrs Fenton also suggested that they plant a tree in the school grounds in Hope's memory. I cried when she said it but agreed it would be a lovely thing to do. Before I knew it Hope's class teachers, Joanne Robertson and Helen Claire, had made a collection to buy a cherry tree and arranged for it to be planted the day after the memorial.

People around me, who I hadn't really noticed before, offered unconditional support.

As Gracie stirred in bed next to me I turned to face her, pushing her mousey brown curls away from her face.

No matter how much sleep she had she looked constantly exhausted. We both were.

'Morning, monkey.' She started to rub the sleep out of her eyes and stretched her arms. Gracie gave a little smile before wriggling in closer and burying her face against my arm. I held her, noticing how fragile her little body felt. Her hair smelt like fresh baked bread and I inhaled deeply, wanting to remember the scent forever.

'You know today we say goodbye to Hope?' I stroked her head and spoke softly not wanting to alarm her in case she might have forgotten. Her silent response answered my question. 'We'll go the school and sing some songs Hope liked listening to. Do you remember which song you chose?' I feel her nod her head and am glad for any response. 'What was it again?' I know perfectly well but I really want to hear her speak. I need to hear her voice.

'Twinkle, twinkle.' Gracie's breath feels warm against my arm.

'That's right. Will you sing it with me, girlie?'

Gracie shakes her head furiously and buries herself deeper beneath the duvet.

'Come on, monkey, we can sing it together.' I feel a lump form in my throat at the thought of hearing the song sung by anyone other than Hope. 'OK, you don't have to. It's all right.'

Our conversation is cut short by the shrill ringing of the telephone. Answering it begrudgingly I secretly wish that today could be a private matter for family only.

'Hello?'

'Ah, hi, Lib.' Mike's Aussie voice travels down the line.

'Hi Mike.' Why is he calling me at seven-thirty in the morning?

'I just wanted to check how you guys are holding up?'

'Well, you know. It's going to be a tough day.'

'Sure is.' He pauses. 'Look, tell me to bugger off if you like, but I was wondering if you wanted me and Eva to walk down with you, to the school. I mean, you probably have your family around you but I thought, you know, maybe you might like it if we joined you.'

I've only laid eyes on Eva once since learning that Hope is dead. I found it very hard to look at my dead child's best friend because of the memories that came flooding in. It's easy to forget that Gracie and I aren't the only ones suffering.

'Sure. That would be good. I think Gracie would like it.'

'Well, if you're sure. I didn't want to impose but I thought maybe it might help having friends around you today.'

'Maybe it will. I don't know. It's so surreal, Mike. How did this happen? Why am I saying goodbye to my baby?'

'Ah Lib, don't cry. I'm gonna throw some clothes on and Eva and I will come over. We'll make you guys some breakfast. You need all the support you can get today.'

Hope

I've been picking at my feet for a while. They feel really dry and crusty. I thought maybe by now I would get used to the dark and be able to see but I am still blind like a mole. And that makes sense that I am like a mole because now I think I must be underground. The smell of the earth sometimes is strong, like the coffee daddy drinks mixed with wet grass. I can't decide if I like the smell or not. Sometimes I think I do but maybe I am just getting used to it.

The other thing I am getting used to now is being on my own. I missed Zoe a lot to begin with but now I know it's just me here.

The strangest thing is what happens to me when I'm not thinking about stuff. It's like I don't exist some of the time but then when my brain starts going round I am real again. It feels really weird, a bit like I can time travel but when I'm not here I don't know where I go or what happens to me. It's when I'm time travelling that my body hurts in those places again. Sometimes I think that maybe I have been asleep and that is where all the empty time goes. There's not much else to do here except think.

I do sing songs sometimes to cheer me up or I say nursery rhymes. It stops me being frightened so much and reminds me when I was happy playing with Gracie or my friends.

At school me and Eva made up the groovy club. It was only for people who were part of the girl gang and no one else could join. Definitely no boys. We had a secret password and used to write notes that we would put in our book bags with lists of things we were going to do in the groovy club. That was a lot of fun. I was in charge and Eva was my assistant.

One Sunday when I was bored, and mum and dad were watching football on the TV, I made badges for everyone who was in the club. They were really cool with pink sparkles on. My teachers Joanne and Helen said they were pretty but we couldn't wear them in school, so we would put them on at the end of the day when we were waiting to be picked up from the playground. I wonder if my friends still have their badges? Maybe they have forgotten about me. Eva probably has a new best friend now. I wish I wasn't so lonely.

APRIL 2016

Libby

The first time we kissed I was a gibbering wreck. It had been so long since I'd been looked at in that way and part of me still felt guilty being with anyone other than Danny.

He'd kindly offered to come over and spend New Year's Eve with me. He understood how difficult that time of year was. Everything was still so raw.

It had been only two years since I'd lost Danny and learnt that Hope was dead and that time had passed slowly. Gracie had started school and was going daily, leaving me with a lot of spare times on my hands.

I still missed Danny every day. He was the love of my life and the father of my children. Without him nothing would ever be the same again.

Eventually the other village inhabitants learnt to give us space. The vicar still came to visit, despite the frosty reception he received. I couldn't understand why he wouldn't leave us alone. There was no way I was going to suddenly find God and start going to church.

He came about once a month, and always brought a lollipop for Gracie. It was sweet of him and eventually I softened. Robert stopped quoting the bible and kept the subject matter light. Never again did he ask me to forgive Amit.

Once he asked if I thought Gracie might like to go to church one day and watch the choir sing but I declined. No matter how nice he was I would never let my little girl out of my sight, even if it was to pay a visit to a church with a vicar. We would sit together and have a cup of tea before he'd make his excuses and leave again. Eventually, I realised that he had helped to get people to forget what had happened to us. He was on our side but I couldn't understand why he persisted, especially since I'd been so unfriendly.

After Danny died, I couldn't carry on with the business. It had been our thing and without him it didn't make sense. So, in order to scrape a living, I started baking cakes for special occasions. I'd never been very good at making the sponge but had always been a dab hand at making them look pretty. With a little help from Betty Crocker, and word of mouth, I started to build the business up. The spare bedroom was turned into a work kitchen I could use to produce the cakes and practice my sugarcraft in. You wouldn't believe the amount of equipment it takes to make a wedding cake.

After baking cupcakes for a school fete and, I discovered it was the perfect job for me. It meant that I could work from home and always be around to collect Gracie from school. I made it a rule to try not to work at weekends so that she and I could spend time together but that didn't always work out.

Paul and Clare were wonderful. They helped so much financially. I think I would have lost the house if it weren't for them and, although in some ways being there without Danny and Hope was sad, it kept them alive to us. I wasn't ready to let them go and say goodbye.

Mike had been a pillar of strength during the first few years. Having lost his own wife, he related to the pain I was suffering. It was good to have someone else I could talk to about my grief. Not only were we both single parents but our girls were both only children.

Eva had always been very sweet to Gracie and when she learnt that Hope had gone she took it upon herself to look after Gracie. I think it helped Gracie to have Eva around. She missed Hope's company so much and Eva was the next best thing to her sister.

The four of us spent a lot of time together visiting the park, going to pizza restaurants and generally buggering about killing time. In some ways Mike was quite an over-bearing man. He would always order for us all without checking what we actually wanted. Initially it annoyed me, he was so unlike Danny in that way, but then I started to find it endearing, attractive even,

Mike came over at least twice a week and we sat chatting while the girls went upstairs or outside to play. I felt part of a family again so when he kissed me it didn't seem strange. It felt good. We were both lonely and got on well so the transition from friends to a couple was simple.

I would never feel for him what I felt for Danny but I realised I didn't have to. I needn't compare them. Circumstances were so different with Mike. We were looking for company and we found each other.

I insisted that we took things slowly as much for the children's sake as our own. Both Gracie and Eva had had their fair share of heartache and I had resolved not to be the cause of any more. Mike and I had to tread carefully when explaining things to them. Eva got it immediately and was very encouraging. Gracie was a bit slower on the uptake but didn't seem at all bothered by the development. If anything, she was pleased to be seeing more of Mike and Eva.

I'd given Mike a key so that he could come and go as he pleased. My cottage and garden were bigger than his place so we naturally congregated here.

When he came in that evening, he was smiling like a Cheshire cat. I asked him why he was looking so pleased with himself.

'I didn't want to tell you about it until it was all sorted but I've gone and booked a holiday for us all, Lib.' From his back jeans pocket he removed a piece of printed paper and handed it to me. On it is a picture of a beautiful villa with a pool. 'I thought we could all do with some sunshine. It's booked for the May half term.' His eyes are wide and sparkling with excitement. 'So what'd you say?'

'It's gorgeous. Where is it?'

'Algarve, so the weather should be good.'

'The kids will be so excited. What a lovely idea.' I go over to where he is sitting, plonk myself down on his lap and wrap my arms around his neck. 'I could get used to this.'

MAY 2016

Hope

I feel sad all the time now. I remember telling Zoe that Daddy would come and save us but I don't believe that any more. It's been so long I've been here. I feel like I must be older but I don't know if that's true. Without being able to see the sun and the moon I don't know anything. It might be Christmas day or even Easter or something.

If it was Easter and I was at home Mummy and Daddy would have helped me go on an egg hunt around the garden. It's funny how many eggs the bunny always leaves. There are always two big ones at the end of the hunt. One for me and one for Gracie and they are always the same so we don't fight. The Easter bunny is clever like that.

Thinking about chocolate is making me hungry. I wonder if I am really good if maybe I might get to eat some again one day. Just a little bit. That would be really good. Maybe Zoe is somewhere eating chocolate now. I hope so. If she got away, then I think I can. But I still don't understand where she went or why she got out when I am still stuck here.

Sometimes I like to pretend that I am playing hide and seek and I'm in a cupboard waiting for Gracie to find me. We used to play that game a lot. I am much better at it than she is. Even Mummy and Daddy can't find me most of the time. They stand near where I am and I hear them saying 'I wonder where she is?' and I have to put my hand over my mouth so they don't hear me giggle.

But now I wonder if maybe they think I'm hiding. Maybe I am. I can't remember what happened. Did they lose me when we were playing a game? Maybe I haven't been here for that long after all. Or maybe this is like *The Lion, the Witch and the Wardrobe* and I'm stuck in a cupboard somewhere. But then I think about the voice and I know that's not right.

I wonder if I might get another friend soon? It was a surprise when Zoe arrived so maybe I'll get a new friend one day. That would be nice.

Libby

After an easy flight and a relatively short drive we arrive at the villa, which is perched on a hill with breath-taking views down to the coast. The house itself, Villa Montanha, is a stone building that has been painted in faded peach, reflecting the warm sunshine that bounces off the gravel drive that leads up to it.

The girls both jump out of our silver hire car and run towards a plump woman who was standing there waiting to greet us. She has thick grey roots and is wearing a lime green sundress that looks as old as the hills that surround us. The hot sun beats down onto my bare shoulders as I get out of the sweaty car fanning myself.

'Family Kelly?' She smiles broadly at us and I don't have the heart to correct her.

'I'm Mike Kelly. Lina, I presume?' His bright orange short-sleeved shirt sticks to his back as he shakes her hand. I still think of Mike as short. Danny was at least three inches taller than him.

'I show you round?' Her accent makes her sound almost Russian.

'No need. We can work it all out, can't we, girls?' Mike calls to the children who have disappeared around the back of the house to see what there is.

'OK, OK.' She shrugs, happy to leave us to it. 'You have problem you call me. I come. My number in villa.' And with that she shuffles off down the drive, her black plastic flip-flops slapping the gravel beneath her feet.

'I wonder if all the locals are that easy-going,' I raise an eyebrow before lifting a heavy piece of luggage out of the boot.

'I'll do that, Lib.' Mike rushes to my aid and carries the bag to the front door. 'Let's go and see what our new home is like, shall we?' He slips the keys in the lock and pushes the door open.

Inside the villa is spacious and light. The lobby leads to the kitchen on the right, which has a terracotta stone floor, with Shaker units that I immediately coveted for my own kitchen and a large Belfast sink. A bar counter divides the cooking area from the dining room, which has a round metal table and four chairs. The layout had been designed to perfection.

I follow Mike as he returns to the lobby and leads me into the sitting room on the other side. On the far side of the room is a large, contemporary open fireplace. It's hard to imagine it ever gets cold here, though. The ceiling to floor windows show off the incredible view of the countryside that rolls down towards the coast, and overlook the pool, where we see the girls are already playing, dipping their feet in the water and splashing each other. I've not seen Gracie look this happy for so long and I am overwhelmed with joy. For a moment I imagine it's Hope there with her, instead of Eva.

I will never love Mike the way I loved Danny but I want Gracie to be happy and to grow up in a family environment. He's a good man and that's what counts.

'You all right, doll?' Mike puts his arm around my shoulder and I rest my head against his.

'I am. It just is odd feeling happy. I can't help it. I feel guilty. They are dead and here I am enjoying the sunshine. I still miss them both so much.'

'I'm sure that's normal. I felt the same way after Emma died. It'll get easier.'

'Thank you for being so understanding.'

'You are most welcome.' He holds my head in his hands and kisses my forehead. 'Now let's go down there and start enjoying the pool. I'm sweating like a nun in a sex shop.'

'Can I tell you something?' I speak softly, looking into his eyes.

'Sure. Anything?'

'I'm not so sure about that orange shirt.' A smile spreads across my face.

'Hey, this is one of my favourites!' He takes a step back and looks down at himself as I crease up laughing. 'Maybe you've got a point.' He admits chuckling and starting to unbutton the sweat-drenched shirt.

'Last one in the pool has to do the washing-up.' I call out, letting my dress drop to the floor and dashing towards our luggage in search of my swimming costume.

'Come on, Mum!' Gracie appears in the doorway looking pissed off. 'We've been waiting for you for ages.'

'Coming, monkey.'

'Do you know where my–' but before she's had a chance to finish her sentence I have removed her costume from the bag and thrown it playfully in her direction. 'Thanks, Mum.' She is beaming as she rushes back out of the house, leaving her sandals discarded in the hallway.

'Kids.' Mike laughs dropping his shorts and rushing out wearing only his boxer shorts.

'Hey, that's cheating!' My words mingle with the echo of his laugher that bounces off the walls and fill me with happiness.

Libby

Having spent a wonderful relaxing week soaking up the sunshine, Mike and I put the girls to bed on our final night in the villa and treat ourselves to a romantic supper on the porch.

Like any good Australian he is an accomplished barbeque cook and rustles us up herby pasta salad and some large grilled prawns.

The sweet Portuguese white wine washes it down nicely and we sit back, beneath the dome of stars enjoying the stillness. Occasionally a bat appears and cuts through the calm night hunting for food.

'Thank you for a fabulous week. I haven't felt so relaxed for ages.'

Mike sits opposite me, the silver light from the swimming pool reflecting on his face.

'Yeah, it's been good, hasn't it?' He holds a glass of wine in his hand and swirls the contents around. 'I've been thinking.' He puts the glass back on the table and leans over. 'I think we should move in together.' He lets the idea sink in before continuing. 'We have both had our share of rough times. I don't want to be on my own any more. I want to be with you. I want us to live together and for the girls to always have each other. Look, I know it's early days, but we've known each other for a long time. I wanna be with you, Lib. We're good together and we make sense.'

'I still miss him, you know.'

I look down at my hands and my eyes are immediately drawn to my wedding finger. I am still wearing my wedding ring.

'That's natural. I'm not trying to replace Dan. He is the father of your kids. I just want us to be happy.' Twisting the ring round and round I decide enough is enough.

'OK,' I say taking my wedding band off and putting it down on the table, 'let's do it.'

'Really? As easy as that?' he looks incredulous.

'Why not? I have to let go of the past. I miss Hope every second of every day and I will never get over her loss. But I owe it to Gracie to be happy. She has to be my focus now. She loves having you, and Eva around. So do I.'

'I thought you'd tell me to go take a leap.'

'I don't know which one of us is more shocked but we've had such a lovely week. Why does it have to end there? We all deserve some happiness. I know that Danny would want me to be happy.' My wedding ring has left a tan mark on my finger. I can't erase my marriage to him so easily. 'You are a good man, Mike. You're a great father to Eva and you've been my rock. I don't need to think twice. Let's do it.'

'You don't know how happy that makes me, Lib.' He reaches over the table, takes hold of my hand and kisses it. 'This is going to be a new chapter for all of us.'

I nod, knowing he is right but not knowing if I am really ready.

Hope

When I was little, like Gracie is, I didn't mind the dark. Gracie doesn't like it and we have to leave the door open a bit so she doesn't cry.

Before she was born, Mummy and Daddy said they would get me a nightlight if I wanted but I said I liked the dark because it was cosy and I couldn't see anything that would scare me.

Now, I don't like the dark and I wish that when they said they would buy me a light I had said yes. Because now I spend all my time in the dark and it makes me think about the time I spent at home, in my room. I used to like it there but now I know I won't ever like the dark again.

Instead of not seeing horrid things I think that they are probably all around me. And I think that I am still being watched. Not knowing who is watching makes me feel really scared.

Sometimes I think I am like James, in *James and the Giant Peach*, trapped in a fruit and a big, hairy spider is outside trying to eat its way in. I keep thinking it wants to eat me and it is saving me until last, like I do when Mummy makes a roast and I leave the Yorkshire pudding until last, because it is my favourite.

Mummy always gives me extra ones if I eat all the rest of my food and I always do because I love Yorkshire pudding so much. Mummy's is the best and the one they gave us at school with our Christmas dinner wasn't very nice.

It makes me feel really hungry thinking about my favourite food. After eating a roast at home we would always get ice cream for dessert. My favourite is chocolate but Gracie likes strawberry best, so Mummy has to keep two tubs in the freezer. And it's funny because Gracie always asks for dessert but never finishes it so I usually get to eat two bowls of ice cream. Daddy and Mummy roll their eyes when I slide her bowl over but they don't stop me from eating it.

Daddy says he doesn't like waste but I think that they are just being kind to me. I can't really remember what that feels like now because it has been so long since I saw them. It's like I can't even picture their faces that well any more. The memories are going a bit blurry. Like I am looking at them through a fog. I hope they don't fade away forever and I hope they haven't forgotten about me.

JULY 2016

Libby

'I'm pregnant.' The words sound foreign to my ears.

Mike stands there motionless letting my announcement sink in. I'm not sure either of us remembers to breathe.

It's been a hot day and the girls are upstairs asleep.

Since returning from the Algarve we decided that Mike and Eva would move into my house and would sell theirs. Once the house is sold we can then decide if we want to stay in Mill Cottage or if we'll look for somewhere new to start our lives together.

Mike drops his bag onto the floor and a smile creeps across his face.

'Ah, Lib, that's wonderful.' He dashes across the room and sweeps me up into his arms.

'Is it?' The idea still hasn't sunk in properly.

'Isn't it?' He lowers me back down so my feet are on the ground and takes a step back.

'I don't know. This is not what we planned.'

'Sometimes you've just got to go where life takes you.'

'Life has taken me to some pretty shitty places over the last few years, Mike. I don't know how many more surprises I can take.'

'This isn't like what happened to Hope and Danny. This is something totally different. This is a good surprise.' I see the hurt in his eyes.

'We've only been together for a few short months. We've only just moved in together. This is bonkers.'

'So what do you wanna do then? Get rid? Is that what you're telling me?'

'Don't talk to me like that. Like I'm some sort of monster that goes round having abortions left right and centre. It's not fair. It's a shock, Mike. I just need some time to get my head round it.'

'How far gone are you?'

'I don't know. Maybe eight weeks. I thought we were being careful.'

'Accidents happen.' He shrugs, which annoys me as I turn away and slump down onto the sofa. Mike comes and stands behind me and starts rubbing my shoulders. 'Go and have a bath. Relax for a bit. You feel really tense. We can talk about it after.'

'It's too hot to have a bath.' I sit forward moving away from his massaging hands.

'Jesus, Lib. What do you want me to say? This is a surprise to me too, you know.' Mike storms out of the room and heads into the kitchen. 'I'm getting a beer,' he calls out gruffly.

'Don't be cross,' I start to soften. 'Please come and talk to me.'

Mike reappears in the doorway holding a bottle of beer and frowning. 'I'm not sure anything I say is going to make a difference.'

'Of course it is. I need to know how you feel about it.' I pat the seat of the sofa next to me. Taking a large gulp of beer Mike nods then comes and sits down.

'I'm forty-seven years old. For most of Eva's life I've been a single parent. Did I ever imagine I'd have more children? No. I didn't. But then I didn't know that you and I would end up together and I didn't know I could be this happy again. My place is on the market and we've got a good thing going on. Sure, this wasn't planned but I don't see why we can't do it. You're a good mum. We can offer a child a secure loving home. It's that simple as far as I see it, but I've not been through what you have and it's not my body. I guess I'm saying I'll support your decision – but I think we can make this work.'

'What about Eva and Gracie? They are happy it being just the two of them. Another child, one that would be their half-brother or half-sister might complicate things.'

'True. Or it might be great.' Mike puts his beer down on the table and rests his hand on my knee. 'You've already lost one child, Lib. Do you really wanna lose another?'

I hadn't thought of it like that.

'You know it's Hope's birthday just around the corner.' Sadness blankets me.

'Yes. I know.'

When he rests his hand gently on my belly I know what I am going to do.

OCTOBER 2016

Libby

Mike has been really busy with work and so I've taken over dealing with the sale of his house. A nice elderly couple, who are moving from Kent to be closer to their daughter, have made an offer that he has accepted. It has all happened so quickly.

The morning sickness was dreadful a first. I couldn't leave the sofa without wanting to throw up. It was really severe but the Dr Vogler told me it would pass. It did but not before I'd had weeks of feeling like shit.

When Mike and I sat down to tell the girls, I was petrified. Things had been going so well with the four of us and I was concerned that a new addition would throw it all off kilter. But to my surprise Eva was extremely excited. Her face lit up and she threw her arms around me, saying that she'd always wanted a real brother or sister.

Gracie was more reserved about it all. I got the feeling she thought we were trying to replace Hope. She'd gotten used to being my number one and the idea of a baby coming into our lives made her feel uneasy. Luckily Eva's enthusiasm started to rub off on her and soon she, too, was looking forward to the new arrival.

After lots of discussion Mike and I decided that we wanted to know the sex of the child. We'd had enough surprises and uncertainty already. We thought the knowledge would help us feel in control.

We were both nervous as we sat in the hospital waiting room waiting to be called in for the twenty-week scan. Mike's right knee kept jiggling and I had to nudge him in the ribs to get him to stop. All around us were other pregnant women, stroking their stomachs looking lovingly at their partners. Mike and I couldn't look at each other at all. I felt slightly sick. I'd gone over this day in my head so many times. Whether the child is male or female I knew I would love it but it would have been foolish to deny that I was nervous. Part of me was terrified it would be a girl. A boy would have been easier. It would have been a new adventure having a son. The thought of having another daughter left me feeling uneasy. What if the child looked like Hope? Would that be a good or a bad thing?

Then a slightly overweight Eastern European nurse in blue overalls appeared in the doorway and called us in. I collected my handbag from my feet and Mike and I shuffled out of the waiting room.

Our footsteps echoed as we followed the nurse down a brightly lit corridor.

'In here.' She held the door open and I squeezed in past her, followed by Mike who stood awkwardly while I lay down on the bed and lifted my jumper up over my bump.

'Is this your first baby?' She started tucking paper into my pants so that the jelly wouldn't get onto my clothes.

'No. It isn't.' The gel was cold on my stomach but she didn't bother to warn me. I'd been through it before, though, so it didn't come as a shock.

Then the nurse sat down heavily on a stool, picked up the ultrasound scanner and started to roll it backwards and forwards over my lubricated white skin.

After a minute or two of her pressing down on various areas of my tummy that sound comes flooding out of the machine, like horses' hooves galloping across country fields.

'Baby heartbeat.' She told us, clearly rather uninterested.

Mike moved closer to the machine and peered over me at the black and white image on the screen. The foetus moved, arching its back, like it was doing stretches before a sporting event.

'You want to know the sex?' The grumpy nurse asked.

Mike and I looked at each other to make sure we were on the same page.

'Yes,' I said, 'we want to know.'

'Baby is going to be,' her pause seemed to last forever as she rolled the scanner around, making sure she could see clearly, 'a girl.'

'At least we don't have to buy lots of new stuff.' Mike had his arm around my shoulder as we left the hospital and stepped out into the autumn drizzle. I hadn't said a word since we'd left the ultrasound room. My head was going round and round trying to work out how I felt about the news. 'I reckon the girls will be stoked.' He dug about in his trouser pocket for the car keys. 'Hey, what's up?' He looked over the roof of the car at me and saw the tears gathering in my eyes.

'A girl.' The words came out in a whisper.

'She's gonna be so loved, Lib.'

'What if I can't protect her?' the sentence trailed off into the wind.

'Don't think like that. What happened to Hope...' It was his turn to leave the sentence unfinished as the rain began to come down harder.

'I want us to move.' I shake the raindrops off my nose as I get into the car. 'I'm sorry but I cannot bring up another daughter in that house. Too many memories.'

'I understand.' Mike puts the keys in the ignition and starts the engine.

'Why don't we all move into your house and sell mine instead. The contracts haven't been exchanged yet. It's not too late.'

'My place is too small Lib. That wouldn't work.' Typical man. Always being practical.

'But I can't stay at Mill cottage. Please let's find somewhere new before she is born.'

After a week or so I'd got used to the idea that Mike and I were going to have a daughter. I even started to get excited about it and began going through the baby clothes I had stored in the attic. It was hard seeing things that Hope had worn but a bit of me liked the idea that a part of her would live on through the baby.

Mike and I even discussed names. It wasn't an easy conversation in some ways, because we weren't married and had never discussed it, but I reassured him that the child would have his surname. It seemed right.

'I think we should call her May.' He said one evening as we sat having dinner. 'She was likely conceived in May.'

'I like it,' I pushed my spaghetti around my plate.

'But?' he put his folk down.

'I thought maybe we could call her Faith. As in Hope, Grace and Faith.'

Mike sat back in his chair and looked at me.

'But this kid is going to be a Kelly, Lib, not a Bird.' He said it kindly.

'You're right, of course. It was a stupid suggestion.'

'It wasn't stupid, but I think we need to look to the future, that's all.'

Not wanting to get emotional about it I turned my concentration to eating.

'May,' I said through a mouthful of pasta, 'that's a good name.'

Libby

Mike's house, on Coploe Road, is a small, detached two-bedroom cottage. It is on the far side of the village, right on the outskirts on the incline of a small hill, the only one around for miles. On the outside it has seen better days. The white paint is grubby in places and could have done with a touch up here and there. But the petite front lawn is immaculate. He takes pride in mowing the grass and keeping the weeds away.

Inside it lacks a woman's touch. There are very few pictures on the walls and most of the windows have blinds and not curtains. The sofa was butch and there wasn't a sign of a cushion anywhere. He'd tried his best to make it homely but, like a lot of men, he just wasn't very good at it.

Going through his house gave me an insight to him that I'd not seen before. In his bedroom, at the back of his wardrobe, was a large bag full of items that belonged to his dead wife. He'd even kept her wedding dress. Mike is more sentimental than I'd given him credit for.

I collect the girls from school and we make our way to his house. I leave them munching crisps and drawing pictures in the sitting room while I make a start on Eva's room. She wasn't interested in helping to go through her things and I am secretly grateful. I know very well how girls never throw anything away, and I am glad to be able to have a cull without her interfering.

Her room is a mess of toys and clothes. Armed with black sacks I put things into piles. On one side of the room

I make a bundle of things we would keep and on the other side a large heap of rubbish quickly forms. Since Eva has most of her things now at Mill Cottage I can be merciless with what I discard.

Once the floor is clear and I can actually see the carpet, I get down on all fours and reach under her bed, pulling out handfuls of things she had long forgotten. Crumpled girl's magazines, pencils, books, small plastic toys and bits of Lego all went into the junk pile. Right at the back, against the wall, I can make out one more thing that I have to really reach to get. Coughing from the dust, I sit up holding the object in my hand.

I freeze.

I am holding a small pink plimsoll. It is identical to the pair Hope was wearing when she disappeared.

Dropping the shoe onto the floor I wriggle backwards, on my bum, away from it. There it lies, covered in dust. I half expect it to move. I feel as if I've seen a ghost. The child in my stomach gives a hard kick as if she too feels unnerved.

Frantically I search the room for the pair. If I can just find the other shoe, then everything would be OK. I rummage through the drawers, the cupboard, turn the duvet inside out, pushed the bed away from the wall in case the other plimsoll is lodged there. Nothing. I can't find the pair anywhere in that room.

Desperate, I tear through the pile of rubbish in case it has ended up in there. By the time I've finished hunting, the room is back to being the state it had been in before all of my hard work.

I hold the shoe to my chest and hurry downstairs to talk to Eva. The girls are staring at the TV like zombies, their empty crisp packets discarded on the floor with their shoes.

'Eva,' I do my best to keep my voice calm and steady. 'Can I have a word sweetheart?'

She remains fixed to the television.

'Eva, can you come here please,' I speak louder, 'I need your help with something.'

She turns and looks at me, irritated that I've interrupted her programme. For a split second she looks just like her father. 'Can't I finish watching *Shaun the Sheep* first?' she huffs.

'No. I'll be quick. Just come here for a moment.' I don't want Gracie to see the shoe. She gets off the sofa and stomps towards me. I am getting a taste for what lies ahead and the teenage years.

'What?' she folds her arms across her chest and only half looks at me, while still trying to see the TV.

'Is this your shoe?' I ask holding up the grubby pink plimsoll.

'I dunno.' I haven't got her full attention.

'Well, I found it under your bed.'

'Then it must be.' She's not being helpful and I can feel my rage building but know I need to keep a lid on it.

'I can only find one. Any idea where the other one might be?' I ask in my sweetest voice.

'No.'

'I need you to look at me Eva. This is important.' I spin her around to face me, her eyes wide with shocked.

'I don't know where the shoe is.'

'Are you sure this is yours?' I hold the old plimsoll out to her.

'Maybe.' She examines it with uncertainty. 'I don't remember.'

As much as I want to continue to push the subject I refrain.

'That's OK. Go and watch the cartoons. We'll go home soon.' She starts to walk away still holding the shoe.

'Can I have that back please?'

'Yes.' She hands it back to me, looking at me strangely.

'Thanks. I've just got a few more bits and pieces to do then we'll go. OK?'

Eva shrugs and returns to her position on the sofa as I turn and go back upstairs clinging to the shoe, my head a mess of thoughts.

Libby

After taking the girls to school, I go to see the vicar. I need to talk to someone about my discovery.

Robert is not used to me turning up at his house, so when I knock on the door he is surprised to see me.

'Libby, what can I do for you?' He sniffs loudly. The man seems to have a perpetual cold.

'I need to talk to someone. I'm going mad. Can I come in please?'

Robert looks uncomfortable and suggests we walk around the graveyard instead.

'I found her other shoe,' I blurt out.

'Sorry?' Confusion furrows his brow.

'Hope's shoe. I found the missing shoe. The one they never discovered.'

'Where?' Robert turns very pale all of a sudden.

'In Mike's house.'

'That isn't possible.' He shakes his head.

'But I did,' I remove the plimsoll from my bag and hold it out to him. Above us in a tree a blackbird calls out to his wife.

'How do you know it belonged to her?' Robert is looking at me as if I am mad.

'I just do.'

'Libby,' he turns to me and takes hold of my shoulders with his bony hands, 'Amit killed Hope. The police and the papers said so. The case is closed. You know that. He confessed.'

'But what if he didn't? We've never found her. What if someone else has her?'

Robert takes the shoe out of my hand and examines it. 'I know Mike is not capable of that. So do you. You are pregnant and under a lot of pressure. Go home and put your feet up. Stop tormenting yourself.'

Unable to look him in the eye any more I turn my attention to watching Mr and Mrs Blackbird, who hop about on the ground pulling up worms.

'Amit killed Hope.' Robert says it again stroking the shoe.

'You're right. I'm sorry. I don't know what's come over me.'

'I appreciate you must have been very upset, finding this shoe, but it cannot belong to Hope. You must be mistaken.'

'I don't know what I'm doing. Sorry to have wasted your time.'

'You can always come and talk to me.' He scratches his skull and a shower of white specks falls.

'I'm going to go home and get some rest. Thank you, Robert. Can we please keep this thing between us?'

'Of course.' He smiles showing his aging crooked teeth.

'I'll see you soon. Thanks again.' I wave turning to leave the churchyard.

When I'm sure Robert has returned to the vicarage, I go back to Mike's house determined to find the other shoe. I'd not slept well the night before, tossing and turning, worrying about what my discovery meant.

I didn't mention the shoe to Mike last night. I didn't want to sound like a mad woman. I'd slipped the plimsoll into my handbag, certain that Mike wouldn't find it there.

I walk along the damp street hugging my handbag to my side, feeling the shape of the shoe pressing against my body. The baby has been kicking violently since I discovered it. It's as if she knows that something is wrong.

When I let myself into the cold, deserted house a shiver runs through my body. The place feels like a tomb. I hadn't noticed before now. I've been so busy packing everything up into boxes it had not occurred to me how strange it was to be in Mikes' home, surrounded by objects from a life that does not belong to me. He should be here doing this. It isn't my place to decide what happens to Eva's baby things or his dead wife's belongings.

As I close the creaking front door behind me I remind myself not to be so easily spooked. But finding that shoe has sparked something inside of me.

All the questions I had after Danny died have come flooding back. *What if Amit didn't do it? What if Danny was wrong? What if Hope is still alive? What if I will never really know what happened to her?* I am driving myself mad again, but there is nothing I can do to stop it. Everything I have tried to leave in the past has come crashing into the present and refuses to disappear.

I try telling myself that it is just a shoe and that hundreds of children will have owned the same pair as Hope but the voice inside my head screams *something isn't right.* Doing my best to remember back to when Eva used to come and play with Hope, I wonder if I ever saw her wearing the pink shoes. But my memory will not answer the question. I keep coming back to the fact that Eva can't remember if the shoe is hers. Why can't she remember? Surely she'd know if she owned a pair of shoes like that.

Then I start to worry about what it means that I found the shoe in this house. If it were Hope's shoe, why would it be here? What does it mean?

Taking myself into the kitchen I drink some icy water straight out of the tap. The temperature sets my teeth on edge and the water tastes nasty, as if there is too much iron in it. I guess the tap hasn't been used for a while.

Leaving the empty kitchen behind I move from room to room, checking that I haven't missed something, hoping to find the other shoe. But I don't and the feeling that I had when I left Danny to go to Cornwall returns with a vengeance. In my bones I know something is wrong.

My handbag feels heavy on my shoulder as I climb the stairs to Mike's bedroom. When I discovered his dead wife's belongings in his wardrobe I'd decided I would leave them there and tackle them last. I dread going through items belonging to someone deceased. It reminded me of having to do it with Danny and Hope's things. Of course I couldn't bring myself to throw any of it away and so it was all stored in my attic. When I discovered I was pregnant for the third time I counted it as a blessing that I'd kept everything – as if it was meant to be.

Going through the bag of clothes that once belong to Emma Kelly I feel dirty, like a peeping tom or something. I never met her so it seems strange to be handling her things.

Pushing that feeling aside I take each piece of clothing out and fold it neatly on the floor. Her taste was very different to mine and I start to wonder what she was like. Mike has spoken about her, and I've seen photographs, but sitting here going through the clothes she once wore makes me feel closer to her somehow.

After the bag is emptied and I still haven't located the missing shoe, it occurs to me that perhaps the thing that brought Mike and I together was loss. We've both lost important people in our lives. Not everyone knows what that is like. I worry that maybe our grief is the only thing that connects us – and then I remember the life growing inside of me.

I'm being silly, I tell myself getting up from the floor and putting the folded clothes back into the bag. Since finding the pink plimsoll I've been shaken up. Twin that with the hormones and I'm bound to be all over the place.

I lift the sack and put it back into Mike's cupboard and close it. I don't want to look at those things any more. I've violated the dead woman's privacy enough for one day.

Going downstairs I know what waits for me – The dreaded cellar. I've left it till last because I hate spiders. Mike said he'd got rid of them all when he came and had a clear out at the weekend but I doubt he managed to find them all.

I am still clinging to the plimsoll as I push the door to the cellar open. My large belly makes me feel off-balance as I stand at the top of the stairs peering down into the darkness. I need both hands to negotiate the stairs so I cram in into my pocket. The smell of damp floods my nostrils as I fumble about hoping there is a light switch. When my fingers connect with one I breathe a sigh of relief as a low light is cast down the stairway.

Trying my best not to examine the naked brick walls either side of me for webs, I slowly descend into the basement. When I reach the bottom my eyes adjust to the faint light in the small room. Against one wall I can see some tools hanging up. Below them is a bag of coal, an old broken chair and a few grubby cardboard boxes, bursting at the seams.

On the other side of the room are a few old shelves, home to forgotten items smothered with thick dusty spider's webs. Looking around I don't know where to start. I'm not touching those boxes in case a tarantula comes crawling out. Other than that there isn't much down here. Deciding there is nothing for me to do I turn to leave the room when something brushes against the back of my head. Before I've had time to think I've grabbed a rake that is leaning against the wall and swung it round behind me.

The rusty metal teeth make contact with the back wall and pierce through it like butter. I let go of the rake. My heart is thumping hard when I realise it was only a web I'd brushed against. Feeling foolish I bring my hand up to my chest and catch my breath.

The rake is still sticking into the wall. I try and remove it. The surface it made contact with is a stud wall. Standing on tiptoes I try to peer through the small holes and see what is on the other side. The baby inside me kicks my ribs as if she is trying to tell me something, but I ignore her warning and start to pick at the crumbling holes.

The smell that comes through the wall is unlike anything I've ever smelt before. It is stale, rancid and bitter. The scent is unfamiliar but suggests something rotten lies behind the hollow wall.

Pushing my finger through one of the holes I manage to get a hook and pull a chunk of the plasterboard away. A cloud of dust explodes up into my face causing me to cough violently.

When the coughing fit subsides and despite the foul smell, I return to tearing chunks of the wall down. The splintered plasterboard digs into my palms breaking the skin, but I carry on regardless.

Something is behind that wall. Something hidden and I am desperate to know what it is. Like a woman possessed I continue to pull at the wall, watching as the hole expands with each new tug. My fingertips are bloody and the smell is growing stronger but still I keep going until I hear a sound behind me and spin round.

Mike is standing at the bottom of the stairs watching me.

'What are you doing?' he asks with his head tilted to one side.

'I, well, I–'

'Fancied some DIY?' His chuckle fills the room.

'It was an accident. I made a hole and then, I don't know, I just wanted to see what was behind the wall,' my words come quickly tripping over one another.

'Ah Lib, you shouldn't be doing that in your condition. Come upstairs and I'll get you a nice cuppa.'

'Did you know about this wall?' My hands are shaking as the adrenaline starts to kick in.

'Nope. No idea it was there. Come on, let's get you cleaned up. You're covered in dust.' I can sense that he wants me to leave but it makes me more determined to stay.

'I want to see what's behind that wall, Mike. Are you curious?' I brush some dust of my jumper, unable to look him in the eye.

'Probably just an old chimney breast or something.' He positions himself across the stairs and I instantly feel like a trapped animal. Then it dawns on me.

'What are you doing here? I thought you were at work.'

Mike lowers himself slowly until he is sitting on one of the damp steps and puts his head in his hands.

'Why couldn't you just leave it? That damn shoe. Eva told me about you questioning her.' His voice sounds different now, as if it belongs to someone else.

'I don't understand.' I feign ignorance.

'You had to come snooping about, didn't you?' He shakes his head from side to side and looks at me with dead eyes.

'I'm sorry, I don't understand. What are you talking about?' My hand comes down to my belly and I try to soothe the life growing inside of me.

'We could have been happy, the five of us. Then you go getting all upset about a shoe. It wasn't even Hope's. It must have belonged to Eva. But you wouldn't let it go. You had to keep sticking your beak in where it wasn't wanted.' He stands up and takes a few threatening steps towards me. Moving backwards trying to keep some distance between us I fall through the hole in the wall and land on the sweaty ground on the other side. Scrabbling about like an animal caught in a snare, my hands find something cold and hard and I pick it up, hoping to use whatever it is as a weapon to defend myself.

It takes a moment for my eyes to make out what it is I am holding. My brain cannot process the object in my hand at first. Then I drop it and it crashes onto the floor, setting off an echo which dances around my head.

Petrified and unable to speak I stare down and the human bone I had been holding. Disgusted I push myself away from it and huddle in a corner of the dark dank space.

'You weren't meant to find her, Lib. No one was. It all got out of hand. It was an accident.' Mike stands blocking my exit, looking down at me. The child I am carrying starts doing somersaults and I think I might be sick. Searching the small claustrophobic space I try to look for some way out but what I find instead is the small skeleton of a child lying in a heap on the ground.

'It's not what it looks like. I offered her a biscuit. She was so pretty and I just wanted to give her a kiss but she freaked out. I told her to stop screaming but she wouldn't so I brought her down here. I'm sorry, Lib. I really am. I tried to get her to be quiet, to calm down but she wouldn't listen.'

My eyes can't look away from the remains that lie a few feet away from me.

'I told her, you know, if you let me give you a kiss and a cuddle then you can go home. She liked it, she did. I promise I didn't hurt her. She wanted me. I was really gentle but then she tried to bite me and I had to stop her.'

Tears stream silently down my face as I crawl on my hands and knees towards the bones.

'I just wanted to show her how pretty she was. I didn't want to kill her.'

'Say her name.' I choke through my tears cradling the bones in my arms. Mike just looks away. 'Say it!'

'Zoe.' Mike speaks her name as if she is an angel.

'Who is Zoe?' I drop the bones, confused and revolted.

'She was my first. Such a pretty little thing. Bright auburn hair and these dark eyes you would get lost in. Poor kid was neglected by her mother. She needed someone to love her.'

He makes it sound so pure.

My brains whirls round like a tornado trying to put the pieces together.

'This isn't Hope?' I wipe the snot away from my face, still clinging onto the remote chance that my daughter may still be alive.

'No, silly.' Mike takes a flashlight and a set of keys from his pocket and flips the bunch round in his hand before squatting down to face me. I can smell the coffee on his breath and for a moment manage to forget the smell of death that hangs in the stagnant air.

'Where is she?' I stutter. He turns the flashlight on and points it into the furthest corner.

'There she is.'

The bright light illuminates another pile of small bones. The skull, which lies lopsided on the earthy ground, has a hole in it the size of a fifty pence piece. As I take in the scene of horror I notice a shackle around the leg bone. Only then do I vomit.

'I wanted to love her. She was meant to be mine. She came looking for Eva. But she kept biting me so I had to do something. When I put the chain round her ankle she kept pulling and shouting. I told her to shut up but she wouldn't. She kept pretending she didn't want me to kiss her. She was mine for less than an hour. She's been resting here ever since.' Mike steps through the large hole in the wall and comes over to rub my back.

'Get away from me,' I push him away spluttering through waves of sick that pass over my body.

'Don't be like that, Lib. I told you it was an accident.' He sounds genuinely offended. I look up at the monster trying to recognise the man I thought I loved. 'We've got another little girl to think about now.'

For once the baby is not kicking. She is very still as I look down at the small bump protruding from my jumper. My entire body starts to shake as I wriggle away from Mike.

'You need to take better care of yourself.' He stands up, towering over me, and brushes the dirt from his trousers. 'It's not all about you anymore.'

'If you think for one moment that you are ever going to lay a hand on this child you are wrong.' I try to stand up but my legs won't let me.

'Come on now. That's not very nice.' Mike rests his hands on my shoulders and pins me down, long enough so that he can fasten the shackle around my ankle.

'What are you doing?' Immediately I pull at the thick metal chain trying to rip it from the wall.

'You need to take it easy from now on.' He goes over to Hope's skeleton and runs a finger lightly along one of her bones.

'You can't do this. Someone will find me.' I keep tugging hoping to loosen the shackle.

'Shhh.' Mike approaches and pushes a piece of stray hair away from my face. 'You need to rest. We have to think about the baby.' His eyes fill with a twisted love. 'I'm gonna take good care of you. Both of you.'

Then I remember Gracie.

'You leave Gracie alone. You hear me? You don't touch a fucking hair on her head!' My scream shakes the walls of my prison and dirt crumbles down all around me.

'You'll frighten the crows if you keep that up.' He's trying to sound relaxed but I can tell he no longer feels at ease.

'You're used to intimidating little girls. Not liking dealing with someone who can fight back, are you?' I buck and pull against the chain that is bolted firmly to the wall. 'Fucker!' I scream spitting at him.

He moves away and watches me for a moment, deciding what to do. This is not part of his plan. I've taken him unaware and now he is having to think on the go.

'You just stay here for a while until you calm down. I'll come back when you've learnt how to behave like a lady.'

I stop dead, letting the chains go loose and fall to the floor. I don't want to be left alone in this place.

'See, that's better.' His smile repels me.

'I'll get you something to eat and a blanket and I'll be back soon. Don't want the boss wondering where I am,' Mike calls over his shoulder as he trudges up the stairs. When the door to the cellar closes the room is thrown into darkness and I fall to my knees sobbing uncontrollably.

I don't know how long I'm left alone down there. I have no sense of time. The blackness drowns everything.

When he finally opens the door at the top of the stairs and begins his decent I am ready. I have been waiting for this moment ever since Hope disappeared. I sit on the cold hard ground, with my knees tucked up, a barrier between him and my baby.

Mike shines the flashlight over at me blinding me temporarily. 'There you are.'

'Where is Gracie?' my bottom lip quivers with fear.

'She's fine. Watching cartoons at home with Eva. Told them I was just popping to the shop. I can't stay long.' He lowers a plastic bag to the floor and removes a packet of biscuits and a carton of milk. 'You must be hungry.' He hands the carton to me and I glug down as much of the milk as I can in one go.

'Greedy guts.' He brings his thumb up to my face and wipes the milk from my lips.

It is then that I seize my opportunity. From behind my back I pull out a piece of splintered bone and plunge it into his chest. Mike falls back dropping the flashlight as a large red mark spreads across his jumper. The flashlight rolls around on the floor sending rays of light bouncing around the room before settling.

He coughs and blood splatters out of his mouth. The shock makes his pupils dilate. His eyes are almost black now.

Still holding onto the bloody splintered bone I bring it down into his calf. It cuts through his jeans and sinks into the skin and muscle beneath. Mike lets out a howl that sends blood from his mouth whirling around the darkened room like spray paint.

'You should know, *my* daughter is going to be called Faith Bird. She is never going to know you existed.' I look the monster in the eye.

Half sitting up, he grins through the blood, holding his chest with one hand and his leg with the other. I turn the bone around and using the knobbly end, bring it crashing down into his head. On impact both bones shatter and a second later Mike's lifeless body slumps onto the floor, a puddle of shimmering, crimson blood pooling beneath his smashed skull.

Shaking I drop the remnant of Hope's leg bone to the floor and watch as the puddle of Mike's blood spread across the floor working its way closer to me. Tucking my legs up I try to escape it but the liquid meets my shoes and I feel it soak into the trousers I am wearing.

The baby kicks and I collapse into a fit of tears.

I've been here for hours now, trying to break free from the shackle around my ankle, but it's useless. The thick metal bracelet around my leg will not budge and I am making no progress where I have tried to hack at the wall it is attached to.

I had a scare a little while ago. Mike's body started twitching. I thought maybe he was alive, but when I checked his eyes were wide and glazed over, the crater in his skull too deep for him to have survived. I don't know why he was twitching, but he was. I turned away and buried my face against the wall until it stopped.

Sitting here in this cave, surrounded by death I wonder if I, too, am going to die.

All I can think about is Gracie, left alone with no one to love and take care of her and about the little life inside of me, snuffed out before it had a chance to begin. I cannot allow that to happen. I have to get out of here. I have to survive this.

Lying on the damp ground I close my eyes and try to imagine Hope alive in this place. I will never know what he did to her and I don't want to. For so long I thought that answers would bring me peace. Now I know that isn't true. Stretching my hand out I let my fingers rest on her frail bones. She has come back to me at last.

'I am so sorry, baby.' I stroke the cold skull bone, remembering what her hair felt like. 'No one can hurt you now. Daddy is with you. He will look after you.' Just as I begin to doubt that I will ever be found I hear footsteps on the ceiling above my head.

'Hello! Help! I'm down here. Please, someone, help!' The footsteps stop and I wonder if I imagined them. 'Please. I'm down here. Help me. I need help!'

Then very slowly the door at the top of the stairs creaks open a bit more. Two small silhouettes stand there looking down into the basement.

'Mummy?' Gracie calls down, clinging to her doll.

'Yes monkey, it's me. I need some help.'

'What happened?' asks Eva, standing right next to Gracie, sounding just as terrified.

'You mustn't come down here, girls. Do you understand? You have to stay up there.'

'Why, Mama?' Gracie's little voice is quivering.

'Just be a good girl and do as I say. You need to go and get a grown-up to come and help. I've hurt my foot and I need help getting up the stairs. Can you do that, girls? Can you go and get a grown-up?'

'We didn't know where you were. We waited and waited but no one came.' Eva sounds frightened.

'It's OK. I'm fine. But you need to go and get an adult. All right?'

'Who?'

'Go together and knock on some doors in the village. Do not separate. Stay together. Try Mrs Collins at the B and B or Robert at the vicarage. Tell them that I am in the basement and I cannot move. Tell them to call the police. Can you do that for me, girls?'

Both silhouettes nod in tandem before disappearing.

'Good. Good girls.' I close my eyes and hugging Hope's bones to my chest I allow myself to cry.

Hope

I don't know what is happening but everything that was dark and scary is now turning bright white. I look down and can see myself again. My body isn't hurt and the metal thing around my ankle has melted away.

A bit like magic, Zoe appears. I can see her for the first time. She looks different to what I thought she would. She has ginger hair and dark eyes and lots of freckles on her nose. She is smiling and happy.

'Where are we?' I ask as she takes my hand.

'It's time to go home now.'

'But my family aren't here.' I look around hoping to see them.

'Your dad is waiting.' There is a glow around Zoe and I think she looks like an angel.

In the far distance, against the white fog all around me, I can make out the outline of my father.

'Daddy!' I've never been this happy. 'See,' I turn to Zoe smiling 'I told you he'd come and get us.'

THE END

Acknowledgements

Without a shadow of a doubt, this has been the hardest book I have written. I've always avoided a storyline involving children because bad things should not happen to them, in real life or fiction. But I wanted to write a book about what it meant to be a parent. This is the product of that.

After the immense support I received for *The Optician's Wife* I was terrified that this would be a disappointment. I hope that is not the case. Every book I write is very different and I like the fact that each book takes me on a new journey. I aim to learn and improve with every effort and I hope this approach is evident to you, my readers.

There are so many lovely people in my life that I feel very lucky. All the bloggers who support indie authors and presses, you really help writers like me – Sarah Hardy, Noelle Holten, Maxine Groves, Emma Whelton, Joanne Robertson, Nicki Southwell, Joseph Calleja, Sarah Kenny, Helen Claire, Shell Baker, Amanda Oughton, Susan Hampson, Lorraine Rugman, Peter Best, Emma Mitchell and Alexina Golding to name a few.

My fantastic stablemates at Bloodhound Books are a pleasure to work with. The people who have the difficult job of tidying up my work should be given medals. Crime Fiction

Addict on Facebook and all the admins who work hard to make sure indie crime writers get the recognition they deserve: keep up the good work.

A shout out also to TBC and its members for everything they do.

As always, there is a list of people who I owe thanks to. In no particular order they are, Andrew Barrett for tips on forensics. Kerry-Ann Richardson for advice on police procedure. To Tom Walker for information about anaesthetic. To the Inspector who is too bashful to be named but has been my fountain of knowledge regarding police matters. To Anita Waller for her unwavering support and infinite wisdom. To my wonderful children who put up with me and remain my inspiration. To my husband – you are everything.

Also By This Author

The Optician's Wife

The Quiet Ones

Carrion

Beneath the Watery Moon